HOLMES AND MORIARTY

Also by Gareth Rubin

The Turnglass

HOLMES
AND
MORIARTY

GARETH RUBIN

SIMON &
SCHUSTER

London · New York · Sydney · Toronto · New Delhi

First published in Great Britain by Simon & Schuster UK Ltd, 2024

Copyright © Gareth Rubin, 2024

The right of Gareth Rubin to be identified as author
of this work has been asserted in accordance with
the Copyright, Designs and Patents Act, 1988.

1 3 5 7 9 10 8 6 4 2

Simon & Schuster UK Ltd
1st Floor
222 Gray's Inn Road
London WC1X 8HB

Simon & Schuster: Celebrating 100 Years of Publishing in 2024

Simon & Schuster Australia, Sydney
Simon & Schuster India, New Delhi

www.simonandschuster.co.uk
www.simonandschuster.com.au
www.simonandschuster.co.in

A CIP catalogue record for this book
is available from the British Library

Hardback ISBN: 978-1-3985-1453-9
Trade Paperback ISBN: 978-1-3985-1454-6
eBook ISBN: 978-1-3985-1455-3
Audio ISBN: 978-1-3985-2611-2

Illustrations by Bob Venables

Typeset in the UK by M Rules
Printed and Bound in the UK using 100% Renewable Electricity
at CPI Group (UK) Ltd

For Jacob

Chapter 1

I have sometimes, in these poor reminiscences of my days spent with Sherlock Holmes, attempted to describe the sensations I felt when we were called in by the authorities to decipher an incident that had baffled their finest brains. Such descriptions have always irritated my companion, it must be said, because he insists that the interest in such cases should be in their pure mechanics, not unlike a manual on the correct design of a locomotive engine, rather than the human emotions that were bound up in them. I should, therefore, keep such colour out of the narrative, he says. And yet, no matter the admiration I have always felt for Holmes – the greatest consulting detective that the world has ever known – I have always resisted him on that score.

And so I will relate what I felt in the light of a setting sun two days before the Christmas of 1889.

It was fear. Fear like I had never known.

For the murder of Britain's Minister for War, at a time when all of Europe was on the brink of armed conflict, could have been the spark to set the whole continent alight. War, then, would have engulfed the greater part of the entire world. And I have seen war. I have seen the open gates of Hell.

What stood between us and those gates? It was a sight I would never have dreamed possible: the sight of the ever-righteous Sherlock Holmes and that malevolent denizen of the criminal netherworld, Professor James Moriarty, working together as if they were old friends, rather than two men sworn to each other's destruction. Working together to save all of Europe from catastrophe.

Yes, on a Swiss mountain, as a terrible blizzard raged outside, their minds wrought as one, moulding around one another, creating a hybrid of good and evil: a weapon that would strike our first blow against a danger the likes of which the world had never seen before – and, I pray to God, never will again. As night fell, Moriarty looked to me and held out his hand. I nodded and passed him a fistful of bullets, each one made to send a man to his grave, when—

But I am getting ahead of myself. Holmes always tuts when I do so. 'Everything in order, Watson. Without order, what is there but disorder?' And I must admit he has a point. So I shall return to the chronology in which events unfolded.

*

I have had occasion in my previous reports, most notably that queer affair of the Greek Interpreter, to describe the Diogenes Club, the lair of London's least clubbable men. A gentleman who despises the very thought of society may retreat to its muffled environs and content himself with reading periodicals or heftier tomes in an atmosphere devoid of the slightest sound. Indeed, anyone who so much as acknowledges another human being's presence within the club's public rooms runs the risk of permanent expulsion. In life-or-death situations, the Stranger's Room is reserved for interaction, although any member observed entering or leaving it will still receive a black mark against his name in the club ledger.

In short, it was the perfect place for Holmes's brother, Mycroft (who was, indeed, one of its founder members). Sherlock credits his sibling with a mind often surpassing his own when it comes to criminal detection – a fact that our Secret Service has frequently relied upon, Holmes assures me – but negated in its efficacy by the sheer indolence of its owner.

That inertness was a habit, but at the time that I describe, it had become medical. Mycroft was staying in one of the club's bedrooms, and I had been called upon to see what cure I could advise.

The room was functional and no more than that – the inmates of the club like their furnishings in the Spartan style. If it serves a purpose, then let it be. If it is there to look fine, then chuck it out. So there were a couple of solid chairs, a writing desk and not a single painting, print or bunch of flowers to be seen. We stood at the foot of the bed in which Mycroft lay simultaneously reading a treatise on Asian arachnids in his right hand and a thick volume of Dante's complete *Divine Comedy* in Italian in his left. The club's white-coated steward, who had shown us to the room, muttered a few hoarse words as he hung around for some seconds without reason, glaring at us all, and then sullenly took his leave – at which point, Mycroft's mouth cracked into a thin smile.

'You observe, of course, Sherlock, how Manning has suffered a setback of late?' he croaked. While Sherlock is tall, pale, slim and angular, his black hair swept back, with sharp green eyes and the air of an Indian ascetic who could burst into vivid life at a moment's notice, Mycroft is short and plump, with a darker complexion and strange goatee that make him look a little like a Russian anarchist.

He was wearing silk pyjamas and an Egyptian fez hat, whereas we, who had come in from the thick winter smog – it was such a green-tinted pea-souper that the hansom cabs and street-sweepers were knocking into one another and pickpockets were making enough money to retire – were in heavy, wet gear. Indeed, we were crammed in close enough to feel the steam rising from each other's clothes. And even among my rugby team-mates at the Blackheath club, I was accounted a large fellow, so I had had to truly squeeze myself into the small bed chamber. I wanted to remove my sopping outer garments but simply didn't have the space to do so.

To make matters worse, I had, for the previous week, been attempting a disastrous experiment with side-whiskers, hoping that they would add gravitas to my face – it turned out that they only added gravity – and they too were quite sodden. I resolved to shave them off as soon as we returned to our comfortable rooms in Baker Street. Besides, they had been rather greyer than the fair hair on my head, and I disliked the reminder that I was not as young as I had once been. Even the waistband on my trousers was beginning to feel just a little more snug than it used to.

'I see the obvious,' Holmes replied to his brother. 'That he lost ten bob on a horse at the Kempton Races this morning, his nag having nearly won, and that he is now in dire monetary straits.'

'What?' I uttered. 'How can you tell?'

'Oh, Watson. Surely you noticed his downcast and pet-ulant demeanour when showing us in and how he lingered after his duty was complete – despite it doubtless being a dismissible offence in this institution to solicit a gratuity from members or their guests.'

'It is,' confirmed Mycroft.

'But the rest . . .'

Holmes sighed. 'The grass on his boots – we are mid-December, and green grass is hard to come by except on meticulously maintained grounds. The fact that he had not had time to clean his footwear before coming to his place of employment demonstrates that he came directly from the location where they picked up the vegetation. The torn-up pieces of paper unceremoniously stuffed in his trouser pocket, upon one of which the top of a nu-meral '10' could just be seen, are surely the receipt he was handed by the tout – and I doubt Manning is able to stake ten guineas on any race, so it must be shillings. Similarly, it had to be Kempton for the simple reason that there were no other horse races today; and it is clear that his favoured runner was close to winning because his voice is very strained and hoarse, the man having shouted encouragement until his voice cracked under the strain. He would not have troubled himself to do so if the nag had been at the rear of the pack from the beginning.'

'Good Lord,' I exclaimed.

'Well done, Sherlock,' Mycroft said with a smile. 'Just one detail rather off.'

'And what would that be?' my friend replied with a mild curiosity.

'It was not a horse.'

'No?'

'Oh, Sherlock. Did you not notice? The smell of dog on him. It was as clear as day. The dog track, brother. Manning was at Walthamstow without a doubt.'

My friend shrugged as if unconcerned, although I knew him better than that. 'What is wrong with you?'

'Oh, no more than a head cold, I expect.' Mycroft seemed to relish the chance to remain in isolated bed rest. 'Is there something you can offer by way of medication to ease the pain, Doctor?'

'I can have something dispatched to you. Drink a glass of it twice a day after meals. It should help.'

'Thank you. And Sherlock, I did want to ask a boon.'

'And what would that be?'

'I intend to stay here for a while. But in my house are certain documents that I do not wish to leave open to every burglar from here to Constantinople. Take them to my office in Whitehall. And guard them with your life. They are of the utmost sensitivity at this time.'

'Would some, perhaps, be written in German? Some in Russian, maybe.'

'And French, a few in Italian. A smattering of Turkish. Yes, you guess correctly, brother.'

'It was not too difficult a hazard, given the preoccupation of your colleagues in Westminster.'

I finally began to understand. Over the past few months, stories had begun appearing in the newspapers of ructions throughout Europe. A succession of younger politicians and princelings had been rousing nationalist emotions in their native states. The combined effects had left the Great Powers of Europe on high alert – and increasingly, at each other's throats.

'Quite, Sherlock. Quite. The papers are within my combination safe. Jarrow, my private secretary at my Whitehall office, will know what to do with them.'

'I will ensure their delivery. Is there anything more?'

'No, no.' He returned to reading his two books, as if our very presence had ended with the interview.

'And what is the safe combination?' I asked, surprised by the fact that he had failed to supply the information.

He looked at me with utter bemusement. 'Whyever do you ask?'

'Well, we can hardly open the safe without it,' I suggested.

'Can you not?' He turned to Holmes with the same confusion. 'Sherlock, is that the case?'

'Of course not,' my friend retorted.

Mycroft eyed me as if I had claimed that the moon was a giant fish. 'Extraordinary thing to say,' he muttered to himself.

'Come, Watson,' Holmes began. 'We shall—'

But he never managed to finish the sentence because there was a muffled rap on the door.

Mycroft moaned at the noise. 'Oh no, not visitors,' he complained. 'I am a sick man.'

Not wishing to hear more of his plaintive groans, I answered the knock myself and was quite surprised to see a well-dressed young gentleman – an old Harrovian, I noted by his tie (for it is not only Holmes to whom the gifts of noticing are given) – with neatly cut fair hair and a pleasant, boyish face. His height and good figure suggested plenty of wholesome exercise – I would have put him on the wing, myself. His mouth opened in preparation of speech, at which sign Holmes grabbed him by the shoulder and wrenched him into the room.

'Young man,' said Holmes, 'it is more than your life is worth to breathe a word outside the bed chambers or Stranger's Room of this club. You would immediately find yourself violently ejected onto the street.'

He looked a little shaken at his treatment but brushed it off. I had the impression that something severe was afoot. 'Mr Sherlock Holmes?'

'Of course.'

'I have sought you out, sir.'

'Naturally. Or you would not be here. I presume the admirable Mrs Hudson took pity upon you and informed you of our location?'

'She did, sir.'

'Sherlock, I am trying to read,' Mycroft muttered, without lifting his gaze from the pages. 'These octopods are intriguing little beasts and require my full attention at the moment.'

Holmes gestured to the young man, who, I suspected, wished to be considered our newest client. 'Make it brief.'

The gentleman looked flustered. 'Mr Holmes, my name is George Reynolds and I am the victim of fraud. But a fraud so strange I cannot even be sure it is fraud at all.'

A slight narrowing of Holmes's lips was the only sign that such a declaration had piqued some interest in my friend. 'How so?'

Young Reynolds ran his hand through his thick hair. 'I am, sir, by profession an actor. I do not claim to be the greatest light of my generation, but I have some ability. I am currently engaged in a production.'

'You play the titular role in *Richard III*, I see, and have performed a matinee performance today.'

The youth stared at him. 'However could you know that?'

'The faint line of grease-paint on your forehead forms a neat ring, indicating a hat or crown worn throughout the play. But more telling is your posture. As an actor, you will have trained yourself to stand as tall and proud as you can, and yet you present yourself slightly stooped at this moment, indicating that you have been bent over for a long time and your back has not yet recovered. What else but a stiff lower lumbar can one expect after three hours curled over with a hunched back?'

At that, the young man blinked and pulled himself straighter. 'Yes, yes, I see.'

Mycroft sighed audibly.

'And what is the fraud to which you refer?'

'It is this, Mr Holmes: everyone else in the production, from the sword-carriers to the queen is a rank amateur. They have no idea what they are about, rarely remember their lines, have dreadful diction and really cannot possibly be considered actors at all.'

Holmes's mouth pursed a little in dissatisfaction at the goods he had been sold. 'Then I pity the audience, but such professional disappointments are hardly within my sphere of interest. Good day.' And at that he propelled the young man towards the door.

'But the audiences are in raptures,' the young chap insisted, pulling his arm free.

'More fool them.'

'But that is the strangest thing of all. It is the same audience each time. About fifteen of them who seem to come on some sort of rota, with about ten each night. There is never anyone else. And every time they come, they disguise themselves to try to look like other people.'

At that, Holmes's hand stayed. 'The audience members wear disguises?'

Young George Reynolds stood taller now, and I noted that his clothes suited an actor well: a little daring in their cut and colour, but ultimately a bit down-at-heel, too. 'We have had a dozen performances. Each time, they have sat in different pairs, or sometimes on their own, wearing anything from furs to washer-woman's clothes to military dress. The men occasionally don beards or pull caps down low in the hope that they will not be recognized. Well, when you are on stage and the limelights are in your eyes, it is not easy to make faces out, but sometimes when I am off-stage I like to stand at the back of the hall to see if the audience are enjoying the show. And I started to notice that it is the same people and no others.'

'A loyal audience that does not wish to be detected. That is certainly more unusual,' Holmes said thoughtfully.

'But that is not all of it.'

'Then pray continue.'

'You may know that the play features a climactic rapier duel between Richard himself and Richmond.'

'I am aware.'

Mycroft threw his volume of Dante and the work on arachnids to the floor, sighing.

'This afternoon, there was a dreadful accident. The blunt tip of my stage foil snapped as I thrust at Mr Gills, who plays Richmond, and I actually stabbed him in the stomach. It wasn't a serious wound, but he was bleeding and quite shocked. But then, as he lay there, he began to panic. Not because of the blood, but because he thought I might quit the production. He was completely beside himself at the idea and made me swear on my life that I wouldn't. He even attempted to stand, so I would think it was only a flesh wound. He collapsed in my arms, though he revived soon enough. Mr Holmes, what can it all mean?'

'An incognito audience and a cast of strangely desperate amateurs.' He clapped his hands and lifted them to the ceiling. 'Mr Reynolds, there may be something to your case. Come, let us retire to Baker Street and discuss it further.'

I heard Mycroft mutter 'Thank God' as we left.

Chapter 2

If there's one thing I like, it's an ill-matched fight. I hate it when it's fair and all one-way-this, then one-way-that, all punches and parries. No, give me a big bloke pummelling a little 'un into the middle of next week and I'm happy as a lark.

I tell you this because this whole rum business started running at the annual Vauxhall Fair – a wide-brimmed bash better known to many as the Villains' Walk-Out, on account of the general atmosphere of cut-purse vice and black-minded roguery. Once a year at Christmastide, you see, the powers-that-be would unchain the gates of the old Vauxhall Gardens, where the lords and ladies once took tea, to allow three days of what you might call 'earthier' entertainment for the likes of me. Out were the dainty little cups of Indian chai and in were the boxing fights and freak shows that those with the Devil in us liked to attend. That's where I saw Merrick, the Elephant Man, and Bess the Geek, who ate nothing but chicken gizzards. I saw Waller, the Shropshire Giant, beat four men to a pulp in the ring at the same time – while their wives, every one, swooned for him and scrapped for the pleasure of wiping him down after. Bonny times, they were. Bonny times.

I told my friend and mentor – you know the one: the tall, thin gent with the sharpest mind for the analysis of criminal plans that the world has ever seen – about how I only really enjoy a fight when it's unfair, and he said he quite understood my position.

'The reason for it,' he told me, 'is that you are an animal, Moran.'

'Thank you, Professor,' I replied. 'I take that as a compliment.'

And at that he stopped off at a chocolate stand, used his ebony stick to ease a couple of evil-faced urchins out of his path and bought himself a steaming cup of the stuff. He took a bit down and looked at me. 'Oh, I do apologize, did you want a cup, too?'

Well, truth be told, I wouldn't have minded one. And it wasn't as if I couldn't have afforded it with or without him – a penny was hardly going to break my bankers (Coutts & Co., like Her Majesty) – but I couldn't buy one then in his wake, or I'd look more like a mongrel following at the heels of his master than a trusted officer in his royal court.

But just why does Colonel Sebastian Moran, Eton, Oxford, late of the 1st Bangalore Pioneers, follow Professor James Moriarty, late of the University of St Andrews, you ask? Well, stay a while and I'll let you in on the truth.

I had some high times at college, but it was the army that turned me into something new. Hunting on the veldt and fighting in the hills: within a month of donning my uniform, the scales had fallen from my eyes and I knew what I was meant for. I had a sabre in my right hand, a pistol in my left, and I was ready to raise hell.

I was decorated, cashiered, mentioned in dispatches and near-as-damn-it discharged, all by turns. And so it went, until I made a few too many enemies along the way and thought it time to seek pastures new. But when a man has built a name as the best shot in the Indian Army, when he has chased down tigers with nothing but a Mongol sword, well, a life working on the stocks market or teaching Greek to snot-nosed brats makes him want to bash his brains out on a wall.

Because my life needs a thrill. And you get no thrills, chum, sitting in a lodging house in Clapham and strolling through the park on Sunday as your 'day out'. Ballocks to that.

And yet I need money. Cards, horses, harlots – all cost cash. And so I have a certain position with the Professor.

I've scoured a few history books and I can tell you, his brain is unique. There's never been one like it. Oh yes, the schemes he works out are things of beauty. Political, smash-and-grab, a little blackmail. Some of them I don't even understand myself until we're at the end and I find we're halfway to out-banking King Croesus but the Peelers can't so much as touch us. And what's my part in all this? Well, I organize the blags: the men, the shooters if it's a hot tickle, the places to lie low afterwards. I keep discipline and lean on people when they need to be leaned on. I make sure they don't poke their noses where they shouldn't.

Yes, all in all, the Professor pays me a packet to have a rollicking time.

So there we were in Vauxhall Gardens. I took a moment to survey the stalls and entertainments. There were terraces and an ornamental lake with some deathtrap boats for hire, and wooden pergolas overhead that looked more like gibbets than the Chinese cribs they were supposed to resemble. And the whole place had a damned seedy air to it that suited the three-day blowout that we were all there for. You didn't need an invitation to the Villains' Walk-Out, you didn't need to know anyone to get in, but you did need your wits about you and a quick hand to catch at your purse. Otherwise, you'd be walking home a lot lighter on geld than when you left your rooms.

It was all run by the Orchard gang. Seamus Orchard, who had inherited it from his dad, Ichabod, had already mounted such a good track record that you could pass from one side of the Regent's Canal to the other purely on the corpses he had dropped into it. Seamus knew his seat from his elbow, all right, and he took no more chance with his operations than a mongoose with a cobra. I knew some of his men by sight – there was a brace of 'em posted at each entrance for a start – and I wouldn't mind having them back me up in any tangle with the Fuzzy-Wuzzies or the Pashtu tribes.

I did note that there were a number of fresh faces among his boys. 'Seamus has been recruiting,' I said. If Orchard was expanding his operations, the guv'nor would have to give his blessing.

'He needs to. There is new blood in the city.'

'Professor?'

'Haven't you heard? Perhaps you have not. The American gangmaster Dutch Calhoon of New York has expressed an interest in setting up a trans-Atlantic operation. It is an intriguing and ambitious prospect, and he is an interesting man – especially so because until a year ago he and his younger brother were generally considered disappointments in the Calhoon family. They had a reputation for being lily-livered when compared to their father, who was known as a Tartar. Dutch is here now, I believe, with his brother. I feel I shall have to meet him at some juncture to discuss his plans.'

I watched the guv'nor drink his chocolate and smirk as he called over one of the street Arabs to hand him the remains of his cup with a grandfatherish chuck on the boy's cheek. He dresses – and walks – like a grandfather, too, all the better to blend into the crowds. It's all shuffling and neat little three-piece suits that look like any other three-piecer on the omnibus from Tottenham Court to Gawd-Knows-Where. Don't get me wrong, I know the value of camouflage as much as anyone: that's why I go for khaki for the veldt and my smart hunting green Harris tweed two-piece from Gieves and Hawkes for Piccadilly.

But there are limits to how I'll present myself in public, and dressing like a man from Balham with one foot in the grave is beyond the pale.

We were passing the largest tent of them all: the fights enclosure – a huge thing made of striped canvas with prints of crossed fists emblazoned on each panel of the material. Even the most witless fairgoer would understand that. Entry was thruppence, which was cheap considering that you got three separate species for the price: there was one area for fights between men, one for dogs against other mutts and one for dogs against bears with their teeth pulled out.

'Shall we watch a bout?' I suggested.

'If you wish,' he granted. 'Although I am not a great admirer of violence when it has no real object.'

I said nothing but followed him through. There were more bullies at the entrance – I saw Five Fingers McGill, who never went anywhere without his girl, Coleen, a nasty little red-haired thing who I'd set against a fully grown orangutan if I wanted the monkey to come off worse.

'McGill,' I said as I walked in.

'Mr Moran,' he grunted. I stopped and fixed him with a stare. 'Colonel,' he corrected himself, a bit sheepish. Coleen sniggered at his back.

A massive black fighter was being dragged out of the boxing ring by his ankles, his nose spread from one ear to the other, while a five-foot-high Chinaman jumped up and down in the centre. To look at the skinny little bloke you'd think he couldn't smash a bluebottle, but I've seen what those Johnnies can do with their feet, their knees and their fists when you're not expecting it. It's like a whirlwind has been chucked into the ring.

Money was changing hands at the ringside. A lot of money, as it happens. The book-men always lived it up at the Villains' Walk-Out, you see, and in the corner I saw Seamus Orchard smiling like the cat that got the cream, because he could already feel his pockets filling up with his ten per cent.

I wandered over to the bear pit. Now *that* was a fight. A big brown bastard staked down but ready to rip the pin right out of the ground so he could get his claws on the dog bouncing around him and snapping at his flesh. Yes, I was in my element – beasts, screaming onlookers and the chance to make a few quid. I grabbed hold of the cove with a chalk board who was setting odds on the cur winning the fight. 'A guinea it takes down the bear,' I said, holding up the gold shiner. He snatched at it. 'Not so fast, me old mucker. What's the odds?'

He watched the dog for a few seconds, and I could see him calculating. Funny how good a Cockney can be at arithmetic when he needs to be. 'For you, guv, three on.'

'Three on? Don't make me laugh. He's nearly choked already.' Well, he grumbled, but we settled on two on, and I folded my arms to enjoy the pagger. 'Ho ho!' I said as the dog took a good chunk out of the bear's thigh. 'The little sod might just do it.'

Chapter 3

Comfortably ensconced in 221b Baker Street, having groped our way through the gloom outside, Mr George Reynolds paced the room with agitation. He had politely declined the velvet-covered chair in which Holmes's clients usually sat in favour of stepping to and fro through the heaps of curious objects that populated our sitting room.

There is something oddly welcoming about the chaos that Holmes imposes on that room – papers, test tubes, strange African tribal objects strewn everywhere. You might have to fight or gingerly pick your way through the clutter, but when you do, you settle in as if you have always lived there. And I had, since I first moved in, felt it as home. Mrs Hudson, our landlady, fussed over us like a mother hen with her chicks, preparing us tasty meals and complaining loudly if Holmes failed to finish one. She never had that issue with me.

The room's two large windows did their best to illuminate it, and the flickering of the gas lamps made our visitor look less than cheerful as he paced. I guessed he was an amiable sort who was under a certain amount of strain. Holmes filled his pipe with the Turkish tobacco that he kept in a Persian slipper by the hearth and sat waiting for the narrative to commence.

'As you are aware, my name is George Reynolds. I grew up in Sussex and my age is twenty-five years. At school, I was rather bitten by a bug for acting. My parents tried to steer me towards something more respectable.' He smiled quite a winning smile. 'But here I am.'

'And your recent history?'

'My parents both died within the past few years, leaving me a very small inheritance, but enough to make my way to London to pursue my dreams of the stage. Since then, I have had some work – nothing spectacular, but enough to rent a little room in Cheapside and buy my bread. Some weeks ago, I had been out of work for a full two months and was beginning to worry because my savings were quite exhausted. I had contacted everyone I knew, asking if they were aware of any productions forming or companies looking to add to their number. None could help. And then, precisely four weeks ago, out of thin air, a godsend.'

'A role?' I suggested.

'And what a role, Dr Watson! I was in my room, counting my pennies for the hundredth time that night, when my landlady called up to me. "Mr Reynolds! Gentleman here to see you."' He imitated an old crone like a master. 'Well, I was surprised. I had never had a single visitor to my digs. I went downstairs, and waiting at the bottom was a little man wearing thick spectacles.'

'Describe him!' demanded Holmes.

'Oh . . . Well, he had an academic sort of air about him. A lover of books, for certain. Little tufts of black hair over his ears, but utterly bald besides that.'

'Good. Continue.'

'"Sir?" I said. "Mr Reynolds?" "Yes." "I am desirous of some friendly words with you, sir." "So I am taken to understand." By this time, I was becoming quite bewildered, because each line he delivered was preceded by about five seconds of him looking me up and down like a farmer buying a cow. I prompted him: "Some friendly words?" He came to and shook his head with a little laugh. "I apologize. You see, I saw you in an opera last year, Mozart's *Abduction from the Seraglio*. A marvel, sir, a true marvel.' I was pleased because I had enjoyed acting in that show. "And when I came to put together the roll of players for my latest production, I knew you were the very man. We begin touring a fortnight hence."'

At that, Holmes lifted his hand. 'Watson?' he said. The thespian broke off, looking to me to explain.

'He is asking if I have noted something in your description of events,' I informed him. 'And yes, I have, as it happens,' I said, perhaps a little arrogantly.

22

'Excellent, then set it before us,' Holmes replied.

'The man could not have been telling the truth. He claimed he was so impressed by your prior performance that he sought you out. If so, why would he have felt it necessary to confirm that you were George Reynolds when you appeared before him?'

Holmes applauded lightly. 'Bravo, Watson. Bravo. Quite incorrect, but heroically done. You see, this strange visitor would have had to confirm it because *The Abduction from the Seraglio* is indeed an opera by Herr Mozart and there is but one non-singing part in the production, that of the Turkish Pasha. Since you, Mr Reynolds, have described yourself as an actor, rather than a singer, it is an elementary deduction that you played this part. In which case, you would have been heavily bearded and wigged, probably with a false nose and thick, dark make-up to look like a Turk. Even for the curtain call, you could not have appeared as your identifiable self, so this gentleman would have been unable to recognize you at night in the sort of poorly lit digs that we can imagine. But there is another simple question that is rather more difficult to answer. It is this: how did he know where to find you? Your address cannot be publicly known, it seems unlikely that your former employers would give it out without your permission and your previous performance was the year before, so he could not have followed you from the theatre – curious as that would be in itself.'

At this, our young companion started. 'Why, I hadn't even thought of that, Mr Holmes.'

'Then it is strong luck that you came here. But pray continue. What then?'

I felt red-faced at my failure but concentrated instead on our latest client's narrative.

'Well, I was pleased as punch, I must say. Normally I would have asked something of the production, but my circumstances being what they were, I launched straight into a more practical enquiry. "I am very grateful, Mr ...?" "Oh," he said. "Bart. Edgar Bart." "I am very grateful, Mr Bart. May I ask if the position is paid?" "Why, of course it is," he said. "At ten pounds per week. Playing every night and twice on Wednesdays." Mr Holmes, that is three times what I have ever been paid.'

'A true lover of the theatre, he must be.'

'He told me that we would have a week of rehearsals, then a fortnight of touring church halls, temperance halls, a couple of inns and small theatres in the West Country, and then a fortnight in the university towns of Oxford and Cambridge. That seemed very fine to me. So we shook hands and I went quite happily to the first rehearsal – what we call a "read-through". And that is when I had my first doubts.'

'Oho?'

'It was as I said: the rest of the cast seemed to have never so much as set foot on stage before. I had to instruct them as to which way stage left and stage right were. None of them knew how to deliver a line, put on make-up or even stand. The battle scenes really would have been carnage if I hadn't stepped in and shown Mr Bart, who was directing us all, how to do it safely.'

'But you got through it all,' I said.

'We did. And we set off on tour, beginning with a week in Exeter. The first surprise were my digs.'

'Not up to your standard?'

'Just the opposite. They were palatial. Fit for a king. The finest suite in the town's finest hotel.'

'And yet you were only *playing* a monarch,' Holmes commented. 'The rest of the cast?'

'In dreary rooms above a couple of inns.'

'You were the main attraction,' I said, attempting to justify the situation.

'That's good of you to say, Dr Watson. But in truth, no one has ever heard of me. I was hardly a crowd-draw. Well, we played the dates and I put it from my mind. But now we're in Cambridge and it's just the same: I'm waited upon better than Richard himself.'

'How have the other actors treated you?' Holmes asked.

'That is just as odd. Actors are usually a friendly bunch, all mucking in together. It's one of the things I love about the stage as a career. But in this case, they've treated me with the same deference that secured me a hotel room in which any lord would have felt comfortable. If I open my mouth, they shut theirs to listen to what I have to say. If there aren't enough chairs to go around, someone will insist that I take theirs. Everything is done to make me as comfortable and content as I could possibly be. And then there is the strange thing about the audiences.'

'That they are always the same people, taking it in shifts, so to speak.'

'Exactly.'

Holmes settled back in his chair and blew a stream of blueish smoke to the ceiling. 'Watson,' he said after a while, 'this reminds me of one or two cases from our past. That of the Stockbroker's Clerk springs to mind.' He was right. It was the case of a young man tempted away from his position in London to a better-paid job in Birmingham, in order that someone could impersonate him at his existing place of employment and carry out a robbery. 'No professional engagements for a while. Tell me about your accommodation before you left for this employment.'

He seemed a little taken aback. 'A perfectly ordinary small room in a boarding house.'

'A room above you?'

'And below.'

'What does your window look out on?'

'A blank wall. Part of another house. An ordinary little house.'

'You have been there long?'

'Six months, I should say. Nothing unusual has ever happened there.'

Holmes puffed thoughtfully. 'If someone had been desperate for access to your room, they could probably have entered it knowing the performance schedule of your previous plays. No, I think we can discount that idea. Which leaves us ... Watson?'

'Holmes?'

'In need of more data. We need data for an hypothesis. Mr Reynolds, we shall look into this affair for you.' Our young histrionically minded friend sighed with relief and was about to speak when Holmes raised his hand. 'However, at this time my mental faculties are largely reserved for the Giant Rat of Sumatra – a truly diabolical piece of work.' Ah yes, the Giant Rat of Sumatra. How that name conjures a shiver even now. When the world is sufficiently fortified for the tale, I will reveal it. 'To say it plainly: I simply do not have the hours in my day for every call on my attention. And so I must stay in London.' Reynolds tried again to interrupt, and Holmes again forestalled him. 'But Watson, I ask you, old friend, to make an initial examination.'

'I will,' I said. Reynolds looked a little doubtful.

'It will aid you if you can join the company in Cambridge tomorrow.'

'You mean . . . acting?' I asked.

Holmes threw back his head and laughed. 'I do not mean in the play, Watson. I rather think you are a little long in the tooth to change career just now. I mean that Mr Reynolds should introduce you as, say, his uncle. That will enable you to mingle with the troupe before and after the shows, and you can thus harvest more information for our investigation. Inform me by letter what you discover.'

I felt somewhat relieved at that. I tried a little amateur dramatics during my medical training, and I must admit that it did not go down in stage history. Indeed, on the opening night I forgot half my lines and was forced to improvise, which upset my fellow performers so much that the show had to be restarted twice. They were very nice about it afterwards, but I knew what they thought and when I got back to my lodgings, I had to pour cold water over my head to reduce the burning in my cheeks.

Young Reynolds checked his wristwatch. 'Damn,' he muttered. 'It's later than I thought. I have to be back for tonight's evening performance.'

'Then hie you back. Thespis awaits. Watson will join you on the morrow.'

Chapter 4

Well, the Good Lord, who I don't believe in, was smiling on me that day, because within five minutes I saw the bear laid out on the sand and the dog standing over him, a lot of gore around his chops. He even looked ready to take on the second bastard – a white one that some enterprising sort must have captured in Canada or even further north. Like his brown cousin, he was tied down with a set of metal stakes driven hard into the ground.

The book-man grumbled, saying the bear was a rum 'un and must have been sauced. But the moment I twisted his lapels in my fists, he handed over the coins. I wiped them and put them in my pocket for a nice evening at the

Bagatelle Club later. There's a little aristo molly there I've been plumping up for the cooking.

'Now, Moran, it is time . . .' the Professor began. But he stopped and cocked his head on one side like a pheasant. Or a stork, maybe, since he's got the tall and skinny look of one. And I stopped, too. I could hear what he was listening for. There were shouts, then screams. I'm fond of both sounds, but not when I can't see the cause. Everyone in the tent suddenly froze. They could all hear it, coming from outside the canvas. And something different: a mechanical sound, like a locomotive getting closer.

Bleeding chaos. That's what it was. Because I didn't have time to blink before the walls of the tent were torn down and people were running. I've seen a fair few military assaults on foot and on horse, but I've never seen five hundred men, women and kids dash for their lives before four steamrollers chugging at full speed. The machines, which were followed by a dozen bullies with chains and clubs, smashed right through the tent. When it was total pandemonium, the drivers jumped down and started breaking everything in sight. One, a big Hindoostani with long moustaches, kicked the bookie down and rummaged through his pockets, taking all the folding money.

'It's a shake-down,' I muttered to the Professor, who must have been the only calm man in sight.

'Of course it is, Moran. But who is running it? That is what I want to know.'

By this point, I had counted a dozen sprites and I was fingering the little six-shot Derringer I always kept about me. A number of the toughs had bulges at their hips or armpits that told me that I wasn't the only one with a shooter, neither.

A lad from the Orchard gang charged in with his cosh ready, but the second he stepped in, he was knocked cold by the Hindoostani. The brown 'un looked down at his handiwork – I give it to the man, I couldn't have done better myself – then spotted us and stopped. It was probably the fact that we weren't panicking that made him suspicious. 'Them,' he boomed. Two of his men – one fat as a rhino, the other skinny as a gazelle, came for us. I went for my barker, but the gazelle jumped me just as I levelled it, and the shot went through the fatso's foot. He yelped in pain but kept coming and charged me, head down. Now I'm a handy sort, but if one sprite binds my arms while the other knocks me down, I'm going to have a time of it.

At that, the big Hindoo swung over. 'Who you?' he said with narrow eyes. Oh yes, he could see we weren't pigeons.

'I . . . I do apologize, sir, most profoundly,' the Professor stammered, sinking to the ground. 'I am no one. Only a bystander. I had no idea even what this fair was when I passed it and felt in need of a cool drink, so came inside.' He clasped his hands together. 'Oh, please, spare us!' he wailed.

The brown bloke turned to stare at me, obviously taken aback by this show of subservience. But then I saw his eyes narrow further as something clicked into place in his mind. 'Cool drink?'

It was, after all, the height of winter. Well, the very

second that he uttered the final syllable, I saw the guv'nor's right hand twist the top of his stick. The steel blade he pulled out was stabbed straight into the big man's buttocks, making him scream. This surprised my gazelle so much that I was able to twist around and give him a swift knee in the stones. A well-placed foot into the rhino's belly next, a scrabble for my shooter and all had turned on a sixpence.

The Professor stood and dusted his knees a little. 'Turn around,' he ordered the Hindoo. I cocked my pistol, and the man got the message. 'Dear, dear. That does look painful. I shouldn't sit down for a fortnight if I were you. Come along, Moran. I think that might help clear a path.' He pointed with his ebony stick to the anchors holding down the polar bear. I chugged over, prised them out of the ground just enough to free our white friend and fired a single bullet into the air to encourage him to rampage in the direction of the exit. Well, the bullies in our way turned the same colour as the bear and then legged it. I cocked the Derringer again.

'Remind me to get one of those,' the guv'nor said. 'They seem useful.'

'A gun, Professor?'

'A bear.'

Outside, the rest of the fair was in a similar state: toughs shaking down stalls, beer carts and bookies; civvies running to get clear; and Orchard gang boys being chucked about like marionettes with their strings cut. A rampaging polar bear in the middle of it all did very little to calm things down. So we jogged along in his wake, happy as finches, heading for the exit until the guv'nor stopped dead. 'Ah yes,' he said to himself. He was staring with those strange grey irises of his at a dark little bloke surrounded by a dozen toughs like he was the eye of the storm. The jackanapes was reading a newspaper, calm as you like, as if he was out for a stroll at Brighton. By his side, a younger cove with a moustache that looked like it had been drawn on in pencil was lighting a cigarette with a fancy lighter covered in tomfoolery. And all the while, floozies were screaming and lambs were bawling loud enough to wake the dead. 'Yes, that seems quite right.'

'Who is he?'

'Who? Why, the brain behind the soirée,' the Professor replied. 'Dutch Calhoon.'

You wonder what sort of crib the Professor keeps? Well, let me tell you. He changes location every few months, and right then he had taken furnished rooms above Aster's Music Hall in Whitechapel. The hall was a bit down-at-heel because a better place had opened nearby and taken all the good acts. Aster was left with a bad sword-swallower and a Bulgarian girl who did something with a boa constrictor that even the French would think twice about.

The Professor liked the set-up because people could visit his rooms without being noticed and he could have a score of our boys lolling around without attracting any attention from the Peelers. We just had to put up with some idiot singing 'Champagne Charlie' every bloody night.

We stalked in through the lobby, where Irish Dan and

fat Jack Robbie were standing guard. The others were in the bar or patrolling the perimeter. Some talentless swine was murdering Beethoven on the pianoforte in the great hall. Oh yes, I like a bit of Beethoven.

We went on up to the apartment. Young Gawain Plowright was on the door that day. A bright lad and a quick shot, we might make something of him. He stood aside, and we were in the haven.

Wherever the guv'nor is always looks like the Admiralty, because there are maps on every wall, with little pins pointing out some operation or other, and charts detailing times and details. Only you or I couldn't read them, because they're in a cipher of the Professor's own and the only key is in his head.

'Tea, Moran. Indian. And bring me my notepaper.'

'Professor?'

'I believe we are on the verge of a rather irritating situation. It must be resolved.'

'What are you going to do?'

'A conference of the Viennese sort. Warring factions rarely contain themselves, and I should be much inconvenienced if the friction between Seamus Orchard and Dutch Calhoon were to spread and endanger my own projects. So: a conference.'

We had spent the day at the Villains' Walk-Out; now it looked like we were going to host the Gangmasters' Jamboree.

Chapter 5

Cambridge is a dear city to me. I spent some days there courting my wife, and the memories it holds are therefore at once bitter and sweet. As I stepped off the train, all those recollections and thoughts whirled into my head. And I was glad for them – even those that are tinged with sadness and loss. Because the pain of grief is the price that we must pay for the warmth of love.

It was around six-thirty, because I had had patients to attend to during the day, and I went straight to the theatre. It was a small back-street affair with seating for perhaps a hundred patrons. The building had once been something else, but it was hard to put one's finger on it – a laundry, perhaps, or waterworks. It was a red-brick edifice, built in the middle of the century, between a Christian temperance mission and a bread factory. Hardly the Royal Lyceum. There was a single play bill outside, no larger than an edition of *The Times*, with nothing but the name of the play above a picture of two young boys wearing medieval costume.

I arrived at the ticket booth, where a young woman looked up from some papers she was studying, clearly surprised to see me. It took me a second to work out why: apart from the solitary bill I had barely noted in passing, there was otherwise no mention of a play about the place.

'A ticket, please,' I told her.

She licked her lips and looked sideways, seemingly in the hope that someone would come to her rescue. I laid a shilling on the counter. She checked again for aid, but the lobby was quite empty. And so she dropped the coin in an otherwise empty box, tore a purple paper ticket from a roll before her and handed it to me.

'Is that the right money?' I asked.

She glanced at the coin in the box. 'Y-yes, that's right.' It was a northern English accent, from somewhere around Leeds, I supposed.

'And the play?'

'It begins in ten minutes.'

The house lights in the auditorium were low but not yet out. I took a seat in the middle, so that I could look around and perhaps memorize some of the faces. I did it as subtly as I could, pretending to find my seat uncomfortable and needing to change it twice. I counted twelve other spectators – four women, eight men. The youngest appeared to be in their thirties, and the oldest were significantly beyond even my own years. The liver spots on their skin were the giveaway signs, which you certainly did not need medical experience to identify. One odd thing that I noted to relay to Holmes was their attitude. Even before the lights cut for the commencement of the play, they were all staring with astonishing focus at the stage before them: not a word was uttered, no caramels were unwrapped. All were still and silent as the grave.

So when the limelights at the foot of the stage flickered on with that familiar fizzing sound, and the velvet curtain rose (it had seen better days, that drape) to reveal George as the titular character leaning against a wooden pillar while Edward IV was crowned, the atmosphere was quite electric.

George had a moderate talent overall, but an ability for the physicality of the part that was quite monstrous. His back was not so much humped as twisted around. It must have been terribly uncomfortable – but, of course, that added to the realism of his delivery. And when it came to his first famous soliloquy – 'Now is the winter of our discontent made glorious summer by this sun of York' – I could have truly believed his noble blood.

I was far from the only one. Through the dark interior, I could make out one or two audience members on their feet in admiration. At the other end of my row, an elderly gentleman was pushing himself up from his seat, his eyes locked on the bright stage as George sneered at the risks he would hazard to seize the crown from his own family. The old man was nearly up when I noticed his companion – a younger woman, perhaps his daughter – glance nervously at me and pull the gentleman back down.

I returned my attention to the play. It was clear that when young George had described his fellow players as 'rank amateurs', he had been treating them with sympathy. Their performances made my medical school treading of the boards seem like Henry Irving at his very best. They could barely remember their lines – three weeks into their play's run – and mumbled so that even the other actors could not hear them. They actually seemed quite shy of the stage (show me an actor who shuns attention, and I will show you a stone that bleeds!).

Why the producer of the play, Mr Bart, had cast them in their parts was quite incomprehensible. I like to think that I am a generous man, but if I had had access to a box of rotten vegetables, I would have been sore pressed not to make my dissatisfaction apparent in the most direct of ways. Well, of course I had not, and I was there for a purpose other than enjoying the drama. So I settled into the seat, appreciated the scenes with George and attempted to close my ears whenever anyone else was on stage.

A particular low point came when George, as Richard, set out to woo the widow Anne as she followed the open coffin of her previous husband. The members of the company playing monks attempting to carry the corpse had not been selected well and were not strong enough for the task. A lot of huffing and puffing by the undersized holy men as they staggered about under the substantial weight of a fully grown man and a solid wood casket conveyed less than an air of dignity to the proceedings; and when one stumbled,

dropping his corner of the coffin to the floor and almost tossing the deceased fully out, thus eliciting a startled yelp from
that dead character, I began to wonder just how successful
this performance was likely to prove. I am no professional
critic of the theatre, but I did feel that even the small sum
I had paid was perhaps more than was wholly warranted.

It turns out that *Richard III* is not a short play. And it
did not feel like one. I was happy when the interval arrived
between the second and third acts. It had been a cruel trick
when the curtain fell between the first and second, only
to rise again immediately, catching me half out of my seat
and making a beeline for what I had hoped would be an
interval bar. I had had to resume my chair and sit through
more barely audible waffling before the true interval came
around. Still, that meant that I had then made it through
half the show without falling asleep. I only hoped that
Holmes would appreciate what I had endured in the name
of gathering his precious data.

When the house lights came up, I noticed that someone
had entered the rear of the auditorium and was sitting
in the back row. He was a jaundiced-looking man, quite
unhealthy in his complexion – insufficient vitamin con-
sumption, I should say – but he was sitting as raptly as the
others, leaning forward enough for his chin to touch the
seat in front of him.

My eyes met his and, to his credit, he did not demur or
look away, but kept steadily fixed upon me. I felt that it
would be to the benefit of our investigation if I could try
to extract information from him. So instead of heading to
the bar, I made my way to this gentleman.

'Good evening,' I said.

He waited a second, as if deciding whether to reply at all. 'Good evening.'

'Are you enjoying the play?'

'It is Shakespeare,' he replied. And I have to say, I wasn't quite certain what that was meant to imply: that Shakespeare is always enjoyable? Never enjoyable? Or simply that he could not think if he was enjoying it or not.

'It is. A good performance, no?'

He gazed back at the curtain. And for the life of me, I was certain that he was trying to penetrate the velvet with his vision, because there was something quite intense about the way he looked at me and then towards the stage. I realized, too, as he broke the connection between us, that I had failed to take full note of his dress and demeanour, as Holmes would have wished. I therefore set about mentally storing all the details. He was still leaning forward, which suggested a far greater engagement with the show than I had felt. His shoes were clean, which implied that he had not walked here but had come by cab. One notable aspect was that while his left hand gripped the top of the seat in front, a circular depression around the base of his little finger implied the long-term presence of a ring, likely a signet ring given his generally smart appearance. No ring appeared there now. He had removed it. I checked then the rest of his appearance: his tie pin was without distinction, but a pin-prick in the plain black tie itself showed that another pin had recently been in place; he wore no wrist- or pocket watch (that in itself being somewhat unusual); and even the handkerchief in his breast pocket carried no visible monogram. Given such evidence, I was of the opinion – and I think Holmes would have congratulated me for the deduction – that the gentleman before me was a man who at that moment wanted to travel incognito.

'The performance is good.'

It was clear that I would be driving the conversation. 'I am impressed by the young man playing Richard. Are you not?'

He sighed. 'Sir, I most humbly advise that if you wish to discuss the performance of individuals within the company, you do so with another patron.'

Now, given the business that Holmes and I pursue – that of consultative detection – being unwanted comes with the territory. Still, it rarely aids an investigation to make too much of a spectacle of oneself, and I therefore decided to withdraw.

'I bid you good evening.' I nodded politely, and he did the same.

The bar was, for sure, a more lively environment. The audience members who had watched as if under a magician's spell were excitedly talking among themselves in a small group while staring at an easel. I sauntered over in what I considered to be a genial fashion to find out what they were all looking at. I was disappointed to see that it was merely the same poster that was outside, which I now realized depicted the famous and tragic Princes in the Tower who were murdered on Richard's orders, although this one was a larger size and printed in colour, which must have cost a pretty penny.

'Oh, that's all,' I said. I thought I had said it under my

breath, but the woman next to me, aged in her sixties, I would have said, and solid as an English oak, gave me an icy sort of look.

'It is John Everett Millais,' she informed me. 'His depiction of the poor Princes in the Tower.' Well, I had never been much for high art, but I knew Millais's name. He had painted a celebrated image of Ophelia drowning, too, I remembered. He must have specialized in tragic Shakespearean characters.

'I see. Well, it's very fine.'

'Fine?' Her voice rose almost to the level of outrage. 'You see the infantile humanity, the love between these two brothers in the face of their oppression, and it is only "very fine"!'

It was a stronger reaction than one might have expected to a theatre play bill. Still, I did my best to placate her by studying the picture quite minutely. And I had to say, there was something about it that was remarkable. On the surface, just two young lads: the twelve-year-old Edward, Prince of Wales, and his nine-year-old brother, Richard, Duke of York. But the painter was a subtle master of his art. The two boys wore black velvet doublet and hose, as if attending their own funerals. A golden garter around the prince's thigh and a golden neck chain and some sort of bird medallion around his neck matched the boys' angelic golden hair. It was an affecting work. But it was hardly the reason for my presence there, and I had to move the conversation on.

'Have you seen this company before?' I enquired.

'I have not.'

'They are trying their best, aren't they?'

She snorted and walked away.

I remained sipping my drink and attempting friendly smiles at those around me. They were not reciprocated, and soon enough the bell tolled to send us back to our seats. The sallow man who had not been minded to chat to me had disappeared.

The second half of the show was in the vein of the first. The scene where the wicked King Richard decrees the murder of his innocent nephews – one of the most famous royal crimes in history – caused one of the supposedly heartless murderers to break down in a fit of tears or stage fright, and one of my fellow spectators to stand and complain loudly. 'Rubbish! Why must we sit through this nonsense? All false, all false!' he exclaimed before being pulled down and hushed by his companion.

I suspect that I groaned a little too audibly, for I noticed one of the other spectators look at me and grimace. I must defend myself, though: Shakespeare, too, would surely have been pained to see such a mockery. Had the original supposed assassins of the two brothers reacted in such a way, the princes would both have lived out their days in splendour, rather than smothered in their sleep and their corpses spirited away to be buried in secret as history recorded.

Finally, Richard's death, which should have been noble despite his wicked nature, was rendered little better than absurd by the prancing about of the Lancastrian soldiers, who took just a little too much joy in their parts.

For polite form's sake, I felt it necessary to clap when

the final curtain came down. Though I need not have been so worried: the rest of the audience was on its feet and crying in joy, as if they had seen Charles Warner and Ellen Terry giving the greatest performances of their lives. The dozen of them sounded like a hundred.

Chapter 6

From time to time, I get talking to some cove in a watering-hole. They don't know the half of who I am, but they can tell I'm no shrinking violet. Tough men, we know each other. And when talk turns to how we became the men we are, and when we first knew how we were going to turn out, I always tell 'em about the Eton–Winchester cricket match of '60. I'd fought my way up through that school with my fists and teeth. It had been a hard road – what, you think your church school with its miners' sons is a place of toughs? Well, ask yourself this: do they have a gun room there? Do they beat their fags with broom handles for arriving late in the morning? Do they run fourteen miles through sodden fields every Saturday in February? No.

So by the time I was cricket captain, there was no bleeding way I was going to let those pansies from Winchester beat us. But they had a weapon, and a good one: Giles McLean had been called up for Kent aged sixteen – and that was two years earlier. A fast bowler, they called him Express Train McLean. Well, I was going to make sure his wheels came off the tracks.

Luckily for me, my father was in the habit of visiting the same Covent Garden 'nunnery' as McLean and got to know his habits. My old man tipped me off when McLean was next expected to visit his favourite goose – a week before the match – and I and a couple of the boys from the first eleven went to pay him a visit 'mid-meal', if you know what I mean. I thought it was fitting that we used our bats. We enjoyed ourselves that night. Much more than he did.

He played again, did McLean, but not for a full year, and by that time the silver cup was sitting nice and snug in our trophy room.

You see, the guff about playing nicely has never sat well with me. I like to hold something up at the end of the day and say, 'I trapped this', or 'I took this from the kid brother of the Duke of Argyll. He was giving it lip in Boodles and now he'll hold his tongue.' The only people who don't mind losing are those who are used to it.

I see McLean from time to time in the clubs when I'm in London, and he's changed. There's a sort of glint in his looks that tells me he's not a pigeon anymore, he's a sharp jackanapes; and he knows my part in making him that way. So he bows his head a little and smiles as if to thank me. Yes, McLean's one of us now.

The Professor convened our hoods' get-together the day after the pagger between the Orchard gang and Calhoon's boys. It was a Monday evening, so the place was shut up, and the sun had set, meaning it was bloody gloomy. We plumped for the main stage as the better location, even though it was freezing.

Orchard and Calhoon had been allowed to bring one sergeant each and they were searched from head to foot as they came in. I had my Derringer in my pocket as Gawain checked them for weapons. He put the contents of their pockets to one side. No shooter or blade was coming into our drum unless it was mine. Calhoon and Orchard were under the guv'nor's protection.

So there we all sat, with the scenery of some naval battle floating above us on ropes, each of us ready to rip the throat out of anyone who looked a bit rum, until the guv'nor spoke. 'Gentlemen, I will be brief. This situation cannot continue. We all have businesses to run, and any friction between you will incur attention from the law, which could jeopardize my own plans. That is intolerable. I therefore propose myself as adjudicator in your dispute.'

'There's no dispute,' drawled Calhoon. His accent was just like a banker I once shot dead on a boat to Southampton. 'I'll be taking over all operations south of your River Thames. You try and stop me, Mr Orchard, and I'll mail your body back to your family.'

Now, give him his due, Orchard held his nerve and

forced a laugh. 'You so much as look at me hard, you colonial molly-boy, and I'll drop your family's bodies off at your hotel. You think you can come over to our patch with what – fifty blokes? And we're going to hand you the crown jewels? I'm going to be a generous man and write off what you did the other night. But here you are.' He reached inside his breast pocket, and I drew my shooter. 'No need, Colonel, no need.' He threw something across the table to Calhoon. 'Ticket for you. Back to New York. Steerage.'

Calhoon picked it up and read it. 'You know, my mom went over steerage. From Amsterdam. Me, I'm going back first class.' He tossed it back.

The guv'nor spoke again. 'You have both made your opening statements to insist upon your power of arms. Now we shall talk like men of business.' I knew he was already getting hot under the collar because his eyebrows were beetling about. That's when you know the danger is up. 'Orchard, I know Calhoon's numerical strength . . .'

'You sure 'bout that?' the American said.

The guv'nor doesn't take kindly to being doubted. He stared at Calhoon like he was going to tear his head off. 'Yesterday, you ate bread and eggs for breakfast at seven forty-five in Room 51 at the Savoy. You did not finish your tea. You read the *Daily Telegraph*, discarding it after a few pages, and took up the *Washington Post*. After that . . .'

'Yeah, I get the picture.'

'Do not make the same mistake again,' the Professor told Calhoon. He shook his head at me, and I uncocked the hammer on my pistol.

Calhoon didn't make the same mistake again. Instead, he and Orchard spent the next couple of hours arguing over territory and different games (girls, blags, strong-arm protection stuff) and threatening to rip each other apart. After a long while, it looked like they had the outline of an agreement. Of course, I would give it about a week before one was broken to pieces in the street and dumped off the nice new Albert Embankment, but that's what happens when you do business with hoods.

One of the boys came in.

'A telegram for Mr Calhoon,' he said, holding it up.

Calhoon opened and read it. 'You got a telephone here?' he asked.

'In the office,' the Professor told him. 'Directly above us. Up the stairs, second door on your left. If you go into any other room, my men will shoot you dead.'

'I'd expect nothin' else, Professor.'

His sergeant – a young Australian bushwhacker who looked pretty handy – stayed behind in the stalls as Calhoon left.

Gawain brought in some tea and set it in front of us.

'I wouldn't mind a real drink,' Orchard said.

'Be quiet,' the guv'nor replied. The Aussie grinned. The Professor didn't like that, either. 'I shall be in my rooms. I have something to attend to.'

He stood and left the room. The bushwhacker turned his attention to me, attempting to stare me down.

'Don't try that with me, laddie,' I said. 'I've vomited out more fearsome beasts than you.' At that, he jumped up out of his seat. I could see his strings were pretty tight. But before he could move, my Derringer was pointing right between his eyes.

'You know how to use that?' he growled.

'I could shoot your mother from here.'

Well, I'll give the bludger his due. He had stones. He kept coming at me. But before his second step landed, the sound of a gunshot was ringing around us all. If you've never heard one, it's like a tree breaking in two, and I love the sound. It runs right up and down my old spine like a cat. Nothing like it.

Only thing is: it wasn't my gun. Wherever the sound had come from, it wasn't even in the room, and before the echo stopped, I was footing it for the Professor's apartment, with Orchard, his batman and the bushwhacker at my heels.

Gawain was in the lobby with his hot rod ready. Now, I knew that lad well, but we had just heard a shot and didn't know where it was from, so I still put my barrel on him.

'No need to level at me, Colonel,' he whispered. I never mentioned, did I? But he always spoke in a whisper, that boy. 'I was nowhere near. I heard something fall up there.' He pointed up the stairs, which led to a little landing with two doors. One was for the office and stood closed; the other was for the Professor's rooms and was open. 'I saw the American go into the office.'

'But did he come out again?' It was the guv'nor's voice, and a second later he appeared in the doorway to his apartment.

I stalked to the office door. But I wasn't going to risk

any of that 'Hello? Is there anybody in there?' malarky. Best way to get a bullet right through the wood and into your gut, that. So I kicked it in and dropped straight to my knee, with the barrel up.

I needn't have bothered, because the room measured about ten feet square, with a big desk at one end covered in ticket stubs and papers; a dying fire in the grate, and the walls covered with calendars and play bills; and there was one man in that room, but he wasn't any danger to anyone now, because his brains were spattered right across the wall like he was trying to decorate it.

Aye, Dutch Calhoon was lying in the middle of the room, curled up like a kid. About half his head was there, while the other half had been blasted clean off.

There was no mystery where the shot had come from, because there was a big Webley revolver on the floor in front of him. I picked it up. It was hot – it had just been fired, no doubt about that, and the cylinder had five bullets left, all manstoppers. I do like those bullets. No messing about with a big manstopper.

Well, a man's just another animal, so I don't mind seeing one dead. But I did think it would be a job to get the brains off the wall.

'Well, well,' the Professor said from behind us. 'I think our little agreement might be void.'

'You saw him come in here?' I asked Gawain.

'Him. No one else. I'll swear to that.'

'And no one came out,' the Professor added. 'I had a line of sight from where I sat.'

There was no one else in the room now, either. The

casement window was open, and I went to it. Being a music hall, the upper floor was very high from the ground – I'd say thirty feet. It was a sheer drop down to the pavement of a quiet dead-end lane that gave out onto Whitechapel High Street. There was only the back door to a tobacconist's on the other side of the lane. Now, a man couldn't climb down the bare wall, but a clever one could get down if he used a rope. And instead of tying it to something in the room, if he looped it around something solid, walked himself backwards down the bricks holding both strands at the same time and then drew one strand with him when he touched the pavement, there'd be no evidence. I've seen it done. The chap has to be damned strong, though, and precious lively, because balancing yourself across two strands of rope is a real tumbler's trick.

But I took a hard look at the room – there was nothing the rope could have been looped around that I could see: no solid column holding up the ceiling; the chairs were too light to bear even a kid's weight; the desk might possibly have done, but it was flush to the far wall and its feet weren't exposed.

I looked up. The roof was a good ten feet above the window, and I thought it just possible that if they had one man on the roof to drop down a rope, a quick man inside the room could shin up it.

Shorty Harlow was outside. There was a window above him on the upper storey of the tobacconist's, not much bigger than a postage stamp.

I whistled to him. 'Anyone come out here?' I shouted down.

'Colonel?'

'Out the window. Has anyone come out?' He shook his head. He was a thick oaf but wasn't blind. A two-man team with ropes and a grappling hook would have caught his eye. 'Did you see anything?'

'Nah.' I stared upwards again. 'Only the bloke inside openin' the winder.'

'What bloke?'

'The one as come t'see the Professor.'

Calhoon, that was. 'Did he say anything?'

'No, guv.'

'How did he look?'

'Look?'

'The expression on his face, you cretin!' He shrugged. 'Did you hear a shot?'

'Yeah. 'Bout a minute after the bloke went back inside.'

'Did you see anything?'

'Only a bird flying about. Blackbird, I think.'

'Close the window,' the Professor instructed me. 'Let me take a look at it.' I did what he said, and he looked at the frame. 'I see. Open it again. Now close it.' I did so. 'Do you notice that?'

I looked closely at the frame. It was a common casement, opening outwards, about three feet square, painted white. The paint was flaking and the pane needed a good clean. Apart from that, nothing. 'I can't see anything, Professor.'

'Not see. Smell.' I sniffed like a lioness testing the air. 'There's something bad in the air. When the window is open, you don't notice it, but close off the fresh air – well, what passes for fresh in this stinking town – and you can't help but smell it.'

I sniffed again. And this time I did detect something. 'What is that?' I asked.

'I do not know. Yet.'

'What does it matter?' Orchard said. 'He blew his brains out. Saves us all a lot of trouble.' I haven't heard a man sound so satisfied since the time Madagascar Jack Holness visited a bordello, found it was run by his mother and got one on the house.

'Perhaps, Mr Orchard. Moran, pull the bullet out, will you?'

'The bullet?'

'Yes,' he said. 'Do you need me to ask again?'

I looked down at what had been Dutch Calhoon. 'I'll have a look for it.'

'Get on with it.'

I prodded the body with my toe. The remaining bit of his head lolled and some more spongy grey brain stuff fell out. They'd need to change that rug. I had to get down on my knees to have a good root about inside his skull. Getting your fingers sticky is part of hunting, but brain is a devil to get out of your cuffs. 'Ah!' I said, as my fingers found something metal. I pulled it out, wiped it off and there it was. 'It's a manstopper,' I said.

'A what?' the bushwhacker asked.

The Professor answered him. 'A bullet. A Mark III .455 Webley bullet, to be precise. It is a hollowpoint round, so that the bullet flattens as it enters the corpus, thus destroying more bodily matter. Hence . . .' He pointed to the wide distribution of Calhoon's brain. 'What bullets does the gun hold?'

I showed him. 'Manstoppers. Identical.'

'Well, I think there is little doubt that this was the gun that killed your master,' he said to the Aussie bludger. 'Is it his?'

'I haven't seen it before.' The shock had worn off and the man was looking angry.

'It would have been hard to smuggle it past Moran when he came in. Not impossible, of course.' I bristled at that, I'll tell you. 'But it is likely he acquired it inside the building. No one could have come in or out, or my men would—'

'I don't want any more of your excuses!' snapped the bushwhacker. 'I'm—'

'As I was saying,' the Professor snarled back, 'no one could have come in or out, or my men would have seen them. And my men are loyal to the very last.' That's true, because any bribes or threats used to get our boys to betray the Professor could never stand up to the severity of the punishment he would mete out to them in return. 'Now, it would be quite impossible for anyone to leave the room without being seen by me, so let us exclude any other possibility. Hmm,' he muttered, 'it's a brutish explanation, but worth examining: Moran, pull up the carpet.' I saw his reasoning and set about it. We had the carpet shredded in no time. No trapdoors, and the floorboards were securely nailed down. 'To be expected. Now, for the sake of thoroughness, the walls and ceiling. Get on with it, we don't have all day.' And we went about the room bashing through the plaster. No hidden doors or cubby holes. For good luck, we smashed up the desk. Nothing.

'He shot himself. You said yourself – no one's been in or out. So it couldn't be anything else,' Orchard piped up. 'Come on, the sport's over. I want to eat.'

'Be quiet.' And the guv'nor's hands went to his temples. He stared out the window like the answer was written on the tobacconist's wall. I could see his brain racing. And then his hands dropped to his sides. 'Ah yes,' he said. And I knew he had it. You can't pull the wool over his eyes for very long. 'Yes, I see. I must congratulate you, Orchard.'

'What?' the cove spluttered. 'Congratulate why?'

'A most ingenious stratagem. And truly, what is most ingenious of all is how deceptively simple it is. Your cerebral development is far beyond my initial assessment of it.'

'I had nothing to do with this, Moriarty!'

'No, no, I'm sure he just took it upon himself to blow his own head open on a whim.'

'I am leaving!' Calhoon's man yelled. And he spun around to march out.

Orchard and his man barred the bushwhacker's way. 'You're staying,' Orchard said in a low voice.

'Get out of my way. Or you'll regret it.'

I could see them all mentally itching for their irons. As it was, the bushwhacker was outnumbered, but he looked like he was ready to take on four fists against his two.

'Moran,' the guv'nor ordered.

I knew what he meant. Right then, the situation was contained, under his control. If the Aussie went rabbit, it was going to be a free-for-all. I went to put my hands on him.

But he knew what he was about, this bushwhacker. And I don't know if it was from shearing all those sheep, but he was a damned sight stronger and more agile than he looked. I hadn't taken so much as a single pace towards him before he had grabbed Orchard's sergeant and thrown him straight at me, like he was tossing a bale of hay. I took the bloke straight in the fizzog, and down we both went. But then my barker was in my hand. I wasn't shooting manstoppers, but the .38s I had loaded that morning would do just fine.

And yet the Aussie was so fleet that my first bullet couldn't mark him. By the time the second was out, he was halfway along the landing and jinking like a scrum half. At the third, he was over the banister. The fourth, and I was out on the landing while he was touching down on the ground floor. The fifth, and he ducked with the luck of the Irish just when my round would have put him six feet under. One left. One left for Colonel Sebastian Moran, the finest big game hunter the Empire has bred in a hundred years. I stood, steadied, breathed and fired. And I hit home, square in his gut. It was enough to drop any civilized man. But civilization hadn't touched the bushwhacker, and he felt at the red on his shirt, looked at his hand, laughed, saluted me and dashed off.

Sodding Australians. We should feed 'em all to those weird tree-bears they have.

'You disappoint me, Moran.'

'I'm sorry, Professor.'

'Well, there is nothing to be done.'

'What will happen now?'

'I expect there will be a council of the Calhoon gang, during which Calhoon's younger brother, Jan, will declare war on Orchard in revenge.'

'It wasn't me,' that cove insisted.

'No?' He paused, considered, then shrugged. 'It matters not either way. Jan Calhoon will – not unreasonably, you must admit – believe that it was. In the grand tradition of the American gangs, he will therefore most likely vow that you will not live out twenty-four hours.' I looked at Orchard. He had a grim look on his mug. 'I would advise you therefore to convene your own council of war.'

'And what will you do?' Orchard demanded.

'Do? I think I shall take supper at Rules, since you ask. I wish you good day.'

And that was the end. Orchard bared his teeth and turned tail. He had preparations to make. Dutch Calhoon had been recruiting pretty quick, by the looks of things, so little Jan might be able to field a decent platoon.

'Who do you think will come out on top?' I asked.

'Orchard has what sportsmen call "the home advantage", but I am aware that the Calhoon gang brings a certain colonial ferocity to its actions. I would therefore suggest equal odds. A pity, since I had preferred not to have a war that will undoubtedly attract the attention of Scotland Yard, but I feel it is now inevitable. And so, to Rules, Moran.'

Chapter 7

George and I had arranged that after the play was over, I would join him 'backstage' and he would present me as his uncle, a lover of the theatre who would reside in Cambridge for the next few nights and watch the play each evening.

I duly found my way to the stage door. Young Reynolds appeared and drew me into the depth of the building. I had never seen the workings of a real theatre and I rather enjoyed it. We passed the stage itself and the ropes, flies, scenery flats and prop boxes were fascinating to see up close.

His face was exhilarated as he took me through to what he told me was the 'green room' – the place where the actors relax and wait. It was a Bohemian-looking affair, with sophas and armchairs cast off from a handful of plays spanning Renaissance, Victorian, Roman and Fairyland in style. The decorations on the wall were similarly eclectic: oils of hunting scenes, *papier mâché* vines and creepers; a wooden executioner's axe. Among all this were the acting company, most of them with small glasses in their hands.

'Everyone, this is my Uncle John,' Reynolds announced as we entered. The conversation died out and there were more than a few blinks from those assembled.

'Your . . . uncle?' one man responded. He was about my own age, and there was something quite sprightly about him, despite his rotund stomach.

'Yes, my mother's brother. This is our director, Mr Bart.'

'Edgar Bart,' he said, shaking my hand with some uncertainty.

'John Watson.'

'I didn't know Mr Reynolds had an uncle.' My brow must have furrowed at such a strange comment. 'But then why would I?' he continued, clearly having noted the reaction. 'Do come in, Mr Watson.'

I did not correct him. There is an advantage to the anonymity afforded by a common name. While 'Sherlock Holmes' would be recognized by many whom we would rather not recognize it, my own is far less likely to have similar results. No need for a false moniker when you are John Watson.

'Uncle John will come to the next couple of shows.'

'Well, that's very good,' Bart replied. And he smiled, but the smile was only on his lips. The tell-tale skin at the corners of his eyes remained unwrinkled. No, this was not a man who thought my presence 'very good'. 'You were on the stage yourself, Mr Watson?'

'Oh no,' I chuckled. 'I was in the army.'

'Ah! A soldier.' At that, his face genuinely shone.

'You were also in service of the Crown?'

'Not in the same way. No, we all serve in some way, of course – apart from those who shirk their duty – but no, my bent has been towards books and history.'

'And the theatre,' added our young client.

'Indeed, yes. Though the history books will always be my first love, as they say.' He had, I must say, a pleasant way about him when he was more relaxed. Not prepossessing, not burning with what you might call 'charisma' – but now that we were on a subject that pleased him, he was good company. 'And may I introduce you to my daughter, Devi.' A handsome girl with waist-length dark hair, whom I recognized as having played the hapless Queen Anne doomed to marry her husband's killer, was handing out glasses of Moselle wine. I said hello, and she returned the greeting before continuing her rounds. 'Do you have children yourself?'

Well, such questions can take me off-guard. For the truth is that even though Providence was kind to me and gave me my Mary, albeit for such a painfully brief time, we were never blessed with the sound of small feet on the staircase, and it is too late for me now. So I told Bart that no, I had no children, and swallowed down my sad contemplations. It was not the time. And no, this is not the place for such . . . No.

Bart and I chatted about this and that. After a while, I began to notice something – Holmes often berates me for my lack of attention, but in this case I am certain he could have done no better, if only because affairs of the heart pass over his head in their entirety. For at one point, the girl Devi offered young George a glass of wine. But it was not the words she spoke when she did so that struck me – it was the way her hand reached out to his arm, then hesitated in mid-air and retreated, self-consciously. And the way George glanced down towards her hand and almost reached out to take it. *Oho*, I thought to myself. And I fought back a smile while I tried to concentrate on Bart's description of the joy of reading Tudor English history.

In due course, the man moved on to talk to others, and young George discreetly took me aside.

'What do you think?' he asked.

'I think for certain that you are a better actor than the others.'

'Well, I don't want to boast, but as I said, yes, that's one of the things that seems so queer about the whole affair. Also, there was hell to pay when I turned up yesterday evening after being in London. Half of them demanded – positively demanded – to know where I had been. I told them that they are not my keepers and I had been to London to visit you because you are quite frail.' I raised an eyebrow. 'I apologize. You are in excellent form for a man your age, I am sure.'

'And a man of my age has seen much of the world,' I

admonished him. 'Including signs of love-sickness in a girl. And Queen Anne is displaying them if you ask me.'

He looked sheepish. 'That's something I didn't tell you. I probably should have.'

'Indeed you should. Holmes and I need to know every aspect.'

'Devi and I have taken pains to hide it from the rest of the company, so I suppose it has become second nature to stay mum.'

'There can be no more secrets from myself and Holmes. They undermine our work.'

'I apologize.'

I could not really blame him. He was a handsome young chap, no doubt excited by his career on the stage, and she was a fine-looking girl. No born actress, from what I had seen of her, but in fact not as dire as the rest of them.

The girl came over to us and we chatted briefly before George was called over to speak to others who seemed to hang upon his every word.

'He has told me about you,' I said quietly.

'What about me?' she blurted out.

I paused. Her reaction suggested something unspoken and – to me, as yet – quite unknown. 'About how you and he have formed an attachment.'

'Oh. That.' And she softened. 'Yes, I think we have.' Now that she was speaking more slowly, I detected a Norfolk accent. It was deep and pleasing to my ear as I usually hear only London voices. She screwed up her lips. 'Are you really his uncle?' I tried to form a reply, to reinforce the falsehood, but before I could she spoke again, more urgently. 'I think you are someone else. Someone who can help.'

I was struck dumb for a moment before I could recover the power of speech. I motioned that we should retire to a corner of the room where we could not be overheard. 'My dear, it doesn't matter if I am George's uncle or not. I am a friend, and I can indeed help you.'

She hesitated. 'So who are you?'

'My name truly is John Watson. But you are correct to doubt that there is a family connection. I work with a gentleman of whom you may know. Sherlock Holmes.'

The girl reacted strongly – but it was not quite the reaction I was expecting. She looked perfectly aghast. 'The detective?'

'That is him.'

She stared down at a table. It was covered in little blotches of spilled drink. 'Then you know all. The Silent Conspiracy.'

I lowered my head so that I could look her in the eye. 'My dear, we know nothing. We are waiting for you to let us in on the game. What conspiracy?'

She lifted her chin and licked her lips, ready, I am certain, to speak. But as she opened her mouth to spill it all, her father clapped his hands to gain everyone's attention.

'Everybody, we have an announcement,' he said. 'We are all aware how honoured we are to have George Reynolds join our company.' I noted that the assembled masses absolutely beamed at the young man then. Rather unnaturally, I thought. 'And we have a gift for him.' I was a little surprised that the present in question seemed to be a rather plain-looking wooden box. It was square, each side measuring about a foot, and six inches deep and had what looked to be some sort of carving on the sides: lines curved from the top to the bottom. It seemed to be teak and was very old, for the wood was dull and cracked here and there. But the veneration that the whole company seemed to pay to this item was extraordinary; one might imagine it to be the Ark of the Covenant, their eyes opened so widely.

For his part, George looked bemused and self-consciously took the item with a polite bow that was reciprocated more deeply by all the men in the room and echoed by bobbing curtseys from the women. George stammered a few words of thanks and shuffled back to me and Devi. Bart came with him.

'Thank you for the box,' George said as he opened it. 'And what's this? Costume jewellery?' He lifted out some pieces of gaudily painted wooden chain.

'I do hope you like it,' Bart said with a smile. And he took his daughter away to talk to others across the room.

'Like it? It's tat,' George muttered to me. And checking over his shoulder to see that none were watching, he stowed it under a rail of costumes.

It was a strange evening altogether, but soon over, as there was to be a matinee performance the next day, which I promised to attend, and we all retired to our digs or hotels for the night.

I was not looking forward to seeing the play for a second time.

Chapter 8

We had good belly-timber at Rules. Over the brandies and cigars, the Professor sent out for the evening newspapers to see who was dead: Orchard or Jan Calhoon.

'Will you explain how Orchard managed to knock off the Yankee?' I asked. I had been waiting all through the meal, but he had made no sign of speaking up.

'Hmm? You mean you don't know? Rather obvious, is it not? Think of the strange smell in the room.'

I thought back to it. There had been a whiff of something nasty, that was sure as shooting. 'I don't see the relevance.'

'It would be better that I demonstrate, but that will have to wait until retail business hours.' He picked up his newspaper again. 'Do you ever feel like a wolf living among sheep, Moran?'

'All the time, Professor. I—'

I didn't get to finish what I was saying because at that second something smashed down onto the table, sending the glasses flying and knocking the lit candelabra to the floor. It was young Gawain, and it didn't take a medic to see that the boy had a nasty gash in his neck that was leaking claret all over the place. The couple at the next table – some viscount and the cock-chafer he had hired for the night – started yelling like it was their dinner that had been broken up, not ours. The guv'nor simply moved his chair back from the table and watched as I pressed a napkin to the wound on the boy's throat. The maître d'hôtel and a squad of waiters ran over, but I gave them a look that told them to back off or they'd be next.

'What happened, lad?' I asked. He lifted his eyes to me and tried to speak. 'Take your time.'

The cottontail at the next table was still bleating. I told her to shut up or I'd shut her up myself. That did the trick.

'Cal ... hoon,' Gawain mumbled. 'Forty of them. Max ... Maxim guns.'

Maxims. Those American Johnnies weren't messing around. The Maxim – what they were calling a 'machine gun' – could wipe out a whole platoon in under a minute.

'What about our boys?'

'All ... dead.'

And at that, he joined them. Poor wee bastard.

Well, with all our men lying in a pool of their own ruby back in the music hall, we weren't looking strong.

'What shall we do?' I asked.

'We shall leave, Moran. The maître d'hôtel will add the bill to my account.' That bloke was cowering in a corner behind some of his patrons. He wasn't going to argue about an unpaid chit. 'Then we shall retire to a safe location I keep in reserve. In time, we will continue with my interrogation of the scene of the event, so that I may make sure that it occurred in the way that I currently hypothesize. Jan Calhoon clearly blames us for his brother's death, and I would say that our survival is therefore predicated on understanding the truth of this matter.'

Chapter 9

I spent the following morning pleasantly strolling in the grounds of some of Cambridge's colleges. It does a fellow's heart good to see young people so full of life. Of course, those who had spent a little too long in the city's famous inns the previous night looked more like death, but when can one over-indulge the Bacchanalian instincts if not when one is young and free?

At two o'clock, I trundled along to the theatre for the matinee. It looked no more impressive by daylight. I was about to walk in when a dirt-encrusted vagrant with a mop of white hair burst out of the building and grabbed hold of my jacket lapel. 'Let go!' I demanded, raising my stick ready to strike him.

'For God's sake, Watson, this is not the time!' Holmes snapped back at me, tearing off his wig. 'Our client has been abducted; I will swear to it. The company has gone – their digs have been cleaned out, except for Reynolds's, which is full of his belongings. He did not go willingly.'

He dragged me into the empty building. It smelled musty, and dust swam in the air. The stage, which had been full of sound and life, now seemed eerily vacant as we went back to the dressing rooms – there were all the wooden swords, the banqueting tables, the cheap, faded costumes that would not be worn that day. And something else, tucked away in a corner.

'It is the box they gave George,' I said, pointing to it.

'A gift? Interesting.' He made a beeline for the item and held it to the sunlight.

As I gazed at the dull wooden case, the carving on it that I had noticed the previous night now began to take form and shape. Yes, the lid had the imprint of a copse of trees, most branches spreading up and out from a single sturdy trunk at the centre – its roots forming the curving lines down the side of the box, as if planting themselves into the ground. A few smaller trees appeared around it, their branches entwining with the first. Among them was a medieval-looking church with a square tower that was topped with crenellations like a fort.

'An elegant object once,' Holmes muttered as he ran his fingers along the wood.

'No doubt.'

'And it appears that . . .' He peered closely. 'Yes, there has been some erasure.'

'What do you mean?' I asked.

'In places – look here, for example.' He pointed to a patch on the lid. 'You can make out the outline of a circle, enclosing the faintest relic of some sort of image or symbol.' He bent low. 'No, sadly it is impossible to say what was here.'

'Has someone deliberately obscured it?'

'Possibly, but the ravages of time are at least as likely a culprit. Well, so much for the box. Let us now see the contents.'

The lid was secured with a simple brass catch. Holmes checked the metalwork. 'Fairly ornate without being ostentatious. Eighteenth century, I should guess.' He lifted it. 'Not stiff, oiled in recent times, so we can conclude that some recent owner has been interested in the contents sufficiently to grease the catch.' And then, with both hands, he gently prised up the lid.

Inside, there was only the costume jewellery at which George had turned his nose up the previous evening: a neck-chain made of wooden links and a similarly wooden pendant of what seemed to be a goose, all painted yellow in a rough approximation of gold. The paint was flaking away in patches.

'It must be for his costume,' I said.

'Costume, perhaps, Watson. But not his; it is far too small to go around his neck. No,' he added thoughtfully, 'I wonder if the connection to the play is not quite the one that you have in mind. It is most likely the original. Quite the gift, really.'

He tossed the wooden chain back whence it had come and gathered up the box. 'Come, there is more to learn from this simple item.'

'Where to?'

'Where? Why, to Baker Street, of course.'

We returned to my hotel to collect my effects. 'Why didn't you tell me you were coming up?' I asked as I threw everything into a valise.

'I must apologize, old man. It was a spur of the moment decision.'

'Spur of the moment!' I grumbled.

'Halloa,' Holmes said, and he pulled open the door to reveal a child in the uniform of a telegram boy, who had been about to knock.

'Mr Holmes, sir?'

'I am he.'

The boy tapped his cap and handed over a telegram envelope, before dashing off. Holmes tore the message open. I saw curiosity sweep across his face. 'How very interesting,' he said to himself.

'Holmes?'

'Read it yourself.'

I took the message, emblazoned with the legend 'Cambridgeshire Telegraph Company', from him. Neatly printed were the words: 'Do not fear Moriarty. Soon you will need him. Compose yourself.'

My jaw almost dropped.

'Steady, Watson. Yes, yes, I know. Is Moriarty wound up in this business? If so, I have seen no hint of his terrible genius. If not, what could we possibly need him for? And who has us under such close observation that he knew I would be here to receive a telegram?'

'Is it not from that murderer himself?'

'He would not, I think, refer to himself in the mysterious third person. And he has never been shy, so why contact me in this strange and indirect way?' He paused. 'No, I think there is another who has a stake in these proceedings but chooses to remain for now in the shadows.'

At that, we left the hotel and resumed our journey. In the train carriage, he sat puffing on his pipe – he had brought the big meerschaum – and pondering. But all the way I was – yes, I will admit it – I was worried. Moriarty was no benign presence in our or anyone else's life. We had tangled with him directly on one occasion and indirectly on I knew not how many. The man was the Napoleon of crime, directing so much evil from the shadows while presenting to the world the innocent face of a retiring tutor in mathematics. I have no shame in admitting that when we had gone up against him, our lives had hung in the balance. Holmes had sworn to one day place Moriarty in the dock, and I knew that sooner or later it would be him or us.

The telegram exhorted us not to fear Professor James Moriarty, but how could we not, when his very presence was poisonous to anyone with an ounce of humanity?

Chapter 10

We had spent the night above some Eye-tie's shop just off Hatton Garden. I've had worse billets, and the little Sicilian woman brought us good strong coffee in the morning. After that, we washed and headed back to the music hall.

I scouted the location, of course, leaving the Professor in some tea room. It was dark and raining, but there were still a number of coppers milling about and a gaggle of onlookers, a couple of press-men, too, all pointing at bullet holes in the brickwork like they had found the bleeding Holy Grail. It must have been pretty badly shot up inside.

But it turned out it wasn't the music hall itself that the Professor wanted to visit. It was the tobacconist's next door. I made a polite request to the Russian Jew running the place, who shrugged and said if the gentleman wanted to take a look at his upstairs room, why not? So I went to collect the guv'nor and we were up there, staring out a window not much bigger than a cat at the last window Dutch Calhoon had ever opened, twelve yards across the alley and a little below us.

'Yes, all falls into place,' the Professor said.

'Will you tell me?'

'In good time. We must inform someone else, too. Send for Jan Calhoon. Tell him to meet us in there.' He pointed with his cane. 'In the main hall. With luck, it has been cleared of all the bodies by now, or the stench will be intolerable. Tell him to meet us at five precisely so we can recreate the conditions of his brother's death. You will be unarmed.'

'Unarmed?'

'Unarmed. After I reveal the truth to him, he will no longer try to end my life. And in the meantime, we needs must see an ironmonger. And then a trip to the post office telegram counter.'

I dispatched a street urchin to the Savoy, where the Calhoons had been holed up while they were in England. I sent the Professor's compliments and said we could tell Jan the truth about how his brother was killed. We wouldn't be packing hot rods, so he should meet us in the main hall at five with just two of his men. They could be armed. His other men, those friendly types with the Maxims, would have to wait out in the street.

The urchin – Anderley is his name, and I've used him a few times in the past, he's not as stupid as most – came back with an answer that agreed to the parley but threatened death if we put a foot out of step.

A truly hard man doesn't need to make any threats.

And so the stage was set. The floor of the auditorium was still covered in dried blood and brains from our lads, and the walls had more pock-marks than a Limehouse tart, but at least the bodies had been carted off. A few corpses here and there don't scare me, but they do go off damned quickly, so you're holding your kerchief over your nose for fear of chucking up. The stage had been shot up, too, and the farmyard set marked the spot where several of our little lambs had been slaughtered.

It was eerie in that building. Bullet holes everywhere and the smell of blood and black powder. The smell of a good fight. And echoes through it all from the street outside. I'd taken a sniff about, just in case there were any nasty little surprises waiting for us, but not a dicky bird.

As my wristwatch said it was five exactly, Jan Calhoon came through the wreckage of what used to be the doors.

'Jesus above. You people. You live like pigs.' He drawled like a peasant but was acting big, trying to make it look like he was his own boy, not just his brother's understudy.

'A drink, Calhoon? Moran will make one for you.'

'Like pigs.' He spat on the floor. It mixed in with some blood that was still red and sticky. 'No drink.'

'Then if you will follow me.'

'Not so fast!' Calhoon yelled. And the Australian bush-whacker and another little chum, shorter but solid as a boiler, a Fijian, I'd bet, made their way over and patted us down, as thorough as you like.

'They're not carrying,' the bushwhacker said.

'Just as well for you,' Calhoon blurted out.

'Spare us the theatrics, Calhoon. This may be the place for it, but we are hardly the audience. Now, if you will come this way, I shall explain how your brother was shot dead, although I had no involvement.'

'Get moving.'

Now, I've met some hard men in my time. And I've met some loud men in my time. And they were rarely the same men. This barking little mutt needed drowning in a sack. But we led the way up the stairs to the office. Calhoon's men were directly behind us with their barkers in their hands.

We got to the office. It was a floor above the auditorium that had been raked by the Maxims, and the foot platoon Calhoon had sent in to finish the job had barely touched it, so it was just as we had left it after Dutch had been snuffed.

The guv'nor went in first and stood with his back to the window. 'Come in, come in,' he said.

'I'll come if I want to.' The Yank entered and the two lunks stood guard over us all.

'Now, to business. In the past eighteen hours, you have killed a dozen of my men and, I would presume, even more of Orchard's family and gang.'

'He was—'

The Professor held up his hand to stop the American's mouth. 'I don't care what he was. He is dead. That is the point.' Calhoon shrugged. 'Precisely. And the reason he is dead is that your brother was also forcibly removed from this world.'

'Forcibly . . .? Talk like that, and I'll be doing the same to you.'

The guv'nor just sighed. 'Yes, yes, I've heard it all before. "Kill this, torture that." You must understand that I am consulted every day by persons of your industry and rank. They afford me respect because they are aware that I can do everything they can, only with far greater imagination, scope and efficiency. So please keep a fetter on your tongue. I assure you, I will release it soon enough.' Calhoon looked ready to blow his top, but the Professor continued. 'Now to explain how your brother died. We found him in this office with his brains spattered about the place. No one had gone in or out of the room after him; and no one went in or out of the window, or Shorty would have seen them. In addition, Dutch had a gun by his hand that seemed to be the weapon that killed him.'

'"Seemed?" You mean it wasn't the rod?'

'Oh no, it certainly was that gun. That was the beauty of it. But if you stop interrupting, we shall get to the point. Your brother had come to discuss with me and Orchard how we could come to a mutually beneficial arrangement. During the proceedings, a telegram arrived for him. He immediately asked to use a telephone, so we can surmise that the telegram either requested that he make a call or gave him some information that meant he wanted to make that call. I do not believe it matters which.'

'Get to the point!' The Yankee had no patience. And

no patience makes a bad soldier – a soldier who blunders into things he can't handle.

'He then made the same journey that we made, up the stairs to this office. Very soon after, we all heard the shot and rushed in to find him dead.'

'Are you saying my brother killed himself? Because if you are, I'm gonna—'

'Oh no, your brother was murdered. No doubt about it.'

'But how, for crying out loud, if that was the gun and there was no one in here?'

'The key to it is the odour that I noticed inside the room.'

'Odour?'

'It was the odour of *sal ammoniac*. An especially unpleasant smell.' He took out his kerchief and polished the silver tip to his cane, before replacing the wiper. 'But what is interesting about it is how it got into the room. Because I am not in the habit of releasing such unpleasant fumes in my office.'

'So spill.'

'Your brother brought it in.'

'Why the hell's he gonna do that?'

'He did not realize that that was what he was doing. This afternoon, I paid a visit to the local post office. I have a connection with the postmaster: I once aided him in a little contretemps with a priest of the Greek Orthodox tradition. He checked his records, and no telegram had been dispatched to this address, or indeed any address, for a Mr Calhoon.'

'It was a dummy?'

'Not just a dummy, but a dummy impregnated with *sal ammoniac*. And I have no doubt that the telegram instructed your brother to burn it after reading.' I remembered there had been some embers in the grate. 'The horrendous smell motivated your brother to open the window. Did it not seem strange that, on a winter's evening, he had the window open? Well, the fumes gave him little choice.'

'What then?' Calhoon demanded.

'Then? Why, then the killer shot him.' And he pointed with his cane to the window of the tobacconist's where we had stood a few hours earlier. 'Not the easiest shot, angled down like that, but a skilled marksman such as Moran could do it without too much trouble.' He was right. At twelve yards, I could have picked off a mouse. And manstoppers were just the thing for the job.

'But the gun. It was by his hand.'

'You,' the guv'nor ordered the bushwhacker. 'Lie down there. On your back. That's where his body was.' The Aussie grimaced.

'Just do it,' Calhoon told him.

The man did as he was told, sliding his gun carefully into an armpit holster – but he made sure we saw the retaining strap was unbuckled so he could get to it any time. The Professor walked around the desk so that he was facing the tobacconist's shop. He had Calhoon's other man, the Fijian, to his side, and waved his cane.

At the signal, Anderley appeared at the tobacconist's window and pushed the end of a long, pencil-thin iron rod that we had bought at the ironmongers out towards us. It reached about halfway between the two buildings.

'What's th—'

'Just wait.' Anderley screwed the second section of the rod into the first, so that it poked right into our room. The tip touched down about two feet from the Australian's palm, right beside my ankle. 'Now, you recall the black bird that Shorty saw flying that night.' He waved his cane again, and Anderley carried out his second duty. He produced the big Webley, threaded his end of the steel rod through the revolver's trigger guard and let it go.

The gun rattled at speed down the metal, coming to a stop with a thump just out of reach of the bushwhacker. Now, I can tell when an animal suddenly twigs that he's walked full square into a trap. And that Australian's face was full of it. The guv'nor pulled the blade out of his cane and stabbed the Fijian sharp in the gut. At the same moment, I grabbed the Webley and let the Aussie have two chambers. I don't care how strong a man is, two manstoppers to the chest from a yard away will end him. I put two more in the Fijian, who was wrestling with the Professor. And down he went.

And then there were three: me, the Professor and Jan Calhoon.

'I'll pay you fifty—' he whispered.

And then it was just me and Professor Moriarty.

Chapter 11

It took us four hours to regain our comfortable lodgings. The redoubtable Mrs Hudson fussed and clucked over us and provided boiled eggs and toast with hot tea to keep out the chill. After our repast, which was amiably followed by brandies to further inure us to the weather, I opened a novel. I wanted something to take my mind from the subject that had gripped it for the previous few days. Holmes, however, could never relax. He spent two more hours chugging away at his pipe and staring into space. Just as I was reaching an amusing chapter where the hero of my novel had become unintentionally engaged to an Arab princess, Holmes leapt out of his seat as if he had been stung.

'Yes, of course!' he yelled. 'Oh, Watson, how simple it all is. But how to test the theorem? Ah, but that, too, is elementary. We need the lid of the box.' He rushed into his bedroom, where he had laid the cracked old box, and, without a single thought, swept a jumble of textbooks, glass phials, beaker stands and the like from the table where he did his chemical experiments, replacing them with the wooden item. He plucked up a magnifying glass and slowly bowed his head down to the lid, examining it from no more than half an inch above the surface. 'Yes, yes. A schoolboy could do it.' And he opened at once all the drawers in the table, pulling out an assortment of bottles, before selecting one full of a silvery liquid. This he liberally sprinkled over the lid. 'And now,' he checked his pocket watch, 'an hour for the reagent to do its work.'

That hour felt like ten, as Holmes paced up and down the flat, one minute pulling a book of British history from the shelf, only to hurl it across the room, the next taking up his violin and screeching out four bars of God-knows-what before throwing it down on the sopha. 'Careful, old man. Stradivarius,' I admonished him, but he did not hear a word. His nervous energy was enough to drive a train to Brighton. I gave up and watched him pace, fillet the news-paper without reading a word of it and simply stand at the window, scowling at passers-by because they were not the hour hand of the clock ticking onto the number nine.

Finally, that timepiece did its work, and Holmes cried a wild 'Hurrah!' He rushed back to the wooden box armed with a small lump of charcoal from the grate and a sheet of foolscap paper. 'We have both been schoolboys rubbing brasses in the local church, Watson; well, finally it pays off.' And he smoothed the paper down on the surface of the lid and rubbed the charcoal back and forth across it, focusing on certain points on the paper that I could not identify. In less than a minute, he stood bolt upright, tossed the charcoal over his shoulder and took the paper to the gas lamp, where he once again stared at it through the magnification glass.

'It works, Watson.'

'What have you found?' I asked, finally summoning up the courage to approach him.

'Here, you see? Those little circles on the lid. What they contained was written language. Names, to be precise. The chemical I dropped onto the wood made it swell, reversing the centuries of dry contraction that had led to a thousand cracks. It made the letters legible once more when reversed onto this paper. For sure, these names lay the case wide open!'

I stared through the lens and, as he had assured me, could just about make out small sequences of letters in half a dozen of the circles – the other little discs had been too far destroyed by the years to leave anything identifiable. Most of the circles just had the odd letter legible, but a few had full names: Thomas, Phoebe, Sabine, Jacob.

'Who are these people? Are they important?' I asked, still examining the paper.

Holmes seized me by the shoulders. 'You mean you cannot tell? Surely ... No, no, I see you are not feigning. Well, my old friend, these names signify no less than—'

But he was interrupted by a knock on the door,

presaging the entry of Mrs Hudson with an irritated air about her.

'Mr Holmes, I tried telling the gentleman that he had to wait downstairs and I would see if you were at home to visitors. But he wouldn't stay,' she grumbled.

We both looked behind her. And before us was a man I was quite astonished to see standing in 221b Baker Street.

'Bart!' I exclaimed.

'Well, well, Mrs Hudson,' Holmes replied. 'On this occasion, we shall let it slide. We have business with this gentleman, and by the look upon his face, I believe it will barely wait another minute. Come in, Mr Bart, come in. That chair is reserved for clients. And I have a feeling you are about to place yourself in that category, are you not?'

When clients come to us, they have a narrow range of emotions on their faces. Many are furious, others miserable, some simply befuddled by the bizarre circumstance in which they have found themselves, but as Bart walked, his aspect seemed a unique conflation of despondency, guilt and self-justification.

'I have made an error,' he said eventually. And I could see that he was in mortal fear but attempting to remain stoic. 'A terrible error. And yet I know in my heart of hearts that the cause is a righteous one.' He went to the chair but could not bring himself to sit.

'You will have to explain yourself,' Holmes instructed him.

'Yes, yes, I know that I will.' He stopped. 'Mr Holmes, how much do you already know?'

'How much? Oh, I should say around eight tenths.'

'Holmes?' I said.

'Watson, I must make amends yet again. Yes, I have been playing my hand of cards close to my chest. I shall fill you in momentarily. First, I should like to know one thing from Mr Bart here.'

'And what is that?'

'I should like to know why you have come to us now. I doubt that you are aware of how much I have already uncovered and deduced about your organization, so I discount the idea that you are attempting to save your own skin by coming to me before I uncover the final details and throw you all to Scotland Yard. So tell us: why now?'

'Because my daughter's life is in their hands. She and George are in terrible danger.' The fear that had suddenly burst through in the man's voice struck me cold. The girl Devi. Whoever the puppet-masters were in this case, she was in their clutches. And even in that moment, when there was urgency afoot, I understood what fate had never allowed me to feel: a father's love for his child.

'I never dreamed that anything like this would be the outcome,' Bart insisted.

'Of course. I know your ambitions for my client were only for the highest office.'

Bart placed his head in his hands. 'That is true.'

'Holmes, will you be so good as to tell me what this is all about?'

'Far be it from me, Watson, to tell another's tale. No, this one is for Mr Bart to impart. Tell away.'

Bart looked out the window, up and down the street.

'I shall. But the danger is mounting. For George and my daughter. We must go now.'

'Then lead on and tell us all on the way.'

He agreed. We grabbed our travelling coats and hurried out. A four-wheeler cab was trundling along. Bart lifted his hand to it. 'And now, I shall lay out the true story of the Silent Conspiracy. Some would not credit it as possible, but George is living proof that it is fact.' The cab stopped and he stepped up into it. I placed my foot on the running plate and took hold of the handle to pull myself up.

'Watson!' Holmes grabbed me and threw me to the side. As I fell, I felt the movement of air above me and caught sight of a club swishing through the space where my head had been just a second before. I stared up at the driver as he tried once more to smash my skull. I was out of his reach, but as his hand swung through the air, I saw something: the back of his hand featured a tattoo like a sailor's, with the letters 'EVR' branded thick and heavy across its width.

Inside the cab, Bart was being restrained by a burly figure, who slammed the door closed. Holmes tried to jump up, but the club was swung again and, at the same time, the horses started at a canter, pulling the vehicle from us at speed.

Another cab was coming in the opposite direction, and Holmes ran straight in front of it, forcing the driver to veer to the side so as not to grind him into the ground. 'After that cab!' he ordered the astonished cabby. 'Come on, Watson!'

I ran over as the vehicle wheeled around. To give him

his due, our driver very quickly appraised himself of the situation, and then we were off at the same breakneck speed as the carriage we were pursuing.

Along Baker Street we galloped, bouncing over channels in the mud, spraying oily water onto the paving. Men and boys leapt from our path as the two drivers vied with each other for the maddest pace.

We raced around a corner, almost spinning over with the force, one of our coach lights smashing against that of a delivery van, making the horses pulling that vehicle buck and whinny, and still we went on.

'Can you go any faster?' yelled Holmes, his head out of the window.

'Faster? Only if you want to die here and now!' the driver replied.

'It is already a matter of life and death!'

And at that, the man whipped his horses harder, stinging them into even greater speed.

'Holmes! Will you please tell me what this is all about?' I cried. If I was to die – and it seemed every moment that the chance of that was increasing – I wanted to know why.

'All about?' he shouted back. 'It is about the Crown of England itself.'

My eyes widened. In all my adventures with Holmes, I had never once known him to exaggerate. I knew he was not doing it now.

'Tell me.'

'Think, Watson, think! The play that our bold young client was engaged in, it was no random choice. It was a play that our Mr Bart had probably read, seen and fumed over a hundred times. Some say it is Tudor storytelling to blacken the name of King Richard, others say it is an accurate record of his crimes. Bart and his associates no doubt fall into the second camp. But with one caveat.'

'What caveat is that?'

'Which characters of the play appear on the sole bill promoting the show?'

'Why, the doomed young Edward, Prince of Wales, who should have reigned as Edward V, and his brother.'

'Quite right. And which scene of the performance did you remark to me elicited the strange reaction from at least one member of the audience – whom we surmise were no audience at all – bringing him to his feet in order to angrily proclaim it all a falsehood?'

'The murder of the Princes in the Tower,' I said.

'Exactly. And why?'

'I cannot tell.'

'Because he and his fellows are aware that Shakespeare, knowingly or unknowingly, has lied to the British public for three hundred years.'

'What can you mean?'

'I mean, Watson, that those two boys, the rightful heir to the throne and his younger brother, were *not* murdered in the Tower of London.' He read my astonishment in my face. 'No. They lived. And our young client, George Reynolds, is the direct descendant of the elder of the two.'

'EVR,' I whispered to myself. 'Edwardus V Rex.' I shook my head. 'What was it that you discovered this evening?' I asked, my words almost getting lost in the rumble of the cab's wheels. Cold winter rain was coming down hard now. 'The box. What were you about to tell me when he arrived?'

'Ah! Yes, those names. And the design on the lid.' Holmes braced himself against the side of the hansom as we turned a corner hard.

I recalled the design. 'It was trees.'

'A tree, Watson. A family tree. Denoting the descent of one George Reynolds from Prince Edward – or Edward V as we must now call him.'

'Of course. And the costume jewellery?'

'You had seen that neck-chain before. We both had. It was on the famous painting of the two princes by Millais, encircled around the neck of the deposed Edward. The painting, you remember, was on the play bill. Millais, who I surmise is of Mr Bart's group, used this gaudy prop for the picture, and it was afterwards given to young Reynolds.'

The cab raced on. We were on a major thoroughfare now and were weaving among other traffic. The vehicle we were pursuing showed no sign of slowing, but neither did we and we were gaining on it. Forty yards became thirty. Thirty became twenty.

'But then why the danger to Bart's daughter and George?'

'I imagine our client is refusing to assert his claim to the throne. And his captors cannot have that! Perhaps they have even identified another descendant of Edward V who would be next in line. If so, it would, from their point of view, be better if George Reynolds soon breathes his last – and the same for any person with strong enough affection for him to expose the criminals.'

Our driver hied his horses and flicked his whip. Twenty yards became fifteen, and I began to believe we would have them. Holmes had his head out of the window, demanding greater and greater speed. As we passed a row of shops, the mad driver with the tattooed hand and wooden club looked over his shoulder. Even at that distance, I could see him narrow his eyes ... before he sent his bat spinning through the air at us.

I saw better than Holmes just where it was heading. 'Get down!' I shouted and grabbed him by the waist, wrenching him away from the window and to the careering floor of our coach just as the club thudded through the opening, smashing into the wall opposite and splintering the wood.

'Ha!' shouted Holmes. 'We have him rattled.'

'Is that all you have to say?' I demanded.

'And, Watson, I must thank you for saving my life.'

'Think nothing of it,' I replied, pushing myself up onto the seat. The club was impaled through the side of the coach like some giant arrow shot by a primeval archer.

But far from warning our driver off, the assault seemed only to spur him to even greater speed. Fifteen yards became ten. Holmes opened the door. 'What are you going to do?' I asked.

'Why, I'm going to grab him,' came the reply.

'Don't be insane.'

'It may be our last chance.'

We were galloping through narrow streets now, forcing our two vehicles closer together. Holmes was half-hanging out of the door, bracing himself to jump for the other cab as soon as we were close enough. Ten yards. Five. He crouched, readying his long limbs.

'Holmes!' I cried. 'There!' The coach door had opened, and Bart was fighting to pull himself free of a meaty hand that had hold of him. 'He's trying to escape.'

'You're right! Driver! Try to get alongside.'

Our cabby shifted our heading as Bart made a supreme effort to shake off the heavy man's arm. 'Find them!' he yelled to us.

'Where?' I shouted back.

'Coleridge. The tomb. It's—'

But we never heard the rest, because the tattooed driver saw what was happening and hazarded all to end the message. He had beside him a valise that he hefted at the closer of our two horses, striking that poor beast, knocking him across the wet road. I heard Holmes cry out.

My shoulder crumpled into the side of the cab as we thudded into something hard as a wall, flew up into the air, twisting wildly as if plucked up by a venegeful god, then fell back to earth with a terrible crash and came to a rest. I yelled in shock and pain, but even as I did so I knew that I was getting off lightly. I took a second to let the pain hit, burn like fire and then ebb. I stretched my limbs and decided nothing was broken.

'Holmes,' I mumbled. And I looked around. There was my old friend, huddled up, blood leaking from his mouth. I cast aside the pain I felt and went to him. Something was piercing my palms – shards of glass on the seat, I noticed without interest. I brushed them off and wound my body over to Holmes. 'Holmes!' I said, slapping his cheek for a response. There was none. I tried again, harder. 'Holmes!' It is unmanly, I know, but the thought of losing my dearest friend felt like an icicle through my chest.

'If you keep doing that, Watson, you will do me greater damage than the accident itself.'

'For God's sake,' I muttered. Having half-convinced myself that it was all over, I did not appreciate his humour right then. 'I thought you were . . .'

'Six feet under?' His eyes remained closed, but his mouth creaked into a smile. 'Oh, it will take a little more than that, I think. If Moriarty has failed with a veritable army of thugs, four horses and a road accident have little chance.' His eyelids finally lifted, and with the help of the cabby, who was fortunately uninjured, we were able to stagger out. We gave the driver our names and promised to make good the damage.

'What now?'

'We are bloodied and bruised, but not disheartened.' Well, I could have taken issue with that final claim, but I let it slip by. 'For we have a valuable trail to dog.'

'What trail?'

'Bart said that to find our quarry, we had to find Coleridge. His tomb. I have never been one for poetry myself, but I suppose if they recruited the romantic painter Millais to their order, a romantic poet is no great leap further. Ah, this should do.' There was a stationer's shop on a corner of the street. Holmes, as if the previous two minutes had never taken place, flurried through the store, pulling out pamphlets and leaflets from a row of display shelves and hunting through open crates on the floor. The shopkeeper stood back with his arms folded, somewhat amazed by the performance. Eventually, with a 'Ha!', Holmes leapt down from a shelf jammed close to the ceiling – he having had to climb up there like a gorilla – brandishing a pink quarto pamphlet. 'I shall take this, sir. Watson, pay the man, would you?' And he burst out of the shop while I handed over two and six to the stationer. Then I followed my friend out.

'Yes, just the ticket,' he said, unfolding the pamphlet. A scroll at the top read 'Resting Places of the Great and Good of London'. It was a map of the metropolis with more than a hundred places marked with numbers, and a key in the corner told us who was interred in each. Number fifty-five marked the tomb of Samuel Taylor Coleridge, the great author of *The Rime of the Ancient Mariner* and *Kubla Khan*, in Highgate. 'Watson, we are heading for . . .' And he trailed off.

'Holmes?'

'Does it not seem odd to you?'

'What?' I was somewhat exasperated by the sudden halt in our progress.

'Well, what on earth could our dead-and-buried poetical friend have . . .' And he stopped again. Then he spun on his feet, threw the map aside and charged back inside to an entirely different shelf of books for sale, sweeping a line of them to the floor. The shopkeeper pulled his hair out, and I blamed him not a jot, but Holmes silenced him with a yell. 'A gazetteer, my friend, that is that we wanted!' He brandished one, skimmed through the index and opened the book near the front while I paid the man again. 'Oh, things are so very simple when one does not seek to complicate them. Look.' And he shoved the book into my hands.'

Coleridge. Population two hundred. Hamlet in Devon. Recorded in the Domesday Book as Colrige, mean-ing 'ridge where charcoal is made'. The Church of St Matthew dates from the fifteenth century and sports a fine square tower. Church noted for rare stained-glass window depicting Edward V.

'We had poets and painters on the brain, Watson. We could not see the wood for the trees. Bart instructed us to "find them". Well, we need only take a train from Paddington to do so. And I will lay a pound to a penny that the square tower on the lid of our fine box is the very same one sprouting from the Church of St Matthew.'

Chapter 12

'I had assumed it was Orchard who executed the stratagem. And yet, now I come to consider more coldly, I am
not so sure.'

We'd left the three corpses where they'd fallen and
strolled out of the rear door of the music hall to a new
drum the guv'nor had nearby. Best to keep moving. Yes,
the boys Jan Calhoon had stationed out front would soon
come in and find their boss torn to pieces by two manstoppers and one steel blade. Most would just mooch away,
but there was always a chance a few of them would be
out for revenge, so we needed to lie low until we recruited
some more men. A short walk had taken us to our new
bolt-hole.

'He was, of course, the obvious choice. He knew where Calhoon was going to be and when, and he had more motive than anyone to see our American friend dead. But there are two elements that are out of place. And I do not like elements that are out of place.' A bell slowly clinked outside.

The Professor stood and walked carefully to the sideboard, where a pot of tea was brewing. He poured a cup for himself and dropped in two sugar cubes. The cups had nasty little pink roses on them that made you look like an old woman if you drank from them.

'The first element,' he said, settling into a green leather captain's chair, 'is that Orchard was not an intelligent man. He had a certain efficiency of approach, but not the power of intellectual abstraction that would create such a deceptively simple scheme as the one that ended Dutch Calhoon's life.'

'And the second?' That clinking bell was beginning to get on my nerves.

'The second element is that he would have been utterly terrified of my response, given that Calhoon was, like himself, at least nominally under my protection. As events turned out, I was blamed for the incident on the grounds that it was just the sort of stratagem I would have been proud to call my own. I was what Calhoon would have described as "framed". And I do not believe that was an accident.'

'No?'

'No. I begin to suspect that the ultimate target of the stratagem was myself.'

Well, that was a blazes of a bash. 'I see.'

'I tire of the air down here. No wonder it killed scores of the prisoners. Let us go up. Even the smog is preferable.'

We climbed a metal ladder out of the room. It was rocking a bit as we went, but the guv'nor's sprightly. And then we were out in the night on the deck of HMS *Elysium*, one-time thirty-six-gun Apollo-class frigate, hero of Trafalgar; one-time prison hulk, floating gaol to five hundred men condemned to be sent to Botany Bay for stealing loaves of bread, murdering their wives or trying to burn down their masters' tithe-barns. Most of 'em prayed they'd die on the voyage.

'Let us develop this hypothesis. Someone has calculated to kill Calhoon and place the blame on me, probably leading to my own death. We are therefore speaking of an individual capable of a clever method of murder and a calculating, overarching strategy. He does not have the resources to assault me directly in the way that Jan Calhoon did, which suggests he is not of our world; but he is aware of Orchard and Calhoon, so he has knowledge of it. He does not, even now, when our defences are sorely depleted, want to reveal himself, which suggests that he is vulnerable. And above all, he wishes me great ill.'

The ship creaked.

'A rival of yours?'

'I am unrivalled. And besides, as I said, he is not of our world or he would have summoned up a dozen men to come after me when we put two bullets in Jan Calhoon's brain.'

Chapter 13

We hurried up the stairs to our rooms. Holmes scribbled a note for Inspector Lestrade of Scotland Yard, begging him to follow with as many constables as he could muster, and entered his bedroom to grab his travelling cloak and that deerstalker hat he favours when 'the game's afoot', as he says. As instructed, I took my service revolver and a box of bullets. I was just pulling my own coat from the press when Holmes called out to me.

'Watson!'

'Yes?'

'We have had a guest.' His tone was stern.

'I'm not sure I follow you.'

I went into his bed chamber. He had a fine, large French

looking-glass in one corner that he utilized primarily for assuming the disguises that he used when keeping suspicious individuals under observation. (He was, on the whole, unconcerned with his own natural appearance.) 'What do you think of that?'

I stared. Some unknown hand had written on the surface of the glass in green wax pencil.

Moriarty, Sherlock Holmes.
　　Shall soon be friends, no longer foes.
　　There is more danger abroad than even your deep mind can fathom, Mr Holmes. Prepare yourself for a sea-change.

'Who did this?' I blurted out.

'Surely whoever sent us the telegram in Cambridge intimating the same information. But this missive, if we can call it that, is rather more adamant. Not to mention intrusive.' If he had been merely intrigued by the last message, he sounded disturbed by the appearance of this one.

'Do you think it spells a threat?'

'I am convinced of it. But what type of threat, how widely it is spread, how acute it is – all these are unclear right now.' He checked his wristwatch. 'And we have no time to delve into the matter. We have a train to catch. Let us go, and quickly.'

The journey from London to Exeter should have been a lovely one. The south-west of our land is perhaps the most picturesque – the rolling dales of Yorkshire have a wild drama to them, but the moors and pastures of Dorsetshire, Devonshire and Cornwall put a man at ease. Yet the task ahead meant that my mind had little peace as we travelled through the afternoon, then the twilight and into the night.

All the while, Holmes was brooding. Usually, this would be on the case in hand, but this time it was on the curious and threatening communications alleging that we would soon be working hand in glove with Professor James Moriarty – a man I would sooner see dance what the toughs term 'the Tyburn jig'. Was our shadowy messenger referring to the matter involving George Reynolds, of which we were then in pursuit? Was it another case entirely? Was it the figment of a madman's imagination? Well, we could only speculate.

'And what if our incognito correspondent is correct?' Holmes burst out, quite without warning.

'Correct how?'

'Why, correct that I and Moriarty must somehow ally with one another to see off some great danger.'

'I cannot believe such a threat exists that could make that pact with the Devil necessary.'

'None at all? Plagues of locusts, frogs, boils? Earthquake, volcano or diluvian flood?' He laughed out loud. 'I am sure there is some event within human ken that would fit the bill.'

'Oh, Holmes.' I felt a little aggrieved. 'While you would do whatever was right, I can hardly see Professor Moriarty taking so much as a step out of his path in order to save ten trainloads of innocent people.'

'That, then, is the issue, isn't it? What could possibly bring us together? Well, someone out there in the night knows the answer. And perhaps we will have no choice but to agree.'

I stared out at the passing landscape.

Holmes nudged me awake as we pulled into Exeter St Davids. I must have been lulled into a doze by the moonlit fields. It was just before eleven o'clock.

We descended from the train, our sparse luggage in our hands. 'Come, let us see if there is a police office here,' Holmes suggested.

A porter pointed us to a small office, where he told us they would be. It was next to the left luggage room and had a blue police light above its doorway, but that positive sign was negated by the barred door and lack of lights inside. No, we were on our own until Lestrade turned up with reinforcements.

'Well, Watson, we have your service revolver,' Holmes said. 'Let us hope we need no more than that. Indeed, let us hope we need less.'

'Agreed.'

Outside, we found a solitary, dozing cabby. He sat atop a shabby trap, seemingly converted from a farm vehicle. When I told him where we had to go, he took out a frayed map of the surrounding countryside. 'That's twenty mile,' he grunted.

'However far, we must make the journey.' Well, we agreed an extortionate price, but we would have paid anything at that point. After all, there was a chance that we would be paying with our lives if the affair went badly.

We set off in the gloom. Exeter may be an attractive city by day, but by night it feels oppressive, with streets as narrow as any stalked by Whitechapel Jack. We passed a row of taverns where men and women were being chucked out, rolling drunk, into the gutter.

The only light we had was from the bitter moon, its beams filtered blue through the falling snow. As it hit the ground, the frost scattered like infantrymen, colonizing doorways and filling potholes in the road.

I stared out of the gig. 'It is as if we are the only men in the world,' I said.

We left the city, crossed a brook, joined another road. We passed a tavern. We fell further and further beneath a coat of white. We watched each other.

Mile and mile and mile. Twenty of them to roll through. The horses, not used to the distance, huffed in the cold air so that the lanterns behind them illuminated clouds of damp equine breath every pace of the way. The snow began to settle on them, too, so that I began to plan what we would do if the horses gave out and we were stranded in the lonely countryside under falling snow. It had been worse in the Afghan Hindu Kush, when we had run out of firewood and men had cut off their own frostbitten fingers. But then we were an army together; here, we had ourselves and no others.

Mile and mile and mile. Soreness gave way to numbness.

Eventually we were on the prow of a hill and I checked my watch. It was a few minutes before midnight. The driver stopped and pointed with his whip. He said something I could not hear, he was so muffled in his scarf and greatcoat, with the wind howling around us like a dying creature.

'What did you say?' I shouted to him.

He pulled down his scarf. 'That's the church.'

It was nestled among trees. I opened my bag and looked at the lid of the box George had been given. It was as if the scene had been carved from this very spot: every angle of the tower, every ripple of the ground, the placement of the large tomb, was the same.

And there was a spark of light down there.

'Take us down.'

'I'm not going down the hill. I'll never get up again. Too much snow,' he grunted.

'We paid you to take us there,' I said.

'No, sir. I'm for my bed.'

I was about to remonstrate further when Holmes took my arm. 'Let us walk now,' he said. 'The better to approach without being seen, which might prove vital to our cause.'

I admitted he was right. We climbed out of the trap and took up our bags. I cast mine, with the wooden box, over my shoulder. We watched the cab rumble away, back towards Exeter and what seemed then like the last outpost of civilization. Where we stood, there was only the cold. And the church below, where the light was now moving.

And then there was a second light.

'Let us go down,' Holmes said quietly. 'But not by the

road. We are too exposed here and we do not know who else may come.'

'Through the fields?'

'Through the fields.'

It took us ten or fifteen minutes to descend the hill. As we neared the church, nestled among the trees, we saw it turn from a carving in wood into an imposing stone building, a thousand years old and still standing, surrounded by the graves of villagers and unhappy travellers.

We were moving slowly then, and carefully. Carrying no light, of course, as being spotted was the last thing we wanted. And when we came to the edge of the field bordering the church lane, we crouched behind the hedge. There was no one in sight, and whatever the source of the light had been, it had now gone. All was dark and quiet as the graves before us.

'What do you think?' I whispered. My ears were straining for any sound.

Holmes paused. 'I can see . . . Wait. Do you hear that?'

I heard nothing but the wailing wind. 'No, I . . .' And then I did hear it. A strange, bouncing melody borne by the wind itself. I could barely make it out. 'Where is it coming from?' I muttered.

And then, as if in answer, one by one the tall windows lit up. A bright light within was spreading, and the reds and yellows of the stained glass fell on the white canvas outside, to project bloated and extended pictures of saints and kings.

'It is the church organ,' Holmes said. The moon was as high in the sky as it would be that night. Midnight mass had rung out in that church every year for centuries, but it was not Christmastide then. This service was a stranger and more secret one. 'Purcell.' And then. 'Oh! But of course it is. It is "I Was Glad".'

'I don't know it.'

'No, but it holds a very particular place in the canon of English church music. Come, Watson, let us ...' And then he grabbed me and pulled me down. Around the corner of the building, a new, orange light was spreading. It brightened the white ground and the grey tombstones. It spread almost as far as we crouched but shied away within arm's reach.

Then its source arrived. It was a flaming torch held aloft by a man wearing a vicar's surplice. In his other hand, he held a book open – the Bible, I guessed – and was reading from it as he walked. But he was far from alone. For behind him was another man, wearing the robes of a great officer of the state: the Lord Chancellor, perhaps, or Black Rod. And he, too, was carrying a torch of fire above his head. Two more men followed, these wearing the garb of peers of the realm.

'Quite a gathering,' Holmes muttered.

But the next sight was the one that took our breath away. It was the appearance of our ill-fated young client, George Reynolds, dragged along by a pair of heavy-set men, each carrying a short club. There were around a dozen men and women behind, the light barely falling on them.

'Wait,' Holmes instructed me as I began to stand, ready to spring upon the men holding George. I had grown fond of the boy, and the sight of him being pushed around like a common criminal got my blood up.

'Let me go!' George spat at the man beside him, jerking his arm free. But then the thug stomped back a few paces and pulled another figure into the light. It was a young, terrified-looking woman: the girl Devi. She shrank from the man, and I saw young George grab hold of him, but our ill-fated client was not as strong as the big fellow, who chucked him off with ease and pushed George towards the church door.

'I am armed, they are not,' I insisted under my breath.

'We do not know that.' He was right.

The rear of the procession – for I must call it that, in its strange pretence at dignity – now slipped into the pool of light from the windows. As soon as they were in, I stood and cocked the hammer on my revolver. 'Time to intervene,' I said.

'Brave Watson. Yes. I agree it ...' But he broke off. There was a new, more threatening sound in the air. It echoed all around, bouncing off the wall of the church and buffeted by the winds: baying dogs. And they were coming closer. I whirled around. Holmes did so, too, and then, at the same time, we spotted them: a pack of hounds, their teeth bared, sprinting towards us from a copse of trees halfway up the hill that we had descended. There was a man some distance behind them, and it was clear that he had sent them after us. They were hunting dogs, and we were their quarry. I knew it would attract attention, but I raised my gun and shot into the air to scare them off. The crack from the bullet rang out, then was gone in the wind.

And the only effect on the hounds seemed to be to make them wilder. They were close.

'Shoot to kill, Watson,' Holmes said grimly.

I levelled and fired. One of the hounds fell. The others saw but took no notice. I fired again and another fell. And I aimed once more. Something moved behind me. I spun around, saw a fine coach in the lane, one I had seen before, and a face looking out from between curtains at the window. Something at my side loomed. A club appeared, lit red by the light from the stained-glass window. It came down.

I came to with a painful shake of my whole body. The music had changed. I could not move my hands and looked down and saw them bound with rope. I was in a wooden seat. A pew, a church pew. But everything was askew: I was slumped on my side. And my skull felt like it had been split apart.

'Careful, old man.'

'Holmes,' I muttered. It was as much as I could say.

'They hit us from behind in the dark. Cowardly but effective.'

My eyes began to focus. We were inside the church. The music was coming from the organ, played by a small man in formal attire, while the strange dozen-strong line of men and women we had witnessed outside circled around the quire. And in the centre, atop a bishop's throne, our client sat, a look upon his face that was darker than the fires of Hell.

'What is going on?' I croaked.

'I told you outside that the music was Purcell's "I Was Glad" and that it held a special place in the canon of English church music.' He did not wait for a reply. 'It is the opening music in the service for the coronation of a king. Watson, our client has a strong claim to the throne of England, and these people are determined that he should take it.'

The blood returning to my brain, I glanced around. And then I saw who had cracked my skull: the same man who had attempted it the previous day while driving the cab that had abducted Bart. He stood guard over us, his weapon on a low table beside him. Behind him was the sallow-faced man I had briefly spoken to at the theatre in Cambridge.

The music changed to a work that every Briton knows: 'Zadok the Priest', Handel's soaring coronation anthem. So it was true, these people were staging a mock enthronement. 'What do you think they will do from here?'

'Let us ask one who knows.' And he turned to the men holding us captive. 'What now, eh?' The sallow gentleman initially ignored Holmes's enquiry. But upon the question being repeated, he angrily spun around.

'What we shall do,' he said, 'is announce the accession to the throne of King George V. He is the rightful heir. None can dispute it.'

'And you hope for preferment?' I demanded.

He huffed dismissively. 'Preferment alone would seem a poor salary for my efforts. I expect a little more than that.'

'What did you do with Bart?'

'The sentence for traitors throughout history.' And he

put on his hat. 'I regret only that I must leave you now. Your presence has caused us to delay the ceremony, Dr Watson, and there is but one train left to return to London.'

'You have my name, sir; in return, may I have yours?'

'No, you may not.' From the floor by his feet, he lifted a small brown leather pouch and pushed it to the man guarding us. 'The ether. Then take him straight to the hotel – they will change his mind, you mark my words. They will change his mind beyond what he could ever think possible.' He inclined his forehead to us and departed.

'Who is that man?' I blurted out.

Holmes wore a frown of concentration. 'Oh, Watson, if only you took more interest in the illustrated newspapers beyond those dealing with rugby football matches, you would surely—'

And once again he was interrupted.

'I do not want this!' George yelled at the top of his lungs. The priest was walking around him with a silver crown in his hands.

'George!' Devi cried.

I could see his inner struggle. The girl was clamped between two men dressed in a ragtag of formality. She was terrified for her life.

The mock-priest raised his arms. 'I crown you before the tomb of your illustrious forebear, King Edward V,' he called out.

I stared at a tomb behind the chair that had been decked with silk ribbons. It depicted a man with a shield, with the name John Evans upon it.

'All you were told in school was lies, you know.' It

was our guard, who had found his tongue now that his master was gone. He seemed to enjoy the superiority of his knowledge over us. 'The little prince smothered by Richard? A lie. He lived out his days as John Evans on his half-brother's estate. That's him up there.' He gestured to a stained-glass window, which had a picture of a crowned king. Below was the name Edward V. An effigy on the tomb was staring at the image.

'I believe you,' Holmes said.

The man stood back and focused once more on the ceremony. Young George looked grim as the priest anointed him with holy oil, making a cross with his fingers. The dozen or so spectators – I suddenly recognized them as the audience of the play when I had watched it – bowed their heads. One old woman wept.

The priest stood before George and took the silver crown from a velvet cushion. He held it aloft, turning in a full circle for all to see. The music rang out as a choir of four began to sing Handel's words:

'God save the King!'

'God save the King!'

The circlet was lowered towards George's brow.

And suddenly, it was as if the winds of havoc had blasted in. The door exploded inwards, cracking to pieces and crashing to the floor. The old woman screamed. The priest froze, his hands hovering with the crown inches from our client. Instinctively, George jumped up and smacked it from the man's hand. But this act of rebellion was masked by the bursting in of half a dozen uniformed policemen, their truncheons up and ready to strike.

The man guarding us spat in anger and lifted his club. A policeman leapt at him, the officer's shoulder flying into his midriff and knocking him over. The club in his hand smashed down on the wooden box with the family tree that meant so much, that could set a nation against itself. The wood splintered apart.

There was bedlam as some of the men took up arms, the police rushing to meet them. At their rear, I saw our old colleague Lestrade waiting in the doorway as his tough men took on the revolutionaries. One of those men plucked a flaming torch from its brace on the wall and threw it at the police. But it fell short, on a pile of prayer books and pamphlets. In moments, they were alight.

And as I watched, desperate to join the fray on the side of justice, it became clear that the police needed more hands, for they were being beaten back by the sheer number of opponents.

The man guarding us was wrestling on the floor with the officer attempting to detain him. They were at Holmes's feet, and my friend was just able to twist himself down to pull something from our assailant's pocket. I saw at once that it was a blade. Within seconds, Holmes had cut himself free and then did the same for me. The guard managed to escape and charge away, however.

'There!' I shouted. The priest was running for the vestry door at the rear of the chancel. But he had not reckoned on young George chasing him down and punching him hard in the jaw, knocking him down. The men who had been holding Devi had taken to their heels, and she ran to our client.

But then the wheel turned again. Almost out of no-where, the lackey who had held us appeared behind George with something in his hand that he clamped over George's mouth. Another of their number took hold of the girl and pushed her to the floor. After a few moments' struggle, George went limp as a doll in the thug's arms.

'Ether!' I yelled to Holmes, who was watching in dismay.

'You're right,' he growled.

The tough dragged George out through a transept door with the aid of a comrade, who lifted a glinting knife to the young man's neck in a warning to any who might intervene.

We made for them, weaving through the throng. But too late! The guard was in the saddle of a piebald stallion, while poor, unconscious George lay sprawled and trussed over the horse.

'George!' I yelled, yet even before the word was com-plete, the tough was kicking his heels into the mount's flank and they were away, out through an open gate and along a narrow path.

'Back, we need aid,' Holmes said. We raced back into the church, to find that the fire was not a great one and was isolated on the stone floor. And the spectators of that strange, warped ceremony had all been subdued, quiet as lambs. Devi, meanwhile, was being helped to her feet by one of the constables. Thankfully, she had not been seri-ously hurt. We had, at least, saved one soul.

'Lestrade!' Holmes yelled. 'These devils have abducted an innocent. They are away on horseback.'

Lestrade immediately summoned two of his men out-side. They had all come in a van, drawn by a single huge shire horse, which could not possibly pass through the narrow footpath that the stallion and rider had disap-peared down. The inspector ordered the horse to be set free of the van, and one of his men volunteered to ride bareback in pursuit of the others. Off he went at the best speed that the slow-footed mount could muster.

'The life of their captive is paramount to us, but we have another quarry that is afoot. We will pursue him when we can,' Holmes said.

All we could do was return to the church to wait and explain to Lestrade what had occurred. In time, his con-stable returned, saying that he had lost their trail so had thought it best to pass on the disappointing news. Holmes was subdued. 'Well, Inspector,' he said, 'if we catch our other prize, you may still make the most extraordinary arrest of your life.' We went out to the police van, where the horse was being reattached.

Lestrade, to his credit, remained steadfast, saying: 'We'll get him, Mr Holmes.' He instructed some of his men to stay in the church to keep hold of the score of people they had detained, while one would come with us in pursuit of our man. We jumped in, and the van wheeled away at a trot – although the whirling white around us meant we could barely see more than a few yards ahead. We trusted to the horse to find the way.

In all our adventures, I had rarely taken to a client as I had to George Reynolds. Why I liked him so much, I couldn't say for certain – maybe it was that he was pursuing a rather Bohemian lifestyle that others dreamed of but shied away from, or maybe it was something to do with the fact that he had begun to court his beloved in Cambridge, as I had. Either way, the upshot was that I felt quite futile as we set off once again into the night.

'Worry not, old friend,' said Holmes, reading my thoughts and placing his hand on my shoulder. 'We will see him again, and we will see him a free man.'

Chapter 14

The next morning, the guv'nor announced that there was a private art showing of paintings by Turner at the Royal Academy that he wanted to peep at. Not what I would think of as a bean-feast, but that's his business. Some would have been for lying low right then, but the Professor always calculated the danger instead of feeling it.

So out we bashed and took a Hackney carriage to Piccadilly. Even at nine in the morning, we saw all the lowlifes on the way: the street geese with the pox, their ponces without teeth. Dogs fighting over scraps from eel-sellers. It was the smell that got me more than anything: all rot, nothing dry.

Not a bad place, though, the Royal Academy of Arts.

Good walls for defence, approaches where you can see what's coming. It was all decked out like a tart's boudoir that day, though, with pink silk drapes floating about the place. We stepped in, and some giggle-mug flunkey grovelled low enough to smack his chin on the marble floor, which put my hackles up. I like a bit of deference, but there's a limit.

We took a look around. I can't say painting does much for me, but I could see that the bloke was dimber-damber with his brushes. The seascapes, with those old warships ready to sink down to Davy Jones's locker, had something. We moved on from one room to another, and as we were passing the reception desk, a clerk had a telephone to his ear, one of the modern designs where the ear and mouthpiece are joined together. 'Excuse me, sir,' he called over to us. 'Would you be Professor Moriarty?'

Now, at that my hand twitched to the six-shooter in its holster. The guv'nor discreetly lifted a palm to tell me to cool myself.

'I am he.'

'There is a telephone call for you.' He held out the receiver but didn't seem too pleased with having to do so.

'Thank you.' The Professor held it so I could hear the conversation. 'Moriarty.'

A thin voice, like a kid's speaking from a distance, rattled out. 'Professor, I want you to know that you are embarking on an expedition in which Sherlock Holmes will be your necessary travelling companion.'

At that, the guv'nor's eyebrow twitched. 'To whom am I speaking?'

'All in good time, Professor. But for now, know that Holmes is your enemy by circumstance, not nature. You needs must work together to save yourselves, to save all. It won't be long now. Days, weeks at most.'

'I do not take advice from men who hide themselves.'

'You will know me soon enough, too. Two sides of a coin, Professor. You are two sides of a coin spinning in the air.'

'Absurd.' He looked blazes angry. And it's not often the guv'nor gives that away.

'Is it? Well, as a gesture of good will, I offer you this. You have been seeking a gentleman who recently did you a bad turn. You will find him thirty minutes from now in front of the British Museum in the company of Her Majesty. But hurry – he will not be there for long.'

'Who is he?'

'Let us say that he has judged you and found you wanting.'

At that, the line went dead. The guv'nor handed the phone back to the clerk.

Well, this was a roister-doister bash, wasn't it? It had all kicked off with the Professor asked to intervene in some villains' war, only to find himself in the frame for snuffing one of them. Now there's some other geezer calling up and saying the Professor's got to get pally with Sherlock Holmes to stop some catastrophe he won't tell us about, and the cove who put him in the frame is ready and waiting for us.

The Professor stepped outside and stood rubbing his temples for a full five minutes. I knew when to hold my tongue. Eventually, he moved off again and hailed a taxi, telling the driver to take us to the British Museum.

'Whoever that man is, he knows my movements. We shall see whom he is presenting,' he said to me, though he was peering out of the window. Then he muttered to himself, 'But work alongside Sherlock Holmes? Pah! If so, then chaos has overtaken us.'

Chapter 15

Three hours it had taken us to travel from London to Exeter. Six hours it took us to travel back on the first train. Packed snow, frozen points and a frozen engine-stoker all conspired against us. Holmes was ready to burst with annoyance, and I, too, sank into a grim mood. Lestrade was able to snooze for most of the way, but we had a score to settle.

So when the wheels finally stopped at the platform in Paddington Station, Holmes jumped down with the vim of a leopard, and Lestrade, his men and I had to chase after him.

'For God's sake, Holmes,' I said as we rushed through the station, 'will you now tell me the name of the man we are following?' I had asked him more than once on the way, and each time he had put his fingers to his lips. 'Are we headed to his home? Do you know him?'

He laughed a little. 'Oh, we haven't met – though I wonder if another member of my family has had the pleasure. Quite likely, I should say. But I do know well who he is and, Watson, if you would only read the daily newspapers – or indeed *Punch* – you, too, would recognize him.'

'Well, then, tell me.'

'My dear fellow, I will do better than that.' And he halted at a newspaper stand and snatched a copy of the day's *Times* from the seller. He tore through the pages, dropping them on the damp floor, then triumphantly held one aloft. 'Ha! Not only his identity, Watson, but sportingly, his staff have advertised his precise whereabouts today.'

The page was headed 'Parliamentary Circular', and Holmes's finger stabbed on one entry.

Mr Peter Jet MP, Minister for War: At three o'clock, the minister will have the pleasure of welcoming Her Majesty Victoria Regina to an exhibit at the British Museum of the treasures that he himself discovered on an archaeological expedition to Jerusalem some years ago.

Before I had even read the final words, Holmes was shoving me into a hansom.

It took us all to that majestic building that looks like nothing so much as a great Roman temple. We tumbled out, Holmes in front, Lestrade calling to two bobbies who were standing around watching the crowd for pickpockets.

'There, Watson!' Holmes cried, and he ran through the crowd, sending half a dozen onlookers flying. It was the third time I had set eyes on the small, sallow-faced man. But the first I knew his name. Peter Jet MP was striding into some sort of big glass-sided box.

'For God's sake, Lestrade, get these open!' Holmes yelled, rattling the gates that gave entry to the Museum precincts.

The inspector huffed and puffed his way to us and tried to recover some dignity by ordering a policeman on the other side to unlock them. Not for the first time, his warrant card proved invaluable.

Holmes yelled in triumph as the iron swung aside. But then he stopped, frozen on the spot, a queer frown creeping across his face. His finger pointed ahead and I saw perhaps the strangest sight I ever encountered, even in my many years at the side of Sherlock Holmes.

Chapter 16

We fairly sped through Soho. Not a bad neighbourhood, but right then it was full of the dregs of the city. Put 'em in uniform and send 'em out to the Natal, I say. Get some use out of 'em. If they can't shoot, we can strap 'em together and they'll do as barricades.

When we pitched up outside the museum, some snot-nosed kids told us there was an exhibit of stuff dug up from the ground to gawp at. Is there anything less to my tastes? But this one would be a different sort of affair, because I was happy enough heading there to end this little contre-temps with whoever was shooting at us from the bushes. And it was clear that, whether it happened by the guv'nor's blade or by my rifle, things were going to be settled.

There was a crowd there stuffed to the gills with fools, all waving flags and singing. Some of them half-cut by the looks of 'em. A few government sorts, too, with their lackeys bounding along with red cases full of papers. No whores, which is unusual in London. I suppose around there their clients send out for them, rather than picking them up on the street. Well, apart from Gladstone, of course, he liked a bit of street trade. They should name a couple of alleyways after him.

It was chilly, but at least the air was clear of smog. We had to force our way through, and more than once I saw the guv'nor start to draw his sword-cane before thinking better of it. For my part, I would have used the pistol sooner than you could blink to clear a path. It's their look-out if they can't leg-bail fast enough.

We had nearly reached the main gate when the crowd started shouting more than ever and pointing off to the west. We looked where they were staring. It was the Queen's state carriage approaching. The thing looks like some sort of pudding. It's all covered in gilt and painted carvings. Leaves or cherubs or some such nonsense. I can't see how the damned thing even moves with all that tosh weighing it down. But in it trundled. Six good-looking white stallions pulling it, too. A squadron of Life Guards trotted along in front and behind. I could just make out the old girl inside. She looked like she was sucking a lemon.

Something had been stuck up in front of the museum. It was a big glass box, like a scaled-down version of the old Crystal Palace, all supported by a white steel frame.

Looked like a barracks designed by an Italian imbecile. Full of cabinets and display cases of junk, and a pair of nobs standing about in silk sashes.

I kicked some old biddies out of my path and got to the gate. There was a Horse Guards cornet on sentry. 'Moran, Colonel. First Bangalore Pioneers,' I said, saluting. He stood to and returned the salute. I've never liked their regiment. It only recruits from the aristocracy, so the officers are stuck up and the other ranks are those too dim-witted even to purchase a commission. 'What's that?'

'Exhibition, sir. "Treasures of the Jerusalem Dig", it's called.'

'Is it now?'

'Moran.' The guv'nor gestured with his cane. 'Now I understand.'

'Professor?'

'You recall that our anonymous correspondent said that the gentleman who has been causing us so much difficulty of late had judged me and found me wanting.' I remembered that that was what the geezer on the telephone had said. 'Those words were chosen with care. The man on the left is Jet, the Minister for War. But that man on the right . . .' He pointed with his cane. The cove was an evil-looking, stooped-over bastard with a grey beard you could lose a platoon in. '. . . is Lord Wyneth.'

'Who?'

He grunted. 'Formerly Judge Wyneth. The terror of the Old Bailey. He and I are much acquainted, even though we have never, in fact, been introduced.' He tapped the top of his cane. 'There have been, to my knowledge, four cases before him in which my name was whispered in his ear, although, of course, the prosecuting authorities never even attempted to lay hands on me due to the utter vacuum of proof or living witnesses. Wyneth has recently retired from the bench. It seems he considered he had one last sentence to pass. He is also reputed to be a very fine shot.'

His lordship looked pleased with himself. Well, we would be wiping the smile off his face pretty damned soon.

'What's all that about?' I asked the soldier, pointing to the two blokes.

'Showing it all to Her Majesty, sir.'

The royal coach was coming in through the gate now, and the great unwashed were bawling like they were under assault. It came to a stop, and the minister and our quarry dusted themselves down and waited inside the glass house. It was brightly lit, so was shining like a beacon.

A footman approached the coach, bowed and opened the door for the little woman to step out. She's a tiny, dried-up thing up close. Empress of India? More like the chai-wallah's mother, you'd think to look at her.

Her servant laid out a line of carpet for her to walk on, and she went slowly towards the exhibition glass house, propped up by one of her ladies-in-waiting. Two or three steps, then she stopped. And I could see why.

'Moran,' the Professor said. He had seen it, too.

There had been movement behind our judge. The top of a large display case had sprung up. It must have made a sound, because the two geezers peered over their shoulders. My eyesight is better than a hawk's, and I could see the expression on their faces. It started off a bit curious, then confused, and then it became something else. Something I've only seen on the faces of new recruits dropped into battle for the first time in their lives and facing a thousand Zulu spears. It's sheer blazes terror.

'Colonel!'

I shoved the cornet aside. I wanted to see for myself. The Queen had stopped and was peering bleary-eyed at what was happening. But I saw it plain as day. There was a queer-as-hellfire stream of something that looked liked green water pouring out of the display case that had opened up. Only when I looked closer, the stuff wasn't liquid. It was a river of green spiders the size of your hand. Hundreds of them – no, thousands – pouring out to cover the whole damned floor like a flood. And then the glass house door swung closed.

It hit home, and the bar inside slid down to lock it. I kicked men out of the way and ran to the glass. Behind me, the Queen was being hustled to her carriage by a couple more guardsmen. Inside the exhibit, those hell-ish spiders were crawling over the cases, up the walls and surrounding the minister and Wyneth. For a few seconds – five, ten, don't ask me how many, because I had more on my mind than counting – they seemed to be sizing the men up. Those blokes, for their part, were shouting at each other: Wyneth was telling the minister to stay calm, but Jet was losing his mind. Now, I've known some brute animals in my day, but none so nasty as a spider that spits its venom. So when the first of those ugly things, a fat bastard hanging from the roof, opened his jaws and spewed a few drops of red liquid onto Jet's face, I knew the jig was up.

As soon as the poison hit, Jet clutched his cheek like he'd been slapped. He lifted his hand away, and I could see the skin on his cheek was burned. It wasn't a big burn, but it was blistering and the skin was ragged. He swatted at the spider and knocked it to the ground. 'We must go!' Wyneth barked. And he reached out to lift the bar on the door. But then another spider on the wall spat onto his hand and he yelped in pain like a kicked dog. And he made a mistake then: he hesitated. That's what ended it for him. Because in two seconds, that great pool of spiders was covering the walls and the ceiling, and all spitting their poison at him and Jet. The men were clutching at their eyes and mouths, and blindly trying to swat the little brutes away, struggling to get to the door, but Jet tripped and then they were overwhelmed by the green bastards.

Well, some sights grab hold of you, but a good soldier keeps a level head. *Retreat, chum*, I told myself. No matter what guts you have, if you're outnumbered a thousand to one, you'd better run.

I legged it back to the gate. If the spiders broke out, the old biddies would be an easy meal for them, so I'd be safe enough.

'What do you make of that?' I felt the guv'nor's cane tapping on my shoulder. He sounded interested. Everyone around us was scarpering.

'Never seen anything like it, Professor. Rum.'

We watched the two blokes squirming on the floor. Every few seconds, one of them would lift himself out of the mass of brutes and put his face to the glass. His skin would be bloated and burned, and he would reach out and plead until he was covered up again by the swarm. After a while, I couldn't even tell them apart. They didn't look human. One gurgled for help one last time.

'I have read of such traps. Cyrus of Persia employed an engineer especially to design the most painful forms of death for those who defied him.'

The Queen's carriage sped out of the gates.

'This would have fitted the bill.'

'It would. I do not think Lord Wyneth will cause me any further trouble.'

'No, Professor.'

And then, just as we were settling to the scene, enjoying the sight of our fox bagged and bloodied, we saw three men we knew well enter our line of sight.

It was that blasted Holmes and his lapdog, followed by their personal copper, Lestrade.

'Remain still, Moran,' said the Professor.

Holmes was charging towards the glass, with his little chums behind him. They came to a halt, apparently at a loss for what to do. After a little back and forth between them, they seemed resigned to just watch, same as us. But then, worst luck, that swine Watson happened to glance our way, his jaw dropping open.

'A strategic withdrawal, Professor?' I muttered as that pigeon turned to alert Lestrade to our presence.

'Indeed, Moran.'

And at that, we slipped back into the crowd.

Chapter 17

It was chaos. Women screaming, police running here and there but unable to find anything to do. One constable was about to bash the windows in with his truncheon, but Lestrade stopped him. 'Don't do that, son. Think what those spiders will do if they get out,' he said. So we had no choice but to stand and watch two men die in a way that was as painful and horrifying as any I had ever seen.

But even as they screamed in pain, my eye was dragged away. Because there were two other men whose presence shocked me: Moriarty and Moran. Yes, I should have expected their involvement in this morass of murder, especially with the strange messages we had been receiving, telling us to make friends with that evil man. I called to

Lestrade, pointing them out, but all he could do was tell a couple of constables to go after them, and by that time we had lost sight of the pair.

All around us, terrified onlookers were running home. You can read of that in the newspapers of the time, as reporters were descending like vultures. But what you may not know, for it was not widely reported, was that after the public had been harried from the scene and a police cordon erected, we were left with that horrible glass tomb, with the bodies of the two dead men, their swollen flesh livid red, on display like animals in the zoo. And thousands of the bottle-green spiders pulsing inside. What to do then? How to get the bodies out and deal with the deadly creatures without letting them loose on the streets of London?

It was Holmes who suggested the answer. He has a keen interest in beekeeping and has the protective gear stored at Baker Street. He sent for it, and we carefully sealed him in behind the thick protective cloth and gauze. He made a small chink in the glass and used his beekeeper's bellows to blow huge amounts of smoke into the structure, so as to suffocate the spiders. We carefully observed them as we pumped the smoke in: they indeed keeled over and died in waves. We were at it for half an hour to make sure, before Holmes went in wearing his protective suit. He confirmed the death of all the arachnids and carried out the bodies of the dead men.

We stood over them, the corpses of a minister of the Crown and a senior judge, wondering at what we had just witnessed.

'The great white shark, Watson, is a dedicated killer. It can smell blood half a mile away. Everything about it is singularly honed to catching its prey. Whoever planned this has a twisted and perverse mind. But it is a mind with a singular genius about it, too.'

'I should not describe what happened here as "genius".'

'But we must admit that it is so. For if we want to catch a shark, we must recognize its speed and agility. If we want to catch a murderer, we must recognize his mind. Now, we can presume that the minister's death is linked to his exploits over the past week, but the judge we . . .'

And then he froze. 'My God!' he whispered. His finger rose to point at the corpse of Jet. I looked down at the closed eyes of the dead man, and my heart skipped a beat.

His eyes were opening. His blistered mouth was gaping. And a howl like something from Hell was rising from inside his throat.

'He's alive!' I cried to Lestrade, twenty paces away. I dropped to my knees to stare into his irises and watch for reaction to the light. Lestrade looked blankly at me, then down at Jet, and sprinted over.

I reached to open the eyelids more, but Holmes caught my hand. 'Careful,' he said. 'The poison works on contact.'

The man's skin was peeling away from his once-sallow flesh. Whatever poison the spiders had spat at him had caused the type of horrific blistering I had seen on hospital burn wards. Placing a handkerchief on his wrist as a

132

barrier against any residual venom, I felt for his pulse. It was quite mad: it would beat five times in a second, and then nothing at all for ten.

Holmes, who still wore his protective gloves, was on his knees, too, pulling away the man's clothes to help him breathe. 'Will he live?' he demanded.

'I have no idea. I've never seen anything like it,' I snapped back.

The howl in the man's throat subsided, beginning to mutate into human sound. His lips moved, and his tongue flicked across them, even as his limbs remained still as a fallen tree. The sound sharpened into words, husky and indistinct.

'Back ... I ... back.'

We waited for more, straining our hearing. But there was only a light panting. His pulse was surging and falling away like waves.

'Back where?' Holmes barked at the man. 'Do you know what happened?'

The man's eyes fell on Holmes.

'I ... second life ...'

'What second life? You are Peter Jet, Minister for War. Who did this to you?'

'Bite ... to give another life ...'

'Another life?'

'Where is George Reynolds?' I demanded, frustrated at the man's meaningless words. 'Where have you sent him?'

The man's head rolled to the side, staring at Holmes. 'This is my last ...' he whispered, and the ugliest, most cynical grin appeared on his face. Then the head lolled. He was dead once more.

And yet the horror was not over.

That terrible howling began again. But not from the corpse of Jet. It was coming now from that of the judge, Wyneth, beside him.

Holmes leapt across. This man's eyes, like Jet's, were open but unfocused. And like Jet, the howl sharpened into something like speech. But his lips failed to form words, however cryptic. Holmes shook him and slapped his face. I did not have my medical bag, so there were no drugs I could give him to stimulate life – though I would have had no idea what to give him even if I had had them. I tried compressing his chest, hoping that might regulate his heartbeat. But it made no difference. And then, without warning, his burning hands shot up and reached for my face. Holmes knocked them away before he could grab my flesh. One of the bobbies came to us, looking sickened by the sight.

'We have been gods,' Wyneth whispered. Holmes and Lestrade dropped down beside me to listen closely. 'We have been gods.' And then his head lifted away from the ground as his body jerked. 'Do you hear me?' he cried with all the strength he had left in his veins. And with that cry from the heart, he, too, expired for the second time.

'What on earth can this be?' I asked Holmes.

He looked stern. 'I should say it— Look out!' He thrust me aside and grabbed the constable's truncheon, smacking it down on the ground beside me. He lifted the weapon away to show the crushed bottle-green body of one of the deadly spiders. 'It must have been in his clothing. Watch out for more.' He made a thorough search of both men's clothes, finding a dead example of the deadly creatures, which he placed in a small cardboard box that one of the constables supplied.

Lestrade instructed the policemen to seal the two bodies in two layers of canvas bag, very carefully and minutely stitched up, to transport them to the mortuary.

'Mr Holmes,' the inspector said gravely as he oversaw the lifting of the bodies into the police wagon. 'I have never heard of such a case in all my career.'

'No, Lestrade,' Holmes replied solemnly. 'I am certain there has never been one.'

While I can say without doubt that Sherlock Holmes is one of the best men I have had the honour to know, there is one thing in his character that disturbed me at times. Not his use of the needle and cocaine – though that constantly tugged at my concern, and I wished to Heaven he would give it up – but that he could sometimes miss the humanity of a situation.

So it was this time, as we stood in the drawing room of 221b Baker Street. I was as tense as I have been after a battle, while his eyes shone with excitement. In truth, Jet had been bound for the gallows if we had caught him, so his death was only premature. But the other man, a former judge, had, as far as we knew, been blameless. And that is not even to speak of the life of George Reynolds that still hung in the balance.

Yet, to Holmes, these men were only data in a puzzle.

'Moriarty,' he said.

'And Moran.'

'Yes, Colonel Moran, I saw him there, too. Wyneth, as I recall, once presided over at least one trial in which Moriarty should have stood in the dock. That may well have caused some animosity between them. So, what part do the Professor and the Colonel play in our little drama?'

'Not so little now.'

'Indeed not. A public outrage. It could hardly have been more public and more outrageous. You see, do you not, that whoever planned this did so not only quite brilliantly, but with a desire for publicity. Such a horrendous death must have been intended either as a warning to others or as the culmination of the greatest spite any man has borne in his heart.'

I had to agree. Like any man, there are those who have done me wrong, and I would pay to see them get their comeuppance, but I cannot ever see myself inflicting that degree of suffering on any of them. The trap that we had seen sprung came from quite an animal part of the human brain. After all the villainy we had seen in the past decades, I had thought I was quite inured to human depravity. But there was something unique about this, something somehow *beyond*.

'As to Moriarty and Moran, either of them fits the bill for a weight of spite, but I would hazard that only the Professor has the genius to plan such a trap. And yet!'

'And yet what?' I asked.

'Did you not see? He seemed to be taken as unawares

by the event as any of us. And when the final knell tolled for the two victims, he turned tail and ran. Now, I can believe he would wish to view his handiwork, but if so he would have arranged a vantage point to enjoy it in peace and without the possibility of being apprehended.' I had to agree. Moriarty's behaviour was far removed from his usual conduct. He was not in control of the situation, but a spectator. And a spectator as amazed by the turn of events as we were. 'I rather wish we had our secret observer, who insists that the Professor and I will have to collaborate in the face of some terrible danger, sitting in the client's chair. Then we might get somewhere in this barely penetrable affair.'

I thought back to the previous night's adventure. 'Do you think the police will gain something useful from the people they arrested at the mock coronation?'

'In frankness, no. The puppet-masters strike me as subtle men. But still, we can hope.'

Then, as he was wont to do when he wanted to think over a problem, he took up his Stradivarius violin and played for an hour.

It was a haunting piece, ending on a deep, mournful note that hung in the air. Then Holmes seemed to reach a conclusion and cast the instrument aside into his easy chair. He snatched up pen and paper, scribbled something down, yelled down the stairs for Mrs Hudson and bade her send a boy to take his missive to the offices of the *Evening Standard* to run on his account. He handed over a shilling for the boy taking it.

'Well,' he said, rubbing his hands – it was chilly in the

room, even though the fire was blazing. 'Now we have a trip to make.'

'Where?'

'We want to know about strange spiders, so where better to start than the Natural History Museum?'

Chapter 18

We ducked away into the Underground, returning to the Eye-tie's flat in Hatton Garden, where that Sicilian hussy admitted us without a word, set down some decent grub before us and left us to it.

'Holmes,' the Professor said.

'And Watson.'

'Yes.' And he rubbed his temples again to get the blood flowing to his brain.

I sat there for an hour, smoking and drinking some decent wine. I'd made a good inroad into a second bottle when he spoke.

'He knew nothing of our presence there. He knew nothing of our intention. He knew nothing, I presume, of

Lord Wyneth. Mark how they were only making for the exhibition structure, they were not combing the crowd for us. No, Holmes was on his own quest, and there is a hidden hand that has brought us together.'

'Whose hand?' He mumbled something. 'I didn't catch that.'

'I said, you fool, that if I knew that, we would not be sat here now. But even you must realize that it was whoever telephoned us when we were at the Royal Academy.' Now, I admit that the Professor has a bigger brain than anyone I know, but when he called me a fool, my fingers twitched for the Webley I still had in my pocket. Clever man or no, I could put three slugs in him before he could open his mouth.

'Do it, and you know that your life would not be worth tuppence,' he muttered, brushing me aside. 'I have structures in place to avenge my death, no matter who brings it upon me.' I knew he was playing no bluff. I would leave him be. 'Bring me the evening newspapers. I wish to know what happened after we left.'

I don't like playing messenger boy, but on this occasion I wanted a read of the penny-sheets myself. So I went out and collected the *Evening Standard* and the *Evening News* from the inky boys on the street. I had a quick shufty before tramping back to the drum. The malarky filled up the first six or seven pages of each paper, of course, but I can't say I saw anything I wouldn't have guessed at. *The government was outraged.* Well, it would be, wouldn't it? What with one major member of it shaking himself to death from poison spider bites. *Scotland Yard has assured the Queen that whoever was behind it will be brought to justice*. Well, they hadn't even caught the two of us, and we'd been in plain sight. So nuts to that.

When I shoved the *Standard* in front of the Professor, he grabbed it with both hands and stared like he was reading his own obituary. 'Impudent,' he said. I couldn't understand what he was getting himself in a twist over and said as much. 'Moran, Moran,' he muttered. 'You must be quite blind. Did you not see this?' He tapped his finger down on a box on the front cover. It was an advertisement.

A certain Professor, late of a Scottish university and sometime army coach, would find it to his advantage if he should reply by similar advertisement to explain his presence at the day's event. If he does not, then the worst inference shall be drawn. S.H.

Moriarty pushed a pencil and note pad in front of me. 'Take this down and see that it is printed in the next edition.'

Chapter 19

We crossed the city, stepping from our cab into the wondrous neo-gothic building in Kensington that housed dinosaur bones, seal pelts and every sort of thing that ran, swam or squawked on the earth.

I insisted we have a bite from a pie stand outside – if it were not for me, Holmes would be fuelled by nothing but his nerves. Indeed, over the years, I have often been asked what motivated Sherlock Holmes. The truth is that the more I knew him, the less I understood him. He and I could spend a day together doing nothing but reading – I would work my way through a light novella or perhaps just through the reports of that season's rugger matches; Holmes, meanwhile, would read a scientific paper on the latest developments in the lifting of fingerprints from un-smooth surfaces.

I would believe at the end of the day that we had both had a satisfying time of it, only to see Holmes boiling with rage because no elderly man had knocked on our door with a strange tale about having one of his shoes stolen and mysteriously returned without laces, or no young governess whose children became ill on the first Thursday of each month. Stranger still, I would sometimes look up, expecting him to be quietly puffing on his pipe, only to find that he had disappeared, and the next time I clapped eyes on him was a fortnight later dressed as a sepoy and utterly refusing to tell me where he had been all that while.

I sometimes wondered if we were even friends. But then he would catch my gaze and somehow know that that thought had entered my head. And he would laugh and reassure me: 'Watson, old man, the very firmest. The very firmest.'

But let us return to the pie. I enjoyed it thoroughly, stuffing it down as the winter chill froze my fingers. It was mutton, allegedly, though I would not have been too surprised if the local stray cat population had been low-ered by one on account of that meal. Still, by that point I was starving, and a dry sea biscuit would have tasted like manna from Heaven.

Holmes, having taken no more than three small bites of his own pie while I finished my own, impatiently led the way in. Just as an attendant asked him where he was going, he ducked down a corridor marked 'Private' and raced away, leaving me in his wake.

'You can't go down there!' the poor attendant – a gentleman of advancing years – shouted behind us.

'This way,' Holmes called over his shoulder, ignoring every syllable. I apologized to the attendant and followed, Holmes checking the painted signs beside every door, until he burst through one marked 'Arachnids'.

'Sherlock Holmes, consulting detective,' he announced to a wiry little man who was sat at an untidy desk, peering through a huge magnifying glass at a finger-sized scorpion.

The little man, to his credit, did not seem at all put out. 'How can I help you, sir?' he asked in an Ulster accent. Holmes placed before him on the desk the cardboard box supplied by a constable at the scene of death earlier that day. 'First, sir, is whatever you have in this box dead or alive?'

'Dead.'

'Are you quite certain?' the little fellow asked.

'I am.'

The naturalist sneezed, drew on a pair of cotton gloves, placed the scorpion in a glass display case, and gingerly opened the box. 'Good Heavens,' he muttered to himself. He took a pencil and poked the spider, still enclosed by the cardboard. 'Yes, dead. Thank the Lord.' Then he took up a large pair of wooden forceps and plucked the creature out to place it on the glass platform vacated by the scorpion. He examined it under the magnifying glass, then measured it, muttering, 'Six inches by four' to himself. 'We have one already in the collection. But yes, we would like to buy it. We can offer you—'

'I am not here to sell it,' Holmes replied, cutting him off. 'I want to know what it is.'

'Ah.' The scientist turned the spider over with his tweezers. 'A female. Yes, it's a female.'

'A female *what*?' Holmes asked, exasperation visibly building in him.

The wiry man looked surprised. 'You mean you don't know? But how did you even find it, if you don't know?'

'Oh, my dear man. You will get the shock of your life when you open the evening newspapers. But for now, would you please simply inform me what this spider is and where it comes from?'

The naturalist shrugged. '*Peucetia viridans*. The Green Lynx spider. Distributed across South America. A few sparse populations of a rare subspecies have been reported in Asia, and I believe this is from one of those colonies – it is twice the size of the parent species.'

'And if I wanted to acquire, say, a thousand of them, how would I go about doing that?'

'A thousand?' He blinked. 'What in the name of the Lord would you want with a thousand *Peucetia viridans*?'

'You would be surprised.'

'I would, sir. I mean, these creatures. One or two could kill a small dog. A thousand could kill . . .'

'Two men,' Holmes said decisively. 'In the most painful way.'

The naturalist stood up. 'What is this about?'

I felt it was my time to speak. 'Sir, I am Dr John Watson. This afternoon, my friend and I witnessed two men – a minister of the Crown and a former judge – murdered. And the weapon was a thousand of these creatures. So it would be in the interests of common justice if you would aid us in our quest for the truth and perhaps the perpetrator.'

He blinked again and smoothed his hand over his head. 'You can't buy things like this. They aren't pets. You could only trap a few of them in their natural environment and then breed them in a vivarium. They multiply quickly enough. The females lay up to five egg sacs in the autumn.'

'And how many of these sharp-fanged little beasts do you find in each sac?' Holmes asked.

'There can be up to five hundred.' Well, that was a nasty little thought. 'But don't approach them. The mother guards them with her life. And she spits venom at anything that comes close.'

'We have seen what that venom will do,' Holmes said darkly.

The little naturalist looked from Holmes to me, and to the box. His voice fell. 'Is that what I will read about in the evening newspaper?'

'It is.'

The man sighed and sat heavily into an armchair. 'How can I help?'

'Tell me everything about this animal.'

'We must first consider,' Holmes said as we called in to a Spanish restaurant on Queensgate to dine, 'that whoever laid that trap planned and executed it well. We must presume that the two dead men were both the intended victims. While we are aware of the recent deeds of Peter Jet MP, and it would be a strong coincidence if his death were not connected to the affair that we so rudely interrupted last night,' he paused to swallow a spoonful of gazpacho soup, 'we know little of Lord Wyneth.' His mention of the previous night's exertions reminded me that we had not slept, and I instantly became weary – though Holmes seemed no more affected by tiredness than by his soup. 'So let us, for now, list only our reasonable assumptions: first, that Jet was killed because of his seditious plan; second, that there is a connection with Wyneth that has motivated someone to murder them both. Now, it could be that Wyneth was also secretly involved with the sedition plan, or . . .' He dropped his spoon in the soup and stared out the window.

'Or?'

'Or there is a darker, more complex connection. One we have yet to see.'

'Holmes, you have not even mentioned George Reynolds's name. Have you forgotten him entirely?'

'Have you ever known me to forget a single thing?'

'Frequently, when it comes to common humanity!'

'Old chap, that was rather below the belt. But I admit you have a point: I do sometimes focus on the non-human aspects of an investigation. Well, in answer to your question: no, I have not forgotten our client. But since he is in the clutches of Jet's confederates, and we know not where he is or what he is doing and he can supply no more data than he already has, I have relegated him to the fringes of my mental algorithms. In essence, thinking about him does him no good and actually reduces my ability to free him. But free him we will.'

A little mollified, I finished the liver pâté and toast on my plate. 'Well, we know one connection between them.'

'Hmm?'

'The obvious one. They were both on that archaeological dig. Historical Israel. That is why they were the ones to show off the treasures to Her Majesty.'

Holmes collapsed backwards into his seat. 'Ha! Good old Watson. Thank you for drawing to my attention the simple fact that I had been overlooking in favour of complicated ones. Yes, that is where we must strike next. Now, the first thing to consider is this: two men on that expedition have been killed. So who else was on it?'

We finished our meal and hurried to Scotland Yard. Outside that headquarters of the Metropolitan Police, Holmes snatched the late edition of the *Standard* from a news stand, scanned it, dropped it on the ground in irritation and threw the money at an amazed paper boy. Below a headline that spoke of a clutch of younger European politicians urging their nations towards bellicosity, I saw the following advert:

Professor M. sends his compliments to S.H. He begs the latter to understand that he had no part in the occurrence mentioned. He was present only to pursue a private matter with the judicial individual and was thwarted by events. He asks S.H. to now return to their previous relationship, which involves no communication.

'Do you believe him? He had no hand in what happened?'

'I do,' Holmes replied. 'Not for want of desire – I become more convinced that the historical friction between the judge and the Professor is an element in this tale. Lestrade!' Holmes yelled. The inspector, walking into the building, looked back in annoyance. He was not used to being hailed in such a fashion.

'What is it, Mr Holmes?' he muttered as we caught up with him.

'Have you anyone here, making a statement or such, connected with the British Museum exhibit?'

'We have the curator, one Mr Walsh-Meadows.'

'Take me to him.'

Sometimes it would not occur to Holmes that other people had plans and arrangements of their own. But Lestrade was too busy for a never-ending argument and beckoned over one of his sergeants, whom he instructed to take Holmes and myself to the gentleman he had just named.

A few minutes later, we were in the presence of a surprisingly young and spritely curator of the British Museum's antiquities.

'My speciality is the Holy Land,' he explained. 'This was to be my first major exhibit.' He looked despondent for the loss of exposure rather than for the loss of life, and I wondered how many human beings in London there were with a little bit of Sherlock Holmes in them.

'And tell me,' Holmes began, 'have there been any threats against it?'

'Threats? What sort of ... No, no one ever threatens an exhibition.' Then he thought for a second. 'Do they?'

'Not to the best of my knowledge. Any strange occurrences during the planning?'

'None that I know of.'

'Have you ever seen one of these spiders before?'

'No, I don't think so. Are they native to Britain?'

'Thankfully not. Now, most importantly, please tell me about the expedition itself.'

He explained the history. Some years before, the Museum had sponsored a dig to search for ancient treasures around Jerusalem. They were expecting Roman artefacts as well as Jewish ones, and possibly Hellenic or Ottoman, from the time of those occupations. In charge of a few local porters and labourers were three principal men: Jet, Wyneth and a third man. In recent times, this third individual had chosen to disassociate himself from the expedition, which was why he had not been part of the group intended to welcome the Queen.

Holmes leaned in. 'And what is his name?'

'He is a musician now. Benjamin Ridge.'

'Ridge? I have seen him play Brahms,' Holmes exclaimed. 'A violinist, Watson.'

'A good one?'

'Indeed, quite brilliant. There is something about his playing that is, how should I put it? Reckless. Unconstrained. It abandons formality. Oh, he plays the music that the composer has denoted, but somehow at the same time he almost disregards it to play something better. And at any second, he could veer off into disaster. Yes, he is reckless. Without delay, we must tell him that his life is in danger. Mr Walsh-Meadows, do you have an address for him?'

'I am afraid not.'

'That is a pity. I think we needs must send wires to every concert venue to enquire about the gentleman's whereabouts.'

There was a knock at the door. A constable entered with a ruby-red envelope. *Mr Sherlock Holmes, in the care of Scotland Yard*, the front displayed formally. 'Well, well,' my friend said after opening it and scanning the contents. He handed the letter to me.

14 Larches Lane,
Greenwich

Dear Mr Holmes,
   Since you have failed to take sufficient heed of my previous messages to you, I shall explain in full the dark danger that has the whole world in its grip. I assure you, it is greater than you can possibly imagine. Please call at eight. Do not be late.
   Yours sincerely,
   Benjamin Ridge

'So, one mystery is solved,' said Holmes. 'Now we know who sent the telegram and scrawled the message on my bedroom mirror.'

I rather like Greenwich, on the Thames. I have had a few good evenings playing three-card brag at the Naval College. It would have been a pleasant jaunt down there were it not for the nasty smog that night – and the fact that the strangeness of our invitation had led me to take the precaution of packing my service revolver. Holmes was armed with his weighted cane – one he was adept at using as a weapon, as he had mastered the martial art of *baritsu*.

Ridge's home turned out to be a large villa on the river-front – possibly once the harbourmaster's, by the grand old look of it. It was quite dark, though, so that the only reason we found the front gate was that there was a street-lamp directly in front of it, dropping a circle of orangey light. 'Here we are, Watson,' Holmes said. 'Now to see what awaits us. Be on your guard.'

'I will.'

We strode through the gate. For a substantial house that implied wealth, if not an actual fortune, it was in an unkempt state. The garden was quite overgrown with bushes and weeds even thicker than the smog. The lamp that we had brought cast a light on the front door, which seemed not to have been painted in years – although, to give it its due, the mist from the river probably aged it faster than was natural. At least three of the panes in the upper windows had been knocked out, too. All in all, it had the air of an old man who had given up the ghost and was preparing to meet his maker.

'Rather uncanny, wouldn't you say, old friend?'

'I would.'

Instead of a bell-pull, there was an actual brass bell beside the entrance. Holmes rang it vigorously and stood back to see what effect it would have on the occupants.

None, as it turned out. We waited, and he tried again. Still nothing. 'Well, the welcome is about as warm as the exterior would suggest,' my companion said with a wry smile. 'No matter, let us take a scout about.' And with that, he set off around the side of the building.

It was a square edifice, built, I should say, a century before. The summer sun and winter rain had roasted and battered it as much as they could, but it was still solid as ever – its poor state of decoration notwithstanding. We trod over mossy gravel to sneak around to the rear. All was just as dark and silent back there. From time to time, I caught on the air the distant sound of jollity and celebration from an inn nearby and I rather hankered to join the inmates of that place, rather than skulk around outside this apparently empty mausoleum of the past.

'Aha,' Holmes announced. 'And what do we have here?' He was a yard or two in front of me, and I looked where he was pointing with his cane. It was a ground-floor window, and one of the panes had cracked in. 'Well, let us not stand on ceremony.' He reached through it and slid the catch. 'We are, after all, invited guests. And if the host will not open his doors to us, we must find our own method of entry.' He lifted the window. Luckily, it was a large one and was easy to climb through. I followed, my feet crunching on shattered glass. I stumbled a little. 'Careful, old man,' Holmes whispered. 'Who knows what ghosts are hiding in these crevices?'

I carefully shone my light around what proved to be the kitchen. It had been grand once, with three ranges and what looked to be a cold store at the back. The tiles were frosty, and we nearly slid across them as we explored. Holmes opened the door to the cold store.

'Precious little in here,' he said in a low voice. 'If friend Ridge is in residence, he is not a great gourmand.' He put his hand to the ranges, too. 'Stone cold. Let us go further in.'

We slipped out of the room, taking care to make as little noise as we could. Somehow the air seemed frostier inside that house than outside. I cannot explain it, but it got into the bones more. We found ourselves padding along the servants' corridor. Then out into the hallway – a more domestic affair, with a big old porter's chair by the double front doors, a hat stand made from an elephant's foot and pictures on the walls of musicians and instruments through the ages. Pride of place went to a large oil painting of a Renaissance gentleman playing a violin. As the lamplight fell on it, though, I noticed the strangest thing. It seemed to have been the victim of a violent assault, for the smile on the man with the instrument clamped under his chin had been carved into the canvas with a knife. That rictus grin, the canvas flapping down from it, was quite startlingly grotesque. 'Someone has a terrible grudge,' I muttered.

'I am inclined to agree,' Holmes answered, staring up where my lamp's beam illuminated the act of violence. 'But we must ask ourselves: what does this really mean? And, more importantly, who did it?'

We stole on, through doors covered in what had once been fine, plum-coloured leather but was now cracked and rubbed away, splitting into tiger stripes. We found ourselves in a library, but one which seemed to have been in the middle of a war, for half the books were strewn across the floor, furniture was overturned and a large china vase lay smashed across the fire grate. 'Mr Ridge needs a better class of domestic servant,' Holmes said thoughtfully.

'I fear there is more to it than that.'

'So do I.' He picked up one of the discarded volumes. '*Visions of What Lies Beyond: The Hebrews and the Afterlife*. Ridge has an esoteric bent.' Everything we said was under our breath, as if the spirits in that house would pounce on any word above a whisper.

I plucked up another. *Nicolo Paganini: The Brilliant Player of the Violin Who Most Evilly Sold His Soul to Lucifer*. 'This one is no cheerier,' I said, displaying the title in the lamp's beam.

'Most assuredly not.'

Suddenly, I heard the sound of movement in one of the shadowy corners behind me. I whirled around and aimed my gun, the hammer cocked. A black and white cat strode out, hissed at me and then sprinted away into the house. I lowered my weapon and decided to follow, back into the hallway. I took a single step outside, then froze.

'Don't move.'

It was a threatening low voice to my side. And I had no choice but to obey. Because I felt the steel of a gun barrel against my right temple. I could not see him, but something in the man's voice told me that he would have no qualms about pulling the trigger.

'Mr Ridge?' I asked, keeping my voice calm. 'You asked us to come.'

'Oh no, I'm not Mr Ridge,' came the mocking reply. He grabbed the lamp out of my grip and turned it into my face. 'Now, very slowly, step back into that room.'

I did as he said. My revolver was by my waist, and it must have been masked by the doorframe because the man with a gun on me did not tell me to drop it. As I gently moved backwards, I slipped my hand with the gun around the wall so it was still hidden. He followed me. All I could see was the torch shining in my eyes, burning them, and his revolver pointing at my chest. I took a second pace back.

'Back further,' the voice ordered me. I took another step. And he followed so that we were both in the room. 'And now, very slowly, put your gun on the floor.' I cursed my luck that my weapon was now visible. I hesitated. 'Do it. Or I will shoot you.'

'You may do that, Moran, but the moment you do, I will shatter your skull to pieces.' It was Holmes. He had flattened himself to the wall and had his weighted stick raised above the Colonel's head, ready to do exactly as he threatened. At that, I very slowly raised the barrel of my gun so that it aimed just above the lamp. 'And now you have two weapons on you. So it is time to lower yours.'

'Never,' he snarled back. I knew Sebastian Moran. He was not bluffing.

The black and white cat slunk back into the room. It hissed again at me as it passed, making for the unlit far corner.

Holmes raised his voice to call out. 'You must be here, too, Professor. The Colonel does not tend to stray too far from your sight these days.'

'Oh, I am here, Mr Holmes,' a voice growled from the hallway.

'Then show yourself. Place the lamp on the floor, Colonel. There's a good fellow.'

I moved out of the way, and Moran matched my movement. I saw his silhouette slide to the side. And then, in the doorway stood Professor Moriarty, the most dangerous man in Europe.

'Why are you two here to interrupt my designs once again?' he enquired, his unconcerned tone suggesting that he could have been asking the time of day.

'We are simply out to take the refreshing air in Greenwich,' said Holmes. 'I assure you, interrupting your designs is nothing but an added pleasure.'

'I presume you received one of these, too,' Moriarty replied. He thrust into the lamp's glow a red envelope just like the one we had been sent.

'You presume correctly.'

I was eyeing Moran. The muscles in his hand were twitching. It would take only the slightest excuse for him to shoot me and then take his chances with Holmes. 'Moran, just so you know, if you fire, I promise you I will return the shot even if I have a bullet in my chest,' I said.

'Tough talk, Doctor.'

'"Major". And you are not the only one in the room to have seen action.' At the very thought, my old shoulder wound started to burn, but I made sure he did not see that.

'Do control your underling,' Moriarty said to Holmes. He held a walking cane, and I had a good mind what was concealed within it. 'I am expected at Kensington Palace for a round of whist this evening and should hate to disappoint their Royal Highnesses.'

'I should much prefer to control yours. Perhaps by splitting his head in two,' my friend returned.

'Mr Holmes, you are not my concern this evening. You will be soon, but not this night.'

'And yet you are my concern often.'

'Very gratifying. But there is no advantage to any of us bringing matters to a head like this. There will be a time. And I assure you that it will be of my choosing.'

At that, Holmes allowed himself a chuckle. 'Time, tide and the manacles of Scotland Yard do not wait upon you, Professor. They will be your masters, not your servants.'

There was a tense silence as we all appraised the situation. It was true that we were evenly matched forces and none would escape without a scratch if it came to all-out war. Moriarty was an arrogant swine, but that made us safer; at any time other than that moment, he could design matters so that we would be dangling at the end of his rope. Right then and there, however, the outcome would be anybody's guess.

'And so it seems we are at an impasse,' Holmes said, enjoying Moriarty's discomfiture at his rare lack of control.

'It would be best for you to withdraw.'

'But we have only just arrived, Professor. And we have all of us been invited. The fact that our host managed to find you with a letter suggests that he has some resources – I am sure Scotland Yard, with all its employees and street-touts, would be hard pressed to match his success.'

The cat came back into sight. It was licking and shaking its paws in a strange fashion as it walked.

'I know nothing of the man.'

I watched the cat as it came into the circle of light.

'We know a little.'

'Holmes,' I said.

'Watson?'

'The cat. Look.'

He carefully glanced down. The animal was in the centre of the yellow glow, licking its paws. Attempting to clean them of what was caked into the fur. It was dark red, congealing blood. And a trail of it, in feline pawprints, led back to a distant corner.

'There seems to be more to find in this room,' Holmes said darkly. 'Moran, would you be so kind?'

Moriarty waved his hand in instruction to Moran. The Colonel slowly bent to the lamp and turned it to light the red tracks back to the unlit recesses of the room. The prints ended at a wall case of books.

'Nothing there,' Moran grunted.

'You must learn to look with your mind as well as your eyes, Colonel,' Holmes said. 'The tracks begin there, so there must be a source there. Professor, I propose a brief truce in our game. This situation touches both of us, and we would be best devoting our energies to it, rather than to each other. There will be time enough for that later.'

Moriarty opened his mouth to speak. And the next second told me two things: that Sebastian Moran deserved his reputation as a hunter; and that Sherlock Holmes is no prey.

Moran, quick as a flash, barged his shoulder against me, knocking me to the wall. At the same time, he turned his gun barrel to point at Holmes. But Holmes, having anticipated the move, whirled and dipped his body so that the shot that rang out missed him by an inch, and then the lead-weighted stick in his hand cracked down hard on Moran's wrist. The gun fell to the floor, and my friend picked it up and trained it on he who had just then wielded it. Meanwhile, I pushed Moran aside and aimed my own pistol back on his chest. 'I have you,' I growled, as angry as I had been for years and more than ready to pull the trigger. I had to fight all my urges not to.

I saw in Moran's face pure fury, but he somehow mastered himself so that he remained still as an oak.

'Oh, Colonel. How you have squandered your only credit. Tut tut,' Holmes said cheerily.

'Fool,' Moriarty added.

Moran said nothing, maintaining only a sullen silence. But his looks spoke volumes of hate.

'And now, every card is in our hands. Why don't both you gentlemen walk ahead of us where we can see you? That's the corner to make for. Quick sharp.'

Moriarty, so often urbane, flashed a look at Moran that said he was ready to break his neck, then strode past him to the dark end of the room.

'Move,' I ordered the Colonel and took up the lamp.

Moran shifted a few sulky paces. 'There's nothing there,' he muttered.

'Of course there is,' his master retorted. He poked his cane to the floor and lifted its point.

I shone the light, and the tip of his stick showed red. I lowered the beam. There was a pool of blood mixing with the dust on the floorboards. But what was strange was that the pool did not end at the bottom of the bookcase but seemed to flow right out from under it.

'The source,' said Holmes, 'is behind that case.'

'Are you sure?' I asked.

'Evidently. There is no origin here – that amount of blood means a major wound, and there are no trails to or from the pooling. Save that of our feline friend, of course. Therefore it must be on the other side. You two, shift the case.' Moriarty stood aside, mutely refusing menial work, but Moran relented and attempted to move the case. He was unable to and stood back, glaring at us. 'Then there must be a hidden mechanism.' Holmes waved them aside and placed his gun in his pocket. 'Do not hesitate, Watson.'

'I won't.'

He searched through the shelves, pulling all the remaining books down to the floor. Then he smoothed his hands around the frame of the case. 'Aha,' he said. And he clicked something metallic at the side. 'Not even a mechanism, a simple catch.' He pulled the case, which twisted out on a hinge, into the room where we stood. I tightened my grip on the pistol and shone the lamp beam. Holmes took his gun out of his pocket.

Behind the case was a doorway that gave on to a room the size of a large bed chamber. I need not have shone the lamp nor levelled my pistol as I did, because the room was well lit with a spirit lamp that stood on a square copper table. It illuminated an extraordinary chamber lined with glass display

161

cases, each one full of treasures that must have come from the Jerusalem dig. There were stone jars and tablets, fragments of parchment and what appeared to be musical instruments fashioned from bone and wood. By contrast, a fine-looking European violin rested whimsically among those exotic and simple instruments. And there was something else, something that had once been more majestic than all of them.

On the floor, its skin blistering away from the bleeding flesh just like the other two bodies that we had seen that day, lay the body of a man aged around forty. He had been a handsome one, with dark features and a black-as-coal moustache. His hair was long and wild in a romantic gypsy way, and he wore a brilliant smoking jacket of orange and yellow swirls.

'Too late,' Holmes said, his anger mixed with despondency.

For form's sake, I knelt to him – while keeping the gun pointing at our two captives, who had crept forward to stand in the doorway – and felt his neck for a pulse. Again, in case there was venom on his skin, I felt through a handkerchief. Nothing. Neither did his wrist give the beat of life.

'Man needs a hearse, not a doctor,' Moran sniffed.

'Is it Ridge?' I asked.

'It was.' Holmes felt the man's chest. 'He is still warm. Not so long dead.'

I twitched the gun at Moriarty. 'Oh, Dr Watson. Enough of that,' he replied, brushing some smut from his lapel. 'It is bad enough having to witness the effect of your failures without being accused of originating them. Today I have done nothing more offensive than see some mediocre art. Should I describe it to you? There was a rather poor depiction of Margate. There—'

'I do not think our friends here had anything to do with this,' Holmes said to me, cutting him off.

'Are you certain?'

'Certain? No. But why would they attempt to hide the death and then wait around the house to be discovered?'

'Hmm.' I was not wholly convinced. Holmes had taught me that you could never guess one quarter of what was in Professor Moriarty's mind at any one time. I set about examining the cadaver. A mark on the back of his neck stood out. It was different to the others, more like a pin-prick. And it was fresh. 'Holmes, this is a needle-mark. He has been injected. Within the last hour, I would say.'

'Foul play for sure, Watson. He was to tell us of a great, encroaching danger, but he has been silenced.'

'Would he—'

But I never finished my words because, at that moment, an astounding thing happened. I should, having experienced just such a sight that afternoon, have expected it now. But once more, the eyes of the dead man below me flicked open, his mouth sprang open and he cried out a single repeated word in a cracking and wracked voice.

'Ardeo! Ardeo!'

And even in the midst of the astonishment I felt that a dead man had come back to life, my school Latin bounded about my brain.

I am burning. I am burning.

His terrified eyes flicked everywhere as if he were

watching devils flying around him, and Holmes and I had to grab hold of his limbs to hold him down.

'Keep him still,' I ordered Holmes. I tore off my jacket and placed it under his head to prevent him smashing his skull on the floor.

'*Ardeo!*'

'Ridge!' Holmes yelled at him. 'Ridge, you are alive! Take a hold of yourself!' And at that, the man's gaze suddenly ceased its mad roving and focused sharply on my companion.

'You,' he croaked. 'You.' And at that, my amazement redoubled as he began to laugh a cadaverous laugh.

'Yes, me.'

The laughter faded, and the man's eyes closed a little, but stayed on us. Then they slipped over to our captives. 'And Moriarty, too.'

'I should say you have us at something of a disadvantage, Mr Ridge,' Moriarty replied, as calm as if he had met the man walking in Hyde Park.

'Would you? Like this?' and he chuckled to himself once more, but the laughter turned into a wracking, shivering fit of his body. His eyelids drooped.

'Why are we here?' Holmes asked. But the only answer was a deep sigh. 'Jet and Wyneth are dead. Who killed them? How does it connect with the abduction of George Reynolds?'

Ridge's tongue crept out over dry lips. 'You . . .' A spasm of pain shot through him, and he cried out before sinking back into himself and panting lightly for air.

'Ridge!'

'Questions . . .'

'We must know.'

'Yes, you must.' His voice returned, weak but stable. He turned from Holmes to Moriarty. 'I read your paper on the binomial theorem.'

'Most gratifying,' Moriarty replied. 'Am I to take it we are here to discuss it?'

Ridge smiled. 'If only you knew what is coming, Moriarty.'

'I doubt I should be too concerned.'

'But you should, Professor. For all your cleverness, there are others who are supermen to your *homo erectus*.'

'I care little for your—'

'They will destroy you. They will destroy everything,' he whispered. 'All that you have. All that you think you will ever have. It will turn to dust in your hands, and you will die weeping by the roadside.'

And there was something in his tone, something in the way he spoke, that meant that I, Holmes, Moran and Moriarty all felt the same thing: this man's words were no fool's tale. He was speaking from knowledge. Knowledge as hard and immovable as a mountain.

So for the first time, I saw Moriarty look unsettled. Nervous, even. It was only a flicker, a second, but I saw it pass across his face.

'Who will do so?' Holmes demanded.

'They will know of this already. They know all. They will be . . . coming for you now.'

'Who?'

'The . . .' But something was clouding Ridge's hazel

165

irises. Something seeping across the colour: a stain of red. Blood was filling his eyes, the little vessels bursting, flooding the orbital cavity.

'*Who?*'

'You must . . .' It was a whisper as his breath failed him. 'W-work as one. Or . . . the whole world is . . . is lost. My . . . violin.'

His hands reached out to where his instrument lay in a cabinet, apparently desperate one last time to hold the precious item that had brought him fame and notoriety.

'What will they do? Who did this to you?' Holmes asked.

At that, Moriarty strode over, grabbed the lapels of Ridge's smoking jacket and shook him. 'I will kill them myself. Where are they?'

'Switzer . . . Grunden. Oh, God!' And the pain of suffering behind those final words pierced us all, as the man around whom we were crowded died for a second time. His lifeless body fell to the floor. And this time, there would be no return.

We stood and retreated to opposing sides of the small room. I fingered the pistol in my grip. I trusted the two men before me as much as I would trust a demon.

'Control yourself, Doctor,' Moriarty said. 'Though one does wonder how you gained that title, given your inability to discern a dead man from a living one. Perhaps you consider it an unimportant skill.'

'Remember who has the gun,' I replied. He adjusted his cuffs. 'What now?' I asked Holmes.

'My friend, the future and how we should approach it is far from clear.' He watched Moriarty.

'You cannot seriously be considering Ridge's sugges-
tion that you work with that animal?' I said under my
breath.

In reply, Holmes only stared thoughtfully at the criminal on the other side of the chamber. Then he shrugged.

'More data. I need more data.' He sauntered over to
the cabinet full of primitive musical instruments, with the
European violin among them. All the while, I could hear
Moriarty and Moran muttering to each other – probably
asking themselves just the same questions we had asked.
'Ah, of course he would have a Stradivarius,' Holmes said,
opening the glass door and plucking out the instrument.
With his back to me, he put the bow to it and drew out a
rapid waterfall of notes.

'What is that?' I asked, at a loss for other conversation.

He paused. 'Paganini,' he replied. 'Like Ridge, a
madman. Perhaps a diabolist, too. And yet, can you hear?'
He played another cascade of notes. They ran up and
down scales, pouring from the strings.

'I hear only the music,' I said. 'It sounds like the man
was possessed.'

Holmes spun around to me. 'Oh, he was, he was. He
sold his soul to the Devil in return for his talent. Moriarty,
can you hear it?'

'Parlour games,' that villain muttered. 'I am not interested in playing them.'

'But this game is a deadly one. You must hear something remarkworthy.'

'I do not.'

'Ah, no matter.' And then, quite astonishingly, Holmes

lifted the priceless instrument and dashed it to pieces against the wall.

The wood turned to matchsticks, some wound together by the catgut, others tumbling to the floor in a patter of splinters. I saw Moran coil himself, ready for an assault, while Moriarty furrowed his brow in mild confusion.

Just as I was about to ask Holmes what on earth he was doing, he yelped out 'Ha!' and snatched a sheet of paper that had fallen from the violin's central cavity. 'You must have heard how the sound was off? A Stradivarius with an imperfect tone? Hardly credible. No, there was something within the lower bout that was interfering with the resonance.' He held the page above his head in triumph, then placed it on the table in the centre of the room. I joined him and peered at it.

I felt my eyes crossing as they stared down at the sheet. We were looking at a full page of random letters laid out like normal text. Well, I say 'random', but any military man knows a cypher when he sees one. I stood back and let Holmes exercise that extraordinary mental faculty of his, confident in his ability to see through the cypher and read what had to be a document of unique importance. A minute went by. Holmes remained still as a rock. Another minute. A third. I swear I saw a bead of sweat run down his temple and to his cheek. And then, 'Pah!' He plucked the page from the table, cast it aside and stomped to the side of the room. 'Impossible. A grille cypher. Without the decryption sheet, there is no way of knowing its contents.'

'A grille cypher?'

'An old technique. Bacon was a great proponent. One

has a top sheet with holes cut in it. That sheet is then placed onto the page of code. You read the individual letters that appear through the holes. The text is then—'

'Playfair.' It was Moriarty who had spoken. He was holding the page in his hand.

'What? I asked.

'It is not a grille. It is a Playfair cypher.'

'Are you certain?' Holmes asked.

Moriarty raised an eyebrow. 'Lyon Playfair consulted me on how best to design the system. So yes, I am certain.'

'Well,' Holmes said, 'that is not much better. We need the decryption key phrase. If it were a Vigenère cypher, we could have used relatively simple frequency analysis to break it. But a Playfair is of a different magnitude of complexity. No man can break a Playfair unless he has a year in which to do it.'

'Be quiet,' Moriarty said. And it was not an irritated demand, but a simple request. He needed silence in which to work.

'Do not . . .' I began in annoyance. But Holmes lifted a finger to his lips.

And Moriarty began what I can only describe as a sort of slow mime, lifting his hands here and there, slotting imaginary items onto invisible shelves, writing equations and algorithms in the air with his empty fingers.

How long were we there? I cannot tell. An hour or more, I should estimate, none of us moving a muscle. I found it tiring. Holmes, I think, found it fascinating. Moran enjoyed watching us, as if we were caged beasts.

Until finally: 'The decryption key is: "In the beginning".'

I watched Holmes for a reaction. The only one I could see was a slight stretching of his mouth into the commencement of a smile.

'Bravo, Professor,' he said slowly. 'I imagine there is no other man alive who could mentally crack a Playfair.'

Moriarty hesitated. 'Hmm, there is one other,' he relented. 'Singh of Calcutta. But he is close to death.'

'How close?' I asked.

He opened his pocket watch and looked at the dial. 'A little over four hours. I am afraid I cannot be more accurate. It rather depends on the efficiency of the Indian postal service.'

'Will you favour us with the plain text?' Holmes asked.

Moriarty dictated carefully. He was, I realized, simultaneously completing complex algorithmic calculations as he spoke.

Her Majesty's Foreign and Colonial Office. Report from our man Mercury in the Levant. First of October 1881.

On the orders of the section colonel, I joined the expedition comprising Mr Benjamin Ridge, Mr Peter Jet and Lord Wyneth of Darlington. Our mission – and my presence in particular – were to be kept secret, due to the chance of the Turkish sultan taking anger and the very real danger of direct conflict. The balance in that region of the world is to be maintained until such time as we have the advantage.

We sailed first to the port of Haifa, via Salonika, arriving on the seventh of April. The local Ottoman authorities are indolent and corrupt, so that it took only a little minor baksheesh to be granted safe travel. The Governor of Haifa, indeed, presumed to request that his son be granted a place at Eton from the autumn and offered to pay the fees in silver coins, with a gratuity to ourselves of the same again if we could arrange said request. I assured him that I would put the matter in train.

'That is all the text,' Moriarty said.

'A pity. Evidently the rest of the report is elsewhere,' Holmes commented. 'Perhaps Ridge was unable to secure it or was relieved of it. We can only speculate at this time. But assuredly, the man "Mercury" is an individual we would be happy to encounter.'

Moriarty adjusted his black necktie. 'Well, well, Mr Holmes. We appear to have ourselves a predicament. Everything will turn to dust in our hands, according to Mr Ridge. Are we to believe him?'

'Moriarty, I have seen things recently that hardly seem possible. A member of the Cabinet attempting sedition. A diabolical trap that killed him and another in front of a thousand onlookers. A man who can surreptitiously enter my house and engineer our meeting. And I cannot even guess what you have seen in the last few days. But you are as convinced of the danger as I am. Whatever is coming, I have no doubt that Ridge spoke true when he led us to believe that it is of a magnitude the world has yet to encounter.'

'You have had quite the week-end.' He examined a cabinet of stone tablets. 'But I have seen dangers before. They do not concern me as they concern you.'

'Do not attempt to veil your own fear.'

'Fear? Pah!' At that, Moriarty stiffened and twisted away from us, seemingly to stare at the wall. I was about to speak but, having been silenced by Holmes before when on the verge of interrupting Moriarty's train of thought, I held back. And we waited.

Then Moriarty turned. He and Holmes locked gazes. They did not move, they did not break eye contact. They remained staring silently at one another for minutes that felt like hours. Until Moriarty spoke.

'A catastrophe.'

'It seems so,' Holmes replied.

'A reversal.'

'For certain.'

'Switzerland,' Moriarty said thoughtfully.

'Just so.'

More time swallowed us.

'Technology.'

'Jerusalem.'

A long pause, and then finally, Moriarty's mouth expanded into a smile. 'No, I do not think so.'

'You do not?'

'No, I do not need you, Mr Holmes. The threat is a phantom.' He blew imaginary leaves from his palm.

'Professor . . .'

But Holmes was cut off by an extraordinary sound of hammering from outside in the house. It was the front door, and someone was beating his fists upon it.

'A friend of yours,' Moriarty said. 'Judging from the lack of manners.'

'That way,' Holmes pointed with his revolver. And Moriarty led us with little concern towards the entrance to the house.

I was ready for anything as I threw the door open, my gun discreetly by my side, but was astonished to see a face I knew: Hopkins, a Scotland Yard inspector who was a great admirer of Holmes.

'Hopkins?'

'Dr Watson! There is not a moment to lose. You must leave this instant!' he gabbled.

'As predicted,' Moriarty muttered.

'But why?'

'There is a squad of constables coming right now to arrest you and Mr Holmes.'

'On what charge?'

'Murder.'

'Murder of whom?' Holmes said, striding forwards.

'The man who lives here. Ridge is his name.'

Holmes looked at me sternly. 'It seems Ridge knew this game better than we do: whoever is operating this great conspiracy, they are able to give orders within Scotland Yard.' Then something appeared to occur to him. 'You are here to arrest *us* alone?'

At that, Moriarty slipped from the shadows into the light. I could see from Hopkins's face that he recognized the criminal mastermind.

'Oh yes, Mr Holmes. Just you for arrest.' His voice changed. 'But him, him the lads have been told to take somewhere special. Not on the books, you might say.'

'You . . .' Moran snarled.

But Moriarty lifted a hand to stop him. 'There is little advantage in posturing now, Moran. The resources of the constabulary are substantial and not to be trivialized.' He turned to Holmes.

'Circumstances have changed, Professor,' my friend said.

'They have.'

'Then I take it we have an agreement.'

'Logic would now dictate so.'

My enemy's enemy is my friend? No, no that is not true, no matter how many times you have heard it. But my enemy's enemy is my ally, now that I have seen to be true.

'How long do we have?' Holmes asked the policeman.

'Minutes. No more than five.'

'Then let us spend them usefully.' At double speed, and while Hopkins stood guard outside, we continued our search of the hidden room for anything that could lead us to the dark facts behind our predicament.

'Holmes,' I said under my breath. 'What passed between you and Moriarty?'

'A pact.'

'A pact? With that murderer?'

He placed his hands on my shoulders. 'Old friend, when the world is burning, you pass the pail to whoever will take it. Ridge summoned us both. He must have calculated that the only way to avert the cataclysm he foresaw was to use both our talents.'

'But you and Moriarty . . .!'

'You must realize that no man on this earth is as mathematical in his decisions as James Moriarty. He cares for nothing at all except his survival. He would work with an angel or the Devil to get what he wants. And the pact between us is his best chance.'

'But . . .'

'For my part, it sticks in the craw, but I proposed it because while the danger we face could well turn out to be a phantom, Ridge's belief was that it may also spell the end of life as we know it. Such levels of danger are not unknown: we barely survived the Black Death; the religious wars could have ended the lives of half the population of Europe. Whatever Ridge knew of, I fear it is of that magnitude. So yes, I will walk beside this creature for as long as is necessary.'

'And when it is no longer necessary?'

'Then I imagine we will turn on each other like wolves. Now *that* is interesting, is it not?' Holmes said, pointing to a framed photograph in a cabinet. It was of three men wearing desert exploration gear. And they were all recognizable: Ridge, Wyneth and Jet. 'Yes. Our three explorers.'

'What is interesting about it?'

Holmes glanced at me. 'But don't you see?'

I stared hard. The men were in an arid landscape, before what seemed to be a stone entranceway into a mausoleum. It was a very bright day, as I presumed would always be the case in the Levant. Four pith helmets lay before them. 'I confess that I do not.'

'Three men in the photograph, four pith helmets on the ground. No local labourer would be wearing such an item.'

'There's a fourth explorer,' I said. 'The man taking the photograph.'

'Precisely.' He turned it over. There was writing on the back. 'Jet, Ridge, Wyneth, Mercury. Jerusalem, 1881.'

'Mercury again. Curious name.'

He wafted the photograph in the air. 'Quite possibly an alias of some kind.' But then something else in the cabinet caught his attention, and he drew out a roll of parchment.

It showed a series of stylized pictures in bold colours, like Egyptian hieroglyphs. Reading from the left, the first picture was of a tawny man – a high-born man, it seemed, for he was wearing an animal fur over his shoulders – who was laid out on his back, while a greyer version of him seemed to rise out of his body towards a white disc. In the second image, he was seen kneeling as if before an altar, and beside him there was a green spider, with a yellow disc now present above him. In the last one, he was standing under the yellow disc. There must have been another panel before the first one, but it had been torn away. All one could see of it was a ripped left edge.

Moriarty watched us briefly, then went back to his own examination of the room. If there was to be collaboration, it was not destined to be a warm one.

Under each of the pictures was a series of ink strokes in an alphabet not our own.

'It's Hebrew!' I declared.

'Almost, old man: it is Aramaic.'

'Aramaic,' I said, marvelling at the script of ancient Israel.

'I learned something of the language many years ago

for a case involving the theft of a biblical document. Note, of course, that as a Semitic language it runs from right to left, as do the panels we see.' I looked from right to left, as he instructed. And the actions of the man on the page seemed more sensical: standing, then kneeling, then lying. 'I am somewhat rusty,' Holmes said. 'But if I recall correctly, this first panel is entitled "the lord"; the second is "seek or uncover"; this final one is "knowledge". And this yellowish circle obviously represents the sun; and its white replacement, the moon. It is a pity that the final panel has been violently removed.' He stroked the edge where it had been torn away. 'Ripped, of course, so whoever did it was in a hurry without recourse to scissors or a good knife, which must mean a certain urgency – probably a fear of discovery, given the precious nature of the document. The man who did it was right-handed and wore a signet ring on the fourth finger of his hand: you see the direction of tearing, as witnessed by the fibres of the parchment, is downwards and slightly to the left – and those thin, shallow scores made at regular intervals following the same course but two inches to the right. Though I feel that is all that we can say of it.'

'Then it is time we departed for Switzerland,' Moriarty declared.

'Agreed,' said Holmes. 'And given our current legal predicament, the legitimate methods of transport out of the country are quite impossible. Professor, we shall rely on you.'

'Moran, make the arrangements. Use the Folkestone route. And we must briefly stop at our current lodging.

There is a telegram to dispatch and an item I needs must take with us.' He paused and stared at a picture on the wall of a bucolic country scene. Rosy-cheeked wenches were pouring wine while young bucks played with spaniels. 'Also, take that painting. I like it.'

At that, we left, at speed, from the rear of the house, hailing a cab to HMS *Elysium* and then travelling incognito by train from a suburban station unlikely to be under watch. During the journey, we related what had befallen us in the previous three days. Moriarty reciprocated – although it did occur to me that we had no means of verifying a word he said.

'I don't trust him,' I told Holmes when Moriarty and Moran were out of earshot on the platform at Herne Hill station. 'No matter how much you say he has calculated that it is in his best interest to collaborate,' I insisted, 'what if one day his hatred of you gets the better of him?'

'Of course you don't trust him, old friend. That is because you are a more emotional – a more humane – person than Moriarty. Emotion no more enters into his calculation than the price of fish. Probably less. His mental ledger has shown him that his likelihood of survival and flourishing – in his own strange field of criminal enterprise – is greater if he follows this path. Therefore he will do so.'

'If you say so,' I replied. But I remained sceptical, I must say. I crossed my arms. Holmes seemed not to notice.

'Interesting, is it not? That double death.' Still annoyed, I furrowed my brow and asked him what he was talking about. 'How Ridge and the other victims all seemed to die twice. When we thought they were gone, they came back for a minute, before more permanently giving up the ghost.'

'The human body is full of surprises.' I was not in the mood to continue the discussion and took the opportunity to straighten in my mind the jumble of events that had befallen us in the past days. It was a terrible litany of crimes that only darkened as the trail led on: a young man – still, worryingly, missing – who had come to us with a strange story of a theatre play with a fake audience that turned out to be a ruse to keep him under observation while the perpetrators groomed him to seize the throne. Then, when we came to confront Jet, the supposed mastermind, he had been murdered in quite the most horrifying manner I have ever witnessed, along with another man who seemed to have had a grudge against Moriarty. And now their friend from the archaeological dig was dead, too.

All this I could have taken in my stride, given some of the adventures that I had lived through in my partnership with Sherlock Holmes, but for the presence of Professor James Moriarty. My mind would never be at rest in his presence.

Chapter 20

I've never understood what sea-shaggers like about sailing. You roll about, trying not to vomit your guts up, chewing on maggot-infested biscuits and picking salt out of your ears. Not my idea of a swell time.

The guv'nor has a boat on standby in Folkestone for just this sort of caper, though. It's a sleek 'un, too: faster than anything the coastguard can muster. And it's captained by a bloke drummed out of the Russian navy for excessive brutality – which is going some, I'll tell you.

It's a route we've only had to call on once before, when we had some especially hot tomfoolery to fence in Amsterdam and the Professor fancied escorting it himself. It's not the Cunard Steamship Company. No fancy little French *amuse-bouches*, but it gets you away from Blighty slippery as an eel, and that's what we needed. Even Holmes and his moll were impressed. Well, if the guv'nor hadn't had this ace up his sleeve, they would have been sentenced to five years in the jug. And they would have lasted about five minutes there before some nasty old lag decided to cut their garglers, if you ask me. Oh yes, I know they thought they were the bee's knees in this game, but if it weren't for yours truly and the guv'nor, and the special line of business we were in, they'd have been brown bread before the sun was up.

So there we were, steaming across the English Channel in the dark, tipping straight up, then straight down, looking like we were going to have to swim to dratted Boulogne; the skipper laughing his noggin off in Russky until I told him I'd stop his mouth with a bunch of fives unless he shut up.

The guv'nor and Holmes were talking about the tickle. All the while they were circling each other without making it plain, like young lions do when they think the old pride patriarch is past his best. 'He risked so much, so much that he had built. For a twenty-year grudge. Is that not the most important aspect?' Holmes was saying about Wyneth.

'Explain.'

'I mean this: compare him to Jet, who took no care to absent himself from the bizarre ceremony that Watson and I sat through. He had no need to be there at all. Even less need to attend the performance of the play that Watson had to endure – sorry about that, old friend, there is nothing worse than bad Shakespeare. In those instances, our Minister for War was utterly reckless. In his actions, Wyneth was the same. Watson, do you recall how I described the style that distinguished Ridge as an exceptional violinist?'

His lapdog sat up to attention. 'You said he was reckless,' he barked, asking for a nice pat on the head.

'Indeed I did.'

'You consider scraping badly on a fiddle to be a sign of something untoward and perhaps criminal?' asked Moriarty. 'Should I arrest you here and now, Mr Holmes? I am sure I could gather no more than, oh, forty or fifty of your closest friends and neighbours to volunteer as witnesses for the prosecution.'

Holmes smiled genially. 'He played recklessly, Professor, not badly.'

'Recklessly,' the guv'nor said to himself. And he thought it over. 'Well, perhaps there is something in that.'

At that, Holmes lit up some filthy pipe and the Professor set about rubbing his temples.

Chapter 21

I had not had a good night. The sea crossing would have been a bad one for anyone, but such voyages always, inevitably, remind me of Mary's last. Sometimes I do not even see the connection but suddenly notice that my hand is shaking and my throat is constricted. Then I realize that I am staring into deep water. I have been reading Dr Freud's published papers. In one, the case of his patient Lucy R., I could almost see myself. Without any immediate cause, the patient's body began to misfunction, but the reason was lurking there in the dark – a love that was ever barred to her.

'You mustn't blame yourself,' I have been told over and over again, by everyone from her friends to near-strangers.

But no one else suggested that we travel, no one else insisted that I attend that symposium. She feigned an interest in seeing Madrid just so that I wouldn't feel a hound dragging her there in my wake. So if not myself, then whom *do* I blame?

And for years after, at the back of my mind, there was a niggling realization that the reason I delighted in the adventures I underwent with Sherlock Holmes was not just the excitement and fascination of the cases, but also that they prevented me from turning to thoughts and memories that would have leached life away.

So I had not had a good night.

'It occurs to me that it is your birthday soon,' my friend said, quite without apparent cause. We were on the deck, watching the dark grey waters breaking against the hull.

I was surprised – I could count on one hand the number of times in our twenty-year friendship that he had remembered the date. 'It is, yes.'

'There is to be a revival of *Trial by Jury* at the Savoy. Would you enjoy such a thing?'

'Yes, yes, I like Gilbert and Sullivan very much.'

'Good, then that is agreed.'

Since comic opera is far from Holmes's natural interest, I had the feeling he must have been wracking his brain for something that I would appreciate. Perhaps he had even surmised the reason for my low spirits that night. He was doing his best for me, and I mentally thanked him for it.

Chapter 22

We came into the harbour at Boulogne a couple of hours later, just after six o'clock. The only problem was, there were a few more armed *gendarmes* on the quay than I would like to have seen. A dozen of the sods in their sky-blue uniforms and pillbox hats. And it was clear who they were waiting for. I could have shot half of them from outside the breakwater before they'd drawn their rods, but I would have been hard pressed to reload and do the others, too, before they returned fire. I spun about and what did I clock? Only a bleeding police launch coming in behind us. Jump ship and swim for it? I could have done, but the guv'nor could no more have dived into the briny deep than he could walk on the moon. So I had to stand there, steaming with anger, while our captain brought us in.

'How in blazes did they know we were coming?' I growled.

'They were informed,' the Professor answered, calm as you like.

'I'll wring the bastard's neck.' He didn't reply.

We hove to and the deckhand jumped ashore and tied us up. We sat there bobbing like it was a nice Sunday on the boating lake in Hyde Park.

'*Arrêtez-les tous!*' shrieked the coppers' commanding officer.

Well, I know 'arrest them all' in about fifteen languages, and that was one of 'em. So the second we stepped foot on solid land – staggering a bit with our sea legs – we were clapped in irons like old lags, shoved in some sort of enclosed horse cart and driven away.

'I'll wring the bastard's neck,' I said again, watching out of the window so I could remember our route.

'So you have already informed us, Moran,' the Professor replied.

We were nipping past a stinking fish market where they were chucking the guts on the ground for the stray dogs to gobble; then a gaggle of loafers playing *boules* – they looked just the same as the English type, but with more berets. A swish-looking *boulangerie* – the French have good little finger-fancies, I'll give 'em that, and even though my belly is more used to good meat jerky and rough campfire coffee, I don't mind a bit of pretty Gallic baking from time to time.

We pitched up in front of a big white building, gilded like a china teapot, all sorts of crenellations and such covered in puff-gut pigeons that must have been stuffing down those little finger-fancies. There were *gendarmes* swanning in and out. 'So this is a French cop shop,' I scoffed. 'Soft lot, aren't they?' And in front of it was some big, red-faced nob in another sky-blue uniform, twiddling the ends of his white moustache like it was a kid's toy. We were all ordered out and shoved in through the front doors. I was about to give the Johnny pushing me about a bunch of fives in the gut to let him know who he was dealing with, but the Professor shook his head and I left the bastard alone.

But here was a queer one. Once we got through the front doors, our escort unlocked the bracelets from our wrists, bowed to us and became nice as pie, smiling and showing us the way as the red-faced nob strode ahead. We all piled into his office – well, blow me if it wasn't like the private apartment of the Queen's equerry, with a carpet so thick you could lose a tent in it and even a big-bosomed floozie reclining on a *chaise-longue* as she flicked through some ladies' periodical. The nob went over, kissed her hand and mumbled a few words to her, at which she sighed, gathered up her silk skirts and ske-daddled out.

As soon as she was out, the cove's fizzog changed like the seasons. Off went his smile, and in came a look as if we'd abducted his dog. 'I have done all you asked, Professor,' he whined. 'Please, please may I . . .'

'Oh, do not beg, Parc,' the guv'nor said, sitting himself

on a plush love-seat. He slid the blade out of his sword-stick, and I readied myself for action. But there was something wrapped around the steel, and the guv'nor slipped it off. He held it up to the light. Monsieur Moustache was sweating like a pig in a butcher's shop and tried to grab it, but the Professor snatched it out of his reach. 'Now, now.' He turned it so we could all see what it was. It was a photograph. 'It was quite indiscreet for you to be seen with the consul. I am certain your government would not approve. Not in these times.'

'We were at school together,' he blustered. 'I have told him nothing.'

'Of course you haven't. But still . . .' And he let the photograph flutter to the floor. The Frenchie pounced on it, tore it up and threw it into the fire. As it burned away, he sighed hard. 'Now, what have your British counterparts instructed?'

'You are to be arrested on sight. No one may speak to you. You are to be gagged and sent back in chains.'

'We're not Australians,' I muttered.

'You are to be treated like them. Your Scotland Yard cabled every port in France. I received the message just an hour before you contacted me.'

'Yes, Scotland Yard is not to be trusted.' The Professor stood up. 'Well, our business here is transacted. Now, supply us with luncheon – four courses, followed by calvados.'

'Four . . .? Anything else?' the man spluttered.

'Yes. An armed escort and your personal carriage to take us to Paris.'

Parc fought with himself, but he knew it was a losing battle. 'Yes, Professor.'

'And Parc?'

'Professor?'

'The calvados. An 1862 vintage, I think.'

It was a good few hours of bumping over French pot-holes before we got to Paris itself. The luncheon had been excellent – the guv'nor really knew his brandy – but by then, I was bored to the back teeth and wanted for a bit of sport. So when we'd found a billet for the night, I crept out to the Marais club, a little gaming establishment where I have a line of credit. Into the *privé* room, and I took eight hundred francs at baccarat off an African tribal chief who had never seen a man use a glimmer before.

I do like a glimmer. You have the serving strumpets pour you a glass of golden white wine, like an aged Riesling. You make sure you're the dealer, and when you toss out the cards, you skim them above the glass – that way, you can see their faces reflected in the booze, and you know everyone's hand. Best of all, if one of the Johnnies you're up against gets suspicious, you drink the evidence and no one can prove a damned thing.

Yes, a profitable evening, that one. I invested some of the cash in a decent shaving set. A good-quality badger hair brush and a sharp German steel razor – not so easy to get hold of at nearly midnight, but a good shave is the only thing I always miss when I'm out of civilization. It sets you up for the day. So when first light broke and the other three were stumbling about and moaning about their tired muscles, I was up, shaved, bathed and ready.

Chapter 23

After a day spent travelling from Paris to Zurich and shopping for heavy woollen clothing in the Swiss capital, we continued on the railway up into the Alps. The last leg of our journey was from the town of Interlaken to the high village of Grunden, which you find on a saddle between the Jungfrau and Mönch mountains.

As we stood in the Interlaken station, we got our first good look at the mountain above. To say that it towered over us would be to mischaracterize the sight. In the summer, when there is sun and clear air, it probably towers. But in the winter afternoons, when the light is hardly better than moonlight and sleet rides down the mountainside to whip through the valley and wring its wet hands around you, the Jungfrau has a much more threatening aspect. At such times, it seems ready to crush you down like a schoolboy's boot on an insect. You can imagine that it has a malevolent power that nothing else in nature wields.

We gained some queer looks from the station staff as we boarded the single-carriage switchback train to Grunden, where Ridge's dying words had directed us to discover the truth behind the mysterious threat to us all. Those looks were no surprise, given that we were the only passengers on the once-per-day service; and the day before, only one man – another Briton, apparently – had travelled it. It was an ancient, draughty vehicle with holes in the sides that allowed the frost to form small snow flurries within the carriage. The driver was also the guard, and he explained in a dirty form of Latin – he must have been a member of Switzerland's Latin-speaking Romansh community – that at this time of year the train had to crawl up the tracks, for fear of starting an avalanche. Since we could not understand the Romansh word for avalanche, he had to explain with a pile of the snow that had forced its way into the vehicle. Then he put his finger to his lips and whispered, to explain the danger of loud noises in those months when the snow was packed on the mountainside.

A switchback railway, if you have not ridden on one, is a curious thing. Because a direct ascent would be too steep, it zig-zags up the incline, which is a discomfiting experience – no sooner have you gotten used to the direction of travel than it immediately reverses.

'Christ, can't we just get there?' Moran muttered in

frustration at the stop-go action, which must have trebled the journey time, after we had been at it for forty minutes. 'I'd rather get out and walk.'

'And you would get about a hundred yards before you fell and broke your neck,' Moriarty admonished him.

The Professor had a point. The rocks through which the tracks had been blasted were nearly sheer. A four-man party with ropes and ice axes might have made it up, but they would have taken days, not hours, to do so.

Moran fell silent, though he looked like a simmering pot on a stove: ready to boil over at any time.

So we jerked and slid on upwards. After about fifteen more minutes, we came to an unexpected stop. I had been idly staring back down the way we had come, and not noticed that we had arrived at a plateau, about two hundred yards long and fifty wide. It was a good five thousand feet above sea level, I should say, and somewhat protected from the weather by a curvature of the rock.

As I felt the wheels grind to a halt, I looked out to see that the plateau was not bare. There was something ahead that looked at first glance like a sort of strange garden peppered with rocks. A group of a dozen darkly dressed people were standing at the far end of it, some digging in the ground, others concentrating on something they were carrying between them. It was difficult to make it out through the whirling flakes.

'Whatever is that?' I asked. 'Some sort of garden?'

'Of sorts,' Holmes said grimly. 'This is their cemetery.'

And as the wind dropped for a second, I saw more clearly. The knot of people were mourners. The burden

they were carrying was a body wrapped in a white wind-
ing sheet, and the diggers were excavating packed ice from
the grave they had prepared. The rocks strewn about were
headstones.

The train guard climbed out, removing his cap as his
feet crunched down on the frozen ground.

'Let us do the same,' Holmes said. 'We needs must
know as much of this place as possible.'

'Are you sure?' I countered. 'A funeral is a private thing,
even in a remote mountain village.'

'We shall be respectful.'

Moriarty sighed. 'Do as you wish. We shall remain
here, out of the weather. In my experience, the dead tell
few stories.' He turned the page of a scientific journal that
he had picked up in Zurich. 'In fact, it is a maxim at the
heart of my business dealings.'

Holmes wrapped his coat even more tightly around his
body and scrambled out. I followed.

Mourners in a Swiss village look like mourners around
the world, I should say. A grieving widow choking on
tears, her friends putting their arms around her shoulders
to comfort her. There was no priest here – we might as
well have been outside Christendom entirely, relying on
the pagan gods for protection.

The body was being carried on a rough wooden bier
by four men. Every so often, the widow would brush a
new light dusting of snowflakes from it and then heave
another sob.

'He was young, judging by the age of the woman,'
Holmes muttered. She looked to be in her late twenties,

with youthful cheeks pricked rosy by the cold air. She was handsome with thick dark hair.

'An accident? I imagine they happen frequently around here, especially in these conditions.'

'It could well be. I also suspect there are few doctors in this vicinity.'

The guard glared at us for speaking, although he could have had no idea what our words meant. Admonished, we fell quiet.

There was another chief mourner, by the look of things, other than the wife. A brother, it could have been. He had a dark and angry look about him. As the body was laid beside the grave – the diggers constantly removing the sleet that fell within it – he stepped forward and raised his voice.

He spoke the same muddled Latin as the guard. I struggled to understand at times, and the howl of the air rushing between the two mountains made it even harder, but I picked out words that suggested a terrible crime and the justice that would come. He lifted his open palm to the other congregants and violently closed it into a grasping fist, seeming to grab vindication from the sky.

'Did you comprehend that?' I asked Holmes.

'"They have taken him from us, we will take back," I believe were his words. It loses something in the translation. But you need not know a word of Romansh to see the fury in that man.'

Suddenly, the fellow in question looked directly at us. Until then, I think he had been too engaged in his duties to spot that anyone had left the train. Now he lifted an index finger to point at us and said something too quiet for us to catch. The other mourners turned and stared.

At that, the guard glared at us once more and harried us back into the carriage. 'Private. Not for you,' he said in Latin, clambering back into his cab and starting the wheels turning.

The funeral party watched us rumble away. When we had rolled back a hundred yards and switched direction once more, placing us some two hundred or so feet above their heads, we were able to peer down directly into the icy grave as the body was lowered into it. And the final sight, before it was all veiled from our vision by the white snow, was the brother, staring straight up at us.

Chapter 24

Finally, we were at the village. Well, they call it a village. I've been in more civilized settlements among the Zulus. It was stuck on the mountain saddle, open to the gales and hail that was coming down like cannonballs. I took a couple to the head, and it was like being punched. Not that I cry off a fight – I'm no poltroon – but I prefer one where I can smack the other bloke back.

We were on the platform – there was no station, of course, just a stone block – and looking around the place. It had a log-built shop, thirty-odd houses and what looked like an ale-house within sight.

The train conductor had told us that there was only one place to stay in the village, describing it as an hotel. Well, I assumed that meant it was a goatherd's hut. I've slept out in the wild more times than I can remember, but having the open ground called 'an hotel' feels like an insult.

We tramped along the mud track through the village. I expected them all to come out of their houses and stare, but they were probably all down in the graveyard dropping their mate into the ground, so most of these cabins were shut up. They looked rough, but tight enough on a cold afternoon. Some nasty-looking old biddies stared so hard out a few of the windows it was a surprise the glass didn't shatter.

Well, we came around one snow drift bigger than an elephant and saw the hotel. Blow me down if it wasn't one of the queerest-looking places. It was built right up to the rockface, but the outside looked like an American plantation house in Georgia. It was all white columns and Greek friezes of farm girls, with little patches of snow falling from the carved trollops' knockers. 'Hotel Printemps' was chiselled into the frontage. A pretty name for a doss-house in such a godawful place, if you ask me. Just as odd was that it was built right up against a small, square timber chapel that had seen better days.

Past the hotel, there was a narrow stone trail leading up through a break in the rock. One bloke could squeeze through, but if you met another coming down, then one of you would have to retrace his steps. It looked like it led up to the ridge between the two mountains. There was a signpost, too, with 'Vetus villa' – 'Old village' – painted in black, and a shifty-looking arrow pointing up through the fissure.

I thought the guv'nor would look pleased when he saw the hotel. He didn't.

'It is not what I would expect, Moran. And I do not like what I do not expect. Why is such a thing here?'

'Hillwalkers?'

He grumbled at that. 'There may be some, of course, but it is still a remote community to host such an edifice. What do you think?' But he wasn't asking me. He was asking Holmes. That was a fresh one. And I didn't like it much. I wasn't too keen on fraternizing with the enemy. And no matter what that arrogant cove said about our interests colliding, he was still a running lion to me, and there was nothing I'd like more than to put one right between his eyes.

'I think,' he started up, all swanky, 'the hotel has been here for a year or so. Observe how the paint is peeling from the pillars, which, you will see from the manner in which they are cracking vertically – indicating that they have shrunk, then expanded, in a winter, then a summer – are timber rather than stone. But the owners, whoever they are, have not yet constructed a stone path to it from the railway stop, indicating that they have not been here for very long. Money cannot be the barrier, since the cost of constructing the building in these conditions would be substantial.'

The Professor nodded and walked ahead to the entrance. That had at least been cleared so you could walk in without wading through the damned snow. He strode in like he owned the place.

Now, one thing you should know about me is that I

hear like a cat. A butterfly flits by a hundred yards away, and I know just how many times the little blighter has flapped its wings. So when we were sauntering in, I over-heard Holmes whisper something to his mutt. 'You recall, Watson, when we witnessed that evil mock-enthronement in Devon, that the Minister for War told his lackey to etherise George Reynolds and then take him directly to "the hotel"? Well, I have an inkling that we have just found the hostelry in question.'

'You think that he's here?' the mutt gasped like an old woman.

'I think that there is a high chance that he was brought here. Whether he is still here is anybody's guess.'

Well, well, I told myself. *Better make the guv'nor aware.*

The Hotel Printemps was just as spooking inside as out. The lobby took the best part of a minute to cross, and the last time I saw furniture covered in that much gilt was when I visited the Palace of Versailles for a little muddy business with the French Minister for the African Colonies. There was just as much Louis XIV here. It must have taken two train trips just to get these chairs up the mountain.

It was all one storey, so off the lobby there was a big arch leading to a bar and dining room on one side, a couple of doors that were closed, and two corridors on the other side that must have led to the bedrooms.

The lobby also functioned as the lounge and sported a dozen or so geezers all decked out in good clobber, quietly reading newspapers or chatting nice as you like among themselves while taking tea from silver salvers like they were in a St James's club.

One or two coves in the corner were playing billiards, too. I watched them. One of 'em didn't know one end of the cue from the other so I'd suggest a friendly wager with him later. Just for a few francs. Most blokes I know let them win the first game, then ask for a rematch at higher stakes. Me, I like to let them win twice, then beg them to let me win it back again. And that's when the evening really starts.

The billiards-men walked off. And blow me down but there was something rum about them and when I checked all the others, there was definitely something a bit off, I just couldn't put my finger on it.

The guv'nor marched up to the concierge desk. 'I should like a room,' he said.

'We were not expecting more guests today, mein Herr,' this little Swiss toady in a flunkey's uniform said back to him.

'Then expect one more. A room.'

'I do not—'

'A *room*.'

Well, the toady knew he was up against a tough nut. He was about to say something when a fat French bastard waddled out of the office behind him. He wasn't wearing uniform, so I guessed he was the manager. 'Of course, monsieur,' he said. 'May I have your name?'

'Choose one.'

'Of course, Monsieur . . . Foret?'

'As good as any.'

'Professor?' Holmes piped up.

The guv'nor sighed. 'Rooms for my companions, too.' And he laid out twenty gold sovereigns on the desk. The manager swept them all into his pocket as if this was what he did every Thursday. 'Theirs need not be of the best quality.'

There was a small table with a couple of seats by it so while we waited for the room to be prepared, Holmes went over and picked up a book some guest had left behind. He flicked through it and held it up to Watson. 'Dante's *Divine Comedy*,' he said. His puppy looked like he was all mops and brooms at that. 'You remember this was . . .'

But just then the Frenchie manager put four keys on the desk. 'I have put you gentlemen in the north corridor, which is the modern part of this hotel. The other section is partly built into a number of caves that were inhabited by the ancient people of this mountain. If you wish to attend a church service on Sunday, one will be held in the chapel. It can be accessed through that door.' He pointed to a thin one near the bar. I'll say this for him, his English was better than half the blokes I went to Eton with. 'Dinner is served in the dining room at eight. I shall have your bags sent to your rooms.'

The guv'nor and I had rooms thirteen and fourteen. The Johnny on the front desk said he was very sorry but fifteen had been taken the day before, so Holmes and Watson would be in sixteen and seventeen. As if we wanted to be all in a pretty little line of four. No, I was glad some cove had taken that one, because it meant we had a bit of a defensive trench between us and them.

My room was very fine, I must say, with fresh fruits in a dainty glass bowl on a marble table. I'm at home on the veldt, but that's not to say I don't like a soft mattress and thick carpet when the time is right. And this place was fit for a king: damned big room; rug you could drop an ox into and watch it disappear; its own bathroom, with a big copper bath polished up like a mirror. Not only a pricey-looking marble fireplace, but also one of those modern centrally warming air systems, where a network of internal air pipes blows hot air from a furnace stuffed away in some back room. The air came out of a grille at floor level and rose up so there was a constant waft of heat.

Yes, if we hadn't been on a mission, I wouldn't have minded a couple of days in that billet. Any more and my muscles would have been itching for a bit of a hunt, but forty-eight hours would have been a dashed decent bit of home leave.

I washed in a big china bowl before calling on the Professor. He was sitting on his bed, reading a periodical on astronomy.

'What shall we do?'

He spoke without looking up from his journal. 'Obviously, Moran, we shall investigate why Prince Karl von Habsburg, the third son of Prince Adolfus von Habsburg, is in the hotel lobby playing billiards, when the last intelligence that I had of him was that his father had had to send him to Argentina in disgrace after he had deserted his regiment before a skirmish in the Crimea.' He flicked on to some other article. 'It is no surprise, of course, that that milksop is a coward, only that his father thought he could be anything else.'

I knew just the sort. A wastrel whose father pur-chased his commission so he could look smart in his regimental dress and the strumpets would flock to him. Then, at the first shot, he would turn tail and run like hell.

So we put on fresh, dry clothing and went out. The prince was sitting at a low table in the lobby, staring at a book like it was written in Japanese. The guv'nor nodded to me and withdrew.

'Lord, it's cold!' I said, sounding as hail-fellow-well-met as any you'll find. I didn't actually say it to him directly, just out loud as I rubbed my hands and blew on them. He looked up, though. And I could tell he wanted a friend. Cowards always do. It's the brave bastards who are happy in their own company.

'Cold, you say?' His accent was Hungarian. That branch of the Habsburg Empire, then. He had lips like cushions. They all did, the Habsburgs.

'Yes, damned cold.'

'Yes, yes, it is,' he said, as if it was a revelation handed down by some altar-jockey.

'Would you mind if I joined you?'

'No, no, please.'

I took hold of the chair next to his at the table. 'Roger Hooke,' I said. And I put my hand out.

'Martin Schott,' he replied.

His hand was sweaty as you like. *You couldn't lie your way out of a paper bag*, I thought. 'Pleased to meet you.'

I looked over at the billiards table. 'Difficult game, that. I could never get on with it.'

'Hmm? No, me neither.'

Well, half an hour later, it had been hard enough to lose to him but I'd managed it.

'Stand you a drink to pay for my loss?' I suggested.

'In the bar?'

'Is there anywhere else?' I wanted to get him away from the Hotel Printemps for a while.

He looked like he had swallowed a wasp. 'Well, the village shop sells drinks, but—'

'That sounds fine to me.' I had to push the little prince out through the snow, he was so worried about his stumps getting wet. But we got to the shack and found that it sold a small range of food, household necessaries and a few children's toys. It had a filthy table to one side with four chairs crammed around it for drinks. I lifted two and pushed them out the back – I didn't want anyone taking it on themselves to sit down with us. The shopkeeper, a rat of a man if ever there was one, kept wringing his hands. I can't believe he got many in from the hotel, and he was clocking up how much he could charge us for whatever we ordered.

There was beer or schnapps. Those were the two and only two choices. I ordered both for us before the dimwit to my side could say no. The beer was like water, the schnapps like lava.

I deliberately said nothing. I knew he would speak first, and it would be whatever had been playing on his mind. You mark my words: you want information from a man, you just sit and wait for it to come to you. If you wait long enough and stay quiet enough, it comes.

'Does it worry you?' he blurted out.

'Does what worry me?'

'Why we're . . . here.'

I had seen off the schnapps and now supped some of the bad beer. 'Why, are *you* worried?'

'No. Not at all,' he said.

I sneered. I couldn't help myself. 'Yes, you are.' I put my hand on his shoulder. 'Look, it's natural to be worried.' It crossed my mind that the shopkeeper might just speak English, so maybe I should keep it down. 'What with what's going to happen.' And lowering my voice made him lean in, which helped.

'What do you want from it?' he whispered.

'What everyone else does. How about you?'

'I want to be different.' And he looked down at himself. But different how? Richer? Taller? Less of a poltroon? 'But I worry. Oh God, I worry!' And at that, he actually began to snivel in front of me. 'Is it right? Man's not meant to . . .'

Damned bad luck then. Just as he was about to sing it out, the fat manager from the hotel hurries on in, sweating like a pig because he's had to walk twenty yards. You could smell the grease pouring off him. 'Herr Schott. There is a message for you from your home.'

The lad went white as a sheet. 'A message from home?'

I know a code when I hear one. There was no message waiting for Prince Karl von Habsburg. There was something else waiting for him. I thought about grabbing them

both and smacking it out of 'em, but I was as like to have
the ratty shopkeeper to deal with, too, and the three of
'em against me might just make it an even fight. No, the
guv'nor would want me to keep this quiet.

That fat cove wasn't taking no for an answer and came
and stood over us. He didn't know how close he was to
feeling my fist in his gut. I told myself to calm it and just
gave him a look. And he had more brain to him than the
boy, because he saw what was in my mind and took a
step back. Perhaps I shouldn't have done that, because
he narrowed his eyes like he was squinting right through
me. *Yes*, I thought. *You can see, can't you?*

'I never caught your name,' I said.

'Albert.'

'Albert.' I said it to myself.

We sized each other up for another second. Then he
spoke to the boy again. 'The message, Herr Schott.'

The boy didn't say anything, but got up and left with
him. Out in the slush, I saw this Albert stop and look back
at me. Oh yes, I was on his mind now.

After that, I went back to my room, pulled my boots
off and sat back with a cheroot I'd nabbed from the shop
while the owner's back was turned. It wasn't a bad smoke,
in fact, a bit rough at the edges but it helped me relax.
Next door, I could hear the Professor whispering. It's
a habit of his to whisper to himself when he's working
through a calculation. He sits there rubbing his temples
and muttering away as if the whole world has disappeared.
And he could be like that for half an hour or a whole
night, depending on the calculation he was working on.

No scran, no shut-eye. Just him and a hundred parts moving about in his head.

It's quite a sight, a man still as a statue except his fingers and his lips. And at the end there's no big hurrah, he just stands up and takes himself to his bed. Whatever he knows, he knows. And if he wants you to know it, too, he'll tell you when he's good and ready. It would drive me loco living in my head like that. But our blags need brains and brawn. So I'm stuck with him, and he's stuck with me.

I rested on my back on the good four-poster, looked up and was a bit put out to see a bloody cobweb directly over my face. I thought about grabbing one of the maids and giving her what-for for not cleaning properly, but I wasn't in the mood for a shouting match with some peasant, so I whacked it away with the pillow. Stone me if three big spiders didn't fall out of a fold in the canopy, right onto the mattress six inches from my cheek. I grabbed one of them in my fist before it could scuttle away and smeared the remains on the bed canopy to tell the others what they were in for. They saw which way the wind was blowing and legged it, out through the vent that was part of the piped hot-air system.

Chapter 25

I must say, I did not like being so pally with Moriarty and Moran. Neither did Holmes, but he was more ready to believe that Moriarty's calculation of the odds of him winning alone versus the odds of us all winning together would entice him to throw in his lot with us for the duration. 'You must understand, Watson, that the brilliant Professor sees the world in algorithmic terms. If he does X, the product is Y. If he wants Y to be the product, he cares little for what X actually involves. It is a neat approach to the world. Admirable in some respects.'

'Holmes!'

'Come, come, my friend. I do not say that I admire Professor Moriarty – I only admire the purity of his approach, how he neither doubts it nor attempts to modify it as time and tide affect its application. But enough of that. And do not worry that I have gone native. I have my own thoughts and lines of enquiry that I shall share with him as and when I choose, and not before.'

'A case in point?'

'A case in point, old man, is that while he and Moran are relaxing in their rooms, you and I are going for a little stroll.'

I was pleased that we were not to be handcuffed to them, although I was worried we would miss dinner, which would be a dear price to pay after the long, famished journey we had endured. We walked through the lobby, where a number of well-dressed gentlemen were smoking or taking coffee.

'Did you notice their knuckles?' Holmes asked as he stepped out of the hotel, filled his pipe and struck a match. The sun had set now, so it flared in the dark.

'Whose knuckles?'

'The gentlemen in there.' He nodded back towards the men lounging on settees and tossed the match aside, the strong wind blowing it a few feet away from us.

'No, I didn't notice anything.'

'Bruises, old man. Lots of bruises. I enjoy a boxing bout or two, and it seems that many of those gents do, too.'

That was indeed a curious thing. But there was something more pressing on my mind. 'How can we tell where George is being kept?'

'By waiting, observing and holding our tongues. If he is being held here, they will not tell us. If he is not, they will not know.' As we walked, I gazed up at the Jungfrau. By the moonlight, I could make out a sheet of white peppered with black rocks. A tall wave of white snow slipped down to cover one stony ridge and expose another. A few seconds later, I heard its sound, like a distant explosion of dynamite. So that was an avalanche. I must say, it seemed quite beautiful from a safe distance. 'Is this not the purest landscape, Watson? The white snow and sharp peaks? Could not man be at his most wholesome and natural on these mountain slopes?' I had to agree. I have sometimes fantasized about a quiet retirement to such a place. 'And yet ...'

'Yet?' I prompted.

'There is always an underground river of evil in such lands.'

We made our way towards what passed for the entrance to the village, where the railway line halted. But before we reached the train platform, the path branched away to the lip of the plateau. There was a half-rotten span of fence that signposted a flight of steps descending. 'These, I am certain, will take us down to the boneyard,' Holmes said. Our lamp beam found the top step and seemed to bend downwards, falling with the mountainside. 'Rather like it is lighting the way to Hell, no?' laughed Holmes, in an unusually ironic mood.

'Not the cheeriest thought.'

'You must forgive me, old man. Supping with the Devil, as we now do, puts me in mind of Dante's *Divine Comedy*.' And he fought back a smile that I caught in the amber light reflecting upwards off the snow. Right then, if anyone looked like Lucifer himself, it was Sherlock Holmes.

We approached the top step. I do not know if you have ever stood on the edge of a mountain so high that the clouds form below you, but it is an unsettling experience. The stone steps were encrusted with ice for at least a hundred feet down. Beyond that, our lantern light gave way, and there was only a black mass that must have been the cemetery.

But as I looked more closely, I saw that it wasn't entirely dark. There was a spark moving down there.

'A late visitor?' Holmes conjectured, reading my thoughts.

'It must be.'

'Hmm. Well, let us find out for ourselves. And we shall pray that they are of this world and not the fiery one below.'

There was an iron handrail driven into the rock. Our chapped and numb hands gripped it as well as we could as we stepped down, one by one. Each crunch of our feet into the ice was accompanied by a short skid, so that I gave myself no better than even chances of returning to the hotel that night.

It was the slowest, most tentative hundred feet I have ever travelled. All the while, as we neared it, the spark of light was growing stronger and brighter. At one point, I slipped, and if Holmes's hand had not grabbed me under my shoulder, I might have suffered more than a bruise to my self-image. But with another minute of travel, we were at the level of the graves.

I peered for the source of the light, but it had disappeared just as we reached the cemetery.

'*Salute!*' Holmes called out, loud enough to be heard among the graves, but not so loud that it would be heard in the village above.

And at that, a beam of light suddenly shot out from behind one grave, straight into our faces, to dazzle us. I put a hand up to block it.

'Why have you come here?' demanded a voice in that dog Latin the locals spoke. It was not angry, though, but frightened. It was a woman's voice.

'We seek the truth,' Holmes replied in the same tongue. 'We mean no one any harm.' He took a step forward.

'Stay away!'

He nodded and stepped back again. 'I will. We seek the truth about a crime.'

'Holmes,' I warned. I was unsure that we should be spilling our secrets like this.

'It's all right, Watson. This woman is fearful; what does she fear? Most likely, she fears what we seek out. And she knows more than we do.'

'What crime?' Her voice was less afraid now, more inquisitive.

'Deaths.'

'Holmes!'

'Deaths?' And she emerged into the light from our lamps. It was the widow from the burial earlier.

'Yes.'

She looked at us, still unsure. Then she appeared to make up her mind. 'Look around you.' Something in her tone said that there was more to her meaning than the obvious: that we were all standing in a graveyard. Holmes kneeled and cleared one of the headstones. It bore a man's name and a date a few months earlier. 'Over there.' Holmes looked where she had pointed. Another stone, another recent date.

'How did your husband die?'

In the lamplight, I saw beads of water roll down her young cheeks, then instantly freeze. 'He fell.'

'How did he fall?'

Her voice was weak. 'There was a blizzard. He was climbing the rocks above the village.'

Holmes furrowed his brow. 'Climbing the rocks? Why?'

'I do not know. No one knows.' She clawed her hands through her long, dark hair. 'He had been behaving like a madman for weeks. It was as if he felt . . .' and then she said something I did not quite understand.

'What was that, what did he feel?' I asked Holmes.

'*Like he was wearing silver armour.*' He paused. 'A local idiom, no doubt. But I suppose we can get the gist.' He addressed her again. 'Madam, how did these other young men die?'

She shook her head. 'Alesch was killed.'

'How?'

'A fight in a bar. Two men. In Bern. The police said he began it over nothing. I do not know about Jerun; Sarina will not speak of it. She has left the village.'

'Madam, did these men work together? Were they related? Was there a connection between them?'

And even before she spoke, I knew what her answer would be. 'They all worked at the hotel.'

One look to Holmes told me he had expected exactly the same. 'Yes. Naturally, they all worked there.'

'You think you can buy us!' It was growled at us like a dog. But the words were not the woman's. They rumbled out from a dark corner of the cemetery.

The young man who stepped out – the dead man's brother, I thought, having seen him at the funeral – kicked through the snow into our view. 'You think we are for sale.'

'Whom do you mean by "you"?' I asked.

'You and you. And all the others.' He stabbed his finger at us through the torchlight. 'All the others who have come here. Your money.' He spat on the ground. 'It is only paper.'

Holmes stood firm. He had a way of doing so that was neither threatening nor backing down. 'We are not like the others who have come here. We want to see anyone who has escaped justice brought to justice.'

The woman looked at the man and touched his arm. He shook her away.

'Polin,' she said quietly.

'Do not believe a word they say.'

'Did your friends say anything about what they were doing at the hotel?' Holmes asked.

'Do not answer!'

But she ignored his order. 'Normal work,' the woman said. 'Joel, my husband, worked in the kitchen. Alesch and Jerun were porters.'

215

'Did Joel or the others ever mention anything strange? Anything they were asked to do that was remarkable? Or maybe a strange guest?'

'A strange guest!' Polin sneered, forgetting his own instruction. 'They were all strange. Why would you come here? All these rich men. You are just the same.'

'They . . .' the woman began, but her companion had reached his limit.

'No more!' he instructed her. 'Say no more.'

And at that, he took her arm and guided her forcefully to the steps up to the village. 'Sir!' I said, trying to calm him.

'Stay away from her,' he growled. She glanced sadly over her shoulder but began to climb the steps. I started after them, but Holmes placed a hand gently on my chest to hold me back.

'We must look for another opportunity to speak to her,' he told me. I knew he was right.

We climbed back up – it was safer ascending than descending, even if it was harder on my old knees.

'What do you say, Watson?'

'I say there is something very strange and very wrong about that hotel.'

'That we can agree on.'

We tramped back, arriving just in time for dinner. The dining room was oval in shape and well appointed, seating around fifteen gentlemen. Moran and Moriarty were at the table, finishing their meals. We politely greeted them, and the waiter brought us an excellent dish of mountain lamb in a parsley sauce accompanied by sauteed potatoes.

'The Director of the French National Bank,' Holmes said under his breath as I tucked in.

'What did you say?'

'Over there.' He twitched his fork in the direction of a whiskered chap in his fifties who looked an ebullient sort, ordering another bottle of what he had just finished. 'I once met him at a reception at the French consulate in Porto.'

'Will he recognize you?'

'Considering that he is on his second bottle of Chateau Mouton Rothschild now, and was on his third back then, I doubt it.'

'You do recognize a lot of people.'

'There are a lot of people to recognize. Such as the Russian ambassador to America. The dark fellow opposite our banker friend.' I looked over. An unassuming, small man was reading a book, ignoring the lively conversation going on around him.

'And how do you know the Russian ambassador to America?'

'I did not say I know him. He is reading a book in Russian, the cut of his suit is Bostonian, he asked for a bourbon whiskey and soda and the waiter addressed him as "your Excellency". Who else could he be?'

'He is indeed the ambassador, Alexei Simonyov,' Moriarty said in his strange way that sounded as if he despised every syllable. 'And I can tell you something about him.'

'Something that few men know, no doubt.'

Moriarty ignored the comment. 'A favourite of the

Tsarina since childhood. Some have suggested an improper connection.'

'We understand. Out of interest, how have you been planning to exploit that information?'

The Professor replied as if it was the merest everyday query about the merest everyday action. 'I have not quite decided. Possibly something to do with licences for shipping to pass through the Black Sea. I have a joint-stock company investing in them.'

'I am sure it will be highly lucrative.'

'I can sell you a thousand shares at four shillings per share. A special discount for you.'

'I am sure they are cheap at the price,' Holmes answered him.

'Quite literally a steal.'

'Thank you, I shall keep my money to myself.'

'As you wish.'

At that, Moriarty stood and left, followed by Moran.

'Tell me, do you know anything of the gentleman in room fifteen?' Holmes asked me.

'Nothing.'

'I enquire because you will recall that the only person on the train here yesterday was reportedly a Briton.'

'So?'

Holmes called the waiter over and asked if he had served a British gentleman that day or the previous day. He had not.

'Which leads us to conclude that he takes his meals in his room,' Holmes explained, dismissing the waiter.

'If there is something strange or even criminal about

this place,' I said, 'then it is no surprise that some of the guests wish to remain unknown.'

'That is true. But whenever a man stands out – including by his absence – I want to know why.'

Dinner concluded with a fine pudding of rice soaked in sweet milk and garnished with loganberries, and then a pair of excellent cigars each.

We ambled back to our chambers and, as we passed room fifteen, we heard music from a gramophone within. Holmes stopped. 'It is the second movement of Brahms's Violin Sonata Number One in G Major. The Rain Sonata. A lovely piece.' A piano and violin were playing around each other like birds. 'And now . . .' He tapped the air as if he had a baton. 'That is the rain coming in. Even music has weather.' The gramophone recording crackled.

Holmes rapped on the door with his knuckles. 'It is always pleasant to meet one's countrymen when travelling overseas, is it not, Watson?' he said by way of explanation. 'And are the beautiful notes that we hear a deliberate choice or is the music just coincidence? There is one way to find out.' He rapped again. But the room failed to open to us and there was no sound of movement from within. Short of asking at the front desk for a pass key, there was little we could do to pursue the matter. 'Well, something tells me we shall all meet soon enough,' Holmes said.

It was late morning when I woke. I had a sharp hankering for good English crumpets. Sadly, there were none to be found, but I bucked myself up and Holmes and I strode out to take a wider look at the village.

It was picturesque in a way, with smoke spurting out of chimneys and the snow quite virgin. I would not have wanted to live there, though, the climate nipped at everything you had.

We looked in at the church that abutted the hotel. It was a solid but plain building with a bare altar, no more than six pews and a few memorial stones set into the walls. At the other end of the settlement was the inn, which we had not seen the previous night. It was a grim-looking place that seemed like it had been built as a stone goat-house and had only been turned into a pub as a stop-gap. Seen from the outside, the windows were so small that it must have been pitch black inside every hour of the day. The door banged every two seconds in the wind, its catch having broken off some time ago, by the looks of things. Some filthy straw chucked to the side of the front step suggested just how the floor was covered. We could hear lively voices inside.

'Come, Watson, let us see if we can make some friends among the local people. We might find something of interest.'

We pushed inside. Despite the constant draught, the room was so thick with tobacco smoke that you could hardly see from one end to the other. It took a few seconds for my vision to adjust, at which point a rough room, about twelve yards long with an animal's trough that had been turned into a bar, appeared through the fug. And then I realized what else I was staring at. 'Holmes!' I shouted.

I had seen a serious crime about to take place. A man about my height and age, dressed quite finely, was standing at the far end, with his back to the wall and his hands on his head. To my right, a short man in the garb of a gentleman had a revolver pointed at the stationary man's head. He was squeezing the trigger, and I only had a split second to act. I flung my knapsack at his hand, knocking the gun to the side. It fired into the stone wall, the bullet ricocheting off and hitting the floor with a snap.

'What ...!' the gunman snarled. But he got no more words out before I had grabbed his arm and was wrestling away the pistol.

'Watson!'

'Help me!' I called as I grappled for the gun. The man was small but powerful, and we fell to the floor. Out of the corner of my eye, I saw the man who had been about to be executed run for us.

But instead of aiding me, as I had expected, the man – a swarthy gentleman, I now saw – grabbed my shoulder and started pinning me down, as if I were the one who had tried to kill him.

'Watson, let go!'

It was Holmes's voice, of course, but it made no sense to me. 'But ...'

'Gentlemen, there has been a misunderstanding.' And I felt him pushing away the man and easing my hand from the pistol. 'Watson, there is no danger.'

With Holmes's help, the gunman managed to wrench his weapon away and stood back, pointing the revolver at the floor. Holmes pulled me away.

'Watson, we are in Switzerland. The land of William Tell.' He pointed to an apple that had fallen from the swarthy man's head to the straw beside the wall. 'This was a test of marksmanship. And nerve.'

I stared up, astounded. 'Good God,' I muttered. I had seen such idiocy in the army a few times, but never in civilian life. That didn't make me feel any less sheepish, however.

And if that wasn't bad enough, I noticed then who had witnessed my idiocy. None other than the widow we had encountered at the graveyard the previous night. She stood frozen behind the bar with a glass and a jug in her hands.

The man who had dragged me aside burst into hearty laughter. The gunman, however, looked on me very darkly, and I saw his finger twitching back towards the trigger before he grunted an oath and slipped the pistol into his pocket.

'Your friend is right. A test of nerve!' cried the laughing man. 'What is life with no nerve?' His accent was Italian. 'You, *signiori*, are new here. I speak the truth?'

I pulled myself up. The gunman was still eyeing me as if deciding whether to waste a bullet on me.

'Yes, we are,' Holmes answered.

'Ah, the things you will learn!'

'We are greatly looking forward to doing so.'

Holmes is better at these things than I am. I would have come straight out and asked the man to elaborate. But Holmes started absent-mindedly looking around, as if only mildly curious about the inn. There were three other gents in the room, spectators at the shooting game, and an innkeeper in rougher clothes who had been selling them their sauce.

'Who the deuce *are* you?' demanded the gunman. His accent was American.

'Oh, only two gentlemen like yourselves partaking of the unique nature of this place.'

His features all narrowed. 'Partaking of the *what*?'

'We all know why we are here.'

'Yeah, sure we do. But I ain't . . .'

'Louis, Louis,' the Italian said, as if calming an upset child. 'We are all friends, here for the same thing. I say we all have a drink of schnapps and try again with the shot. But this time, a real challenge. Your eyes closed.'

I was astonished. It was a difficult enough shot when the American could see where he was firing. Blind, it was – at the very best – a roll of the dice. I would not have given a shilling for our Italian friend's life at that point.

'Are you sure?' I asked.

'I am certain.' And he leaned in to me and grasped my arm. 'You will be certain soon.' Then he walked, calm as a summer day, to the end of the room, plucked the apple from the floor and held it above his head. 'Shoot, William Tell.'

'Holmes . . .' I said under my breath.

'Let them be, I think. There is much here that we do not understand.'

There was no doubting that.

The American raised his hand, ostentatiously closed his eyes and pulled the trigger. The barmaid watched without reaction, as if this was something she saw by the hour. A single shot rang out and the apple exploded, the bullet ringing as it struck the stone behind. The Italian burst into laughter again, and the three spectators loudly toasted the success.

The innkeeper placed tumblers in my and Holmes's hands and began pouring clear schnapps. It was very early for hard spirits, but I did not wish to rock the boat. He filled right to the brim, so that there was enough alcohol in each glass to stun a bull. No one made any sign that the amount was unusual, and the innkeeper went to all the other men, giving them the same amount, which they drank down like water. Then they looked at us. There was nothing for it but to follow suit and knock back in a single draught as much as I would normally have drunk in an hour. No wonder they were acting as rash as sailors on shore leave – although I had noticed no actual signs of sottishness. The cheap, home-distilled spirit burned all the way down my gullet, and it was as much as I could do to keep myself from retching. The innkeeper went to refill my glass, but I waved him away. Still, it seemed we had passed the test.

'New friends,' the Italian announced, hugging us into him and then offering his hand. 'Luciano Ado.'

'Edmund Loughton and Charles Pierce,' Holmes replied.

I tried to catch the young lady's eye, but she was studiously missing mine.

'Good. Old friends! Now, we are for ski-racing. Will you come?'

The American looked put out. 'Don't come if you ain't in the mood,' he said. 'It's pretty dangerous, too.' He sneered this last point at me.

'We don't seem dressed for it,' Holmes suggested.

'Then you won't come. Pity.'

Holmes inclined his head to acknowledge the cancelled invitation.

The Italian shrugged and handed a few coins to the innkeeper, and the five of them left. It had been an extraordinary display.

Holmes attempted to engage the innkeeper in conversation, but the man shook his head at anything he was asked. He would fill our glasses and take our money but would not speak. The last I saw of the barmaid was the rear of her dress flitting out into what must have been a storeroom at the back of the place.

'Well, well. A diverting experience. Let us wander more to consider it,' Holmes said, stretching out his legs.

'If you say so.' I confess I was disappointed at having missed an opportunity to engage the young lady in conversation, even if it had been destined to be a stilted one and in a language that I grasped only tenuously.

We left the hut and I glanced up at the mountain. It had been there since the beginning of time and would be there until the very end. That sort of thing gives you pause. I am not a poetic fellow; I'm a medical man and a soldier. I can be gruff at times. But at that moment, looking up at that landmark by which any man or bird could find their course, I felt a little bit of poetry enter my soul.

'Do stop staring and let's get on, Watson,' Holmes said. 'We age like any other creatures and cannot stand here stock still for all eternity.'

I laughed and started shuffling in his wake. But then a

hand clutched at my arm. I looked down. It was a slender hand, even puffed out by a goat-wool mitten.

'Sir, wait. I want to speak to you.' Yes, it was the barmaid. I did my best to keep up with her dog Latin.

'What about?'

Her brow furrowed in a pretty type of irritation. 'What do you think? About the deaths in our village. The . . .' and then she said a word that I did not know.

'*Disappearances*, Watson.' Holmes had obviously seen the lack of comprehension on my face. 'Come, then, madam. Let us speak in private elsewhere.'

'I agree.'

'But first, we must know your name.'

'Ioana.'

It must have been the local form of 'Joanna', a charming name, if you ask me.

We stepped to the side of the hut and waited for her to speak. 'This was a nice place to live,' she began in a quiet voice. 'We were not rich. Never rich. But it was quiet and clean, and the people were good to each other.'

'And then?'

'Then *they* came.' She nodded to the footprints in the snow. 'Or others like them. I wish my husband was here. I pray for him every night in the church to come back.'

I wanted to put my arm around her then, but it seemed wrong. As if she was with her husband in her thoughts and should be left there.

There was silence for a while. 'There must be something quite unique about the Hotel Printemps,' Holmes said gently. 'How long do guests tend to stay?'

'A week, I should say, maybe two. We see them come and go.'

I heard a distant booming like the one the evening before, indicating a sliding down the mountain of the snow shelf. The other two paid it no attention at all.

'Did your husband ever mention anything strange about the hotel?' Holmes asked.

'Strange? Many things.'

'Anything he said he did not understand.'

She considered for a moment. 'When he first started, he said that sometimes people who worked there could not be found. He would need to speak to one and would look in every room, but they were nowhere.'

'Well, old man, we really must find where they got to,' Holmes said to me in an aside. Then, turning back to Ioana, he continued in the Romansh dialect: 'And tell me, the men who come here. Do they always behave like that?' He, too, nodded at the footprints of the men who had just departed to go ski-racing.

'Eventually. They become different.'

'Different how?'

'Many of them are like lambs when they arrive. They always end up like those dogs.'

'I see. A last question, one that may seem odd: did your husband ever mention spiders?'

She looked stunned. 'Spiders?'

'Yes.'

The look of amazement remained on her face as she spoke. 'Once, I found him in our home with his hands over his head, screaming. I asked him why, and he said he could feel spiders crawling up his legs. But there was nothing there. Not one. I thought he must have woken from a nightmare, but it happened again the next week. It came from nowhere.'

'I see. And you said your husband died after a fall.' She bit her lip and sighed. The memory was fresh and painful. 'Did he survive for any time? Did he say anything?'

'He lived for a few hours but could not speak.'

'That is a pity.'

'Holmes,' I remonstrated, feeling that his tone had been unfeeling – as if the man's inability to aid our investigation was the real tragedy.

'But . . .' she began, before halting.

'Yes?' Holmes said, bright-eyed, as he gets when his instincts tell him that a nugget of invaluable datum is within his grasp.

'He . . . he seemed to *want* to tell us something.'

'What was it?'

'I do not know. He could not speak, but he was trying to draw something in the dirt.'

'What?'

And then she drew it herself in the snow. Three separate semi-circles on a horizontal line. And all three within an upside-down V.

'Was he writing?' I asked.

'We do not know how to write, sir,' she said, self-consciously. I felt like a heel for asking without thinking. What need had mountain-dwellers such as they for reading and writing?

'Oh, Watson, no, no, no. These are not letters. Do you

not see? This inverted triangular shape is the mountain on which we stand. This base line is the ground.'

'So what are the semi-circles?'

'I would wager they are the cave houses of the abandoned village above us.'

'The cave houses?' I blurted out. 'But what does it mean?'

'Discovering that shall be our task.' Holmes turned again to Ioana. 'Are those dwellings ever used?'

But before she could answer, the innkeeper appeared before us. I cannot say how he got there without us seeing him. He spoke not a word but lifted a bony finger to point at the girl. Without doubt, it was a warning. Then the finger moved to point back to the inn. And that was a demand.

I guessed that jobs were not abundant in that village, and Ioana was not keen to lose the one she had.

'You have suffered a terrible loss. A tragedy,' Holmes said quickly and under his breath. 'I am here to seek the truth about, and justice for, three deaths in London. I believe I will find the same on behalf of the three deaths here.'

The woman looked suddenly hopeful. 'Please. Please find me the truth.'

'I will do all I can, I promise you.'

At that, she turned tail and went straight back into her place of employment. I was about to have it out with the landlord when Holmes shook his head.

'We are outsiders here, we do not want to make enemies,' he said. 'Not yet, anyhow. We have a more pressing engagement.'

'Which is?'

'Why, to explore those cave houses that seem now to have played a part in the death of Ioana's husband.'

As we walked away, towards the path up to the old village, Holmes reached into his pocket and drew out his pipe. He struggled to light it in the cold wind, but eventually puffs of blue smoke emerged. 'An idea begins to form, Watson. A strange idea, but the only one that, for now, makes any kind of sense.'

'Will you reveal it to me?'

'Not yet, for fear that you will have me carted off to the nearest lunatic asylum.'

For my part, I felt sorry for the woman, Ioana. 'A nice place to live' this had been once. A simple life, no doubt, none of the plays or fine restaurants that populated ours – and none of the corruption, want and hypocrisy that ran wild in ours, too. And they had certainly been none the poorer for it. They had a sky and mountains and each other. What more could they want? Until these outsiders had come calling, not much, it seemed. We can be corrupted by futile dreams. It seemed to me that Holmes and I had something like a moral duty to put right – as much as it could be put right – all that had gone wrong in this hamlet as a result of the arrival of strangers. We were not like these other men, of course, but do we not all feel a degree of responsibility for the actions of our siblings, our countrymen or those with whom we have some other tenuous connection? 'Am I my brother's keeper?' we may ask indignantly – but the answer, for men of good character, is surely 'Yes'.

*

There was a narrow split in the face of the mountain on the other side of the village. A sign pointed up through it and indicated that the old village sat above us, presumably on a plateau like the one where we stood. The path seemed to be twenty yards of a near-vertical scramble.

'A spot of exercise before luncheon will work up a decent appetite, wouldn't you say?' Holmes said, rubbing his hands together to get some blood flowing in them.

'If you say so.' I did not relish the climb as much as he did. 'I barely know why we are attempting this.'

'Because Ridge informed us that this village – and surely the out-of-place hotel – is the source of the great danger grasping the world. So when we discover that a local employee of that hotel has died strangely and directed those who found him to these cave houses, what are we to do but follow his direction?'

'Do you think we will find the truth of his death there?'

'We will not know until we arrive. So let us begin.' And he attacked the stepped trail. Holmes is an agile man and can shimmy up ropes and drainpipes like a cat burglar when he wants to.

'But where is the village?' I asked when we had gained the top.

'That is precisely what I would like to know.'

We were on an uneven ridge, like a smaller version of the one below. But it was quite empty. Just the same brilliant white snow everywhere to blind us in the midday sun.

'There is no other way up from here, is there?' We both peered at the rock face. Here it was quite sheer; presumably a man could scale it with ropes and a chisel to make hand-grips and footholds, but it seemed incredible that an entire village could only be accessed that way.

'Blunder, blunder, blunder.'

I stared at Holmes. Neither he nor I had said the words. I looked down the way we had come, then up at the cliff face. There was absolutely no one in sight. And while the voice had been muffled, it had not been shouted from a distance.

'You fail on so many scores, Holmes, but chiefly on the plane of calculation. Which is why you will never prevail in our chosen demi-monde.'

And at that, a square hole appeared in the packed ice at our feet, enlarging as a trapdoor lifted up and the snow slipped down from the edges into a stone passageway. It revealed Moriarty with a sputtering oil lantern in his grasp.

'Not so much an "old village" as quite prehistoric,' Holmes said as he eased himself onto a stone step jutting from the solid, damp wall and down into the passage itself.

'At least a millennium, I should say,' Moriarty returned. 'There are a number of these dwellings along the ridge. This is the first in which I have found signs of recent life.'

I, too, descended into the passage. I had to stoop to walk along it. A little flurry of snow followed me until Moriarty pulled the trapdoor back into place with a rope.

'Are you here because of the dead man?' I demanded.

'A dead man sent you here? Am I to take it that your clientele now include the deceased?'

Someone chuckled in the gloom. I made out Moran a little further up the passage.

'My colleague is referring to the fact that we are here because the man we saw being buried directed his wife to this location,' Holmes explained.

'I was not aware.'

'Then the question arises: why are you here?'

Moriarty shrugged. 'I do not serve to answer your every query. That notwithstanding, I am here because one of the few local children informed me that he sometimes plays up here but was frightened off yesternight by the distant sight of lamplight. Since it is not a place for midnight revels, I decided some investigation was warranted.'

The passage angled steeply down into the rock. It was cold, but not as cold as outside – in fact, the lack of wind made it feel quite warm compared to the conditions above. The only light we had was from the lantern in Moriarty's hand, which worried me. If he suddenly chose to extinguish it, we would all be blind. I could not guess what he might do with that, but his mind was a constant cauldron of scheming, so he could surely find a way to turn it to his advantage. I held on to the thought that – for now, at least – he had been persuaded that his interest lay with a joint endeavour.

The tunnel was fifteen or more yards long and led to a large, uneven chamber. Humps of light brown rock rose here and there, with more than one dripping stalactite suspended from the ceiling. There was a small depression in the centre with a thin flue above it: a fire-pit, clearly. Dustings of snow were spilling down the rough chimney and settling in the pit. Around the chamber, niches were cut into the walls.

'Give me that,' Holmes said, holding his hand out for the lantern. He held it up, throwing light on the walls.

'Ah, so you notice,' Moriarty said.

'Notice what?' I asked.

Holmes replied. 'There is soot in these candle niches, but the walls are damp, and the soot will be washed away in a matter of hours. So candles must have been lit here recently. All very intriguing.'

'That is more so,' Moriarty said, pointing a finger.

'What are you talking about?' I asked.

'Are you blind? The wall. An iron bracket.'

And I saw that he was right. On the far side of the cavern, there was a metal brace, shaped like a capital H, fixed into the rock wall. Below it, obscured by a ridge in the rock, was a hole, perhaps a yard across. I peered down, but it was black as night and impossible to make anything out. 'Presumably an old bracket for a lamp or such.'

'I must make a more detailed assessment of your cranial development. Such a lack of intelligence must have clear signs.'

I was ready then and there to knock his block off. And I think Moran could tell that I was, because he pulled himself up to his full height and met my eye in an unspoken warning.

'Old friend,' Holmes said, attempting to calm the waters as he, too, looked down into the hole that was quite impenetrable to our gaze and could have been three feet or a hundred yards deep, 'what the Professor is attempting to impart in his cheerless way is that the fixture is clean and new, which in this atmosphere indicates that it is a recent addition; and if there was to be a bracket for a light, it would more likely be suspended from the ceiling in the centre of the room. No, this is for something quite different, I hazard.'

'Of course it is,' muttered Moriarty. 'That is as plain as day.'

'It is to hold a rope ladder,' I exclaimed, taking hold of it. I wished I had thought of it earlier – I had seen such brackets used by regiments of Engineers for that purpose. 'The shape holds the ladder stable.'

'Ah, then this hole must be deep enough to warrant descent,' Holmes said. He struck a match and dropped it. It fell for some seconds before flickering out. 'A pity that we have no ladder or ropes ourselves. We could chance our arms and jump down, but it might be a mile deep with no way out.'

Perhaps it was due to Moriarty's niggling at me and my brain making an effort to prove him wrong, but suddenly I had a flash of inspiration. I went to the entrance of the cavern to collect my bearings. Yes, I was sure I was right. 'It will not be a mile down, Holmes, I can tell you that. I would say it is about twenty yards.'

'And how do you calculate that?' Moriarty replied.

'For the simple reason that we must now be directly above the hotel. You recall that we were informed when we first arrived that some parts of the hotel are adapted from ancient dwellings. This shaft, I wager, descends straight into that part. It must be either one of the ancient internal connections from one level to another or, more likely given that it is perfectly vertical and quite narrow, an air pipe. *That* is how I calculate it, Professor.'

And at that, Holmes positively beamed. 'Watson, we must add "pathfinder" to your military credentials! Don't you agree, Professor?' Moriarty just grimaced and looked away, clearly annoyed at being bested by me. 'No? Well, we will take your congratulations for Watson as read. Now, I think you are right that this is more likely a ventilation shaft that has recently been pressed into service as a method for surreptitiously entering a forbidden and hidden zone of the hotel – the very one that the woman Ioana told us of, in an indirect fashion, when she said that her husband had spoken of his fellow employees suddenly being nowhere to be found. And the newness of this bracket leads us to the conclusion that there is another party, like ourselves, who is interested in what happens there.'

'Do you have any idea who?' I asked.

'I do. There is one mysterious gentleman we have yet to meet in this village.'

'Identify him,' Moriarty demanded.

'Why, the gentleman in room fifteen.'

Chapter 26

After all that, there was nothing more to do in the stinking pit, so we made ourselves scarce. Back out in the open, I was leading the way to the route back down while the guv'nor and Holmes were jaw-jawing about what the plan would be with that French bastard who ran the drum. I was all for chucking him off the bloody mountain but held my tongue. 'It occurs to me . . .' 'The missing element . . .' 'Analytically speaking . . .' Hellfire, they couldn't just come to a bloody decision, could they? Point me at an enemy, and I'll bury him. They seemed stuck on gossiping like old maids.

I held up my fist to tell them to halt and button their lips. They took the order. I knelt down. Now, the mountain ain't the veldt, but a hunter is a hunter and he can see where his quarry is hiding no matter the terrain. And I could see that a few yards ahead of us, the snow was uneven. When the guv'nor and I had come up here, we'd poked about blind to find that trapdoor. But now I could see the outline of another one in the snow. And that told me that it had been opened and closed not so long ago.

I pointed, and even Holmes's lapdog got the message. I drew my barker and told the doggy to lift the door while I covered him – not that I'd mind one bit seeing him take a handful of lead in his belly, but it might make whoever was blasting him a bit cocky, and I wouldn't want that.

There was no need, though. Watson struggled a bit to lift the timber, but there was no sprite waiting under it. Just a wet set of rock steps down. Well, I led the way, jumping down with the shooter ready to give anyone waiting for me the shock of his life. Nothing. Along we all tramped, and I thought it was going to be just like the other one, until my feet trod on something different: wooden planks that made up some kind of walkway. We followed them, making a racket that would wake the dead, what with the heavy boots the fools behind me were wearing.

Ten or so yards in, and we opened out into a cavern again. This one was different from the last one because it was kitted out like a nice little family crib. There was a stove with a pipe up through the rock to take the smoke, a table with chairs around it and a couple of benches. There was a doorway off to another room, and I spied a bed in there, made up with a horse blanket.

Now, anyone can look hard and listen out, but a real

hunter uses every sense he was born with. So don't forget smell – dogs don't, and they'll track better than any man. While all my travelling mates were tumbling in behind me, I took in a whiff and I knew: we weren't the only ones in that cave.

'Come out, or I'll fill your gut with lead,' I snarled at the doorway.

'Do you really think that whoever you are addressing will have understood a single word of what you said, Moran?' the Professor asked. And he switched to Latin. Now, as an Eton and Oxford man, I've had an education equal to any bastard in the Empire. So I could keep up with that. 'My friends and I will not hurt you,' he called out. 'But we have many weapons. So if you do not come out, then you will surely lose your life.'

And sure as sure, we heard a shuffling of feet. Then this short little runt stuck his bald head around the corner. 'Please, gentlemen, I am not a danger to you,' he wailed, blubbing like a kid.

'Of course not,' the guv'nor told him. 'Now, we mean you no harm but if you do not sit quietly on that bench my companion will beat you to death.' At that, he did what he was told. 'Who are you, and is this hovel your home?'

'It is my home, sir. I live here. My name is Andreo. I am a goatherd.'

'Does anyone else live here?'

'No.' He looked around, as if he was checking for anyone else. Holmes started sticking his nose into the pots and pans on the sideboard.

'How long have you lived here?'

'All . . . all my life.'

'What can you tell me about the hotel in the village below us?'

'I do not know anything about it, sir. I do not go there.'

He was meek as a lamb. I hate seeing a man act like a little girl.

'Have you seen anything strange there?'

'I stay here, sir.'

'Where are all your neighbours?'

'They have left.'

'Why?'

'It is hard to live here. They have gone to the . . .' But he stopped, because the Professor had reached out and clapped his hands on the bloke's bald head. He was feeling about with his fingertips, looking down at the Johnny's skull like it was a book.

'Ah,' the guv'nor said. 'I understand.'

'I . . .'

'Be quiet. I understand.' He stood back. 'You are one of *us*.' And he cracked smile.

Now, I could be dead asleep and my reflexes would still catch a poison dart spat at me from five yards away. So when this little bastard sprang up holding a blade that he'd plucked out of the damned air, I was quick enough to smack the shiv out of his hand and pistol-whip him back down, the hammer on my hot rod back and ready to put a round right between his eyes.

The guv'nor hadn't twitched a muscle. He knew he was safe with me around. 'As I said,' he went on, 'you are one of us.'

The cove settled himself and sat back, comfortable as you like. He wasn't even breathing hard. He was a little wolf cub right at home.

'Tell me who owns this dwelling.'

'Johann, the carpenter.' Even his voice was different. Deeper and slower.

'And where is he?'

'I neither know nor care.'

The guv'nor snorted. 'Explain.'

'You ask me about this village.' He examined his finger-nails as if he was thinking about paring them. 'I was born here. I was cast out years ago.'

'For?'

'What do you imagine? A little thieving. A little . . .' and he punched his right hand into his left.

'Why are you here now?'

The cove licked his lips like he was enjoying this. 'Grave robbery.'

'Explain.'

'I watch the village sometimes. Just waiting, because I know my time will come. And, oh, two, three months ago, there was a night like no other.' He paused. The guv'nor nodded to tell him to go on. 'Ah, beautiful, beautiful, it was. Men thrown about. The women too.'

'By whom?' At that, the bloke lifted his finger and turned it down, so that it was pointed towards the village below us. 'The hotel,' the Professor suggested.

'The hotel, *sir.*' He slurred the last word, like he found it funny.

'The staff or the guests?'

'The guests. I see them come, I watch them go.'

'What of your neighbours?'

'They packed and left. The morning of the next day.'

The guv'nor asked him some more, but none of it was worth tuppence. We had no more use for him, and I didn't like the idea of him hanging about where I couldn't see him. I wanted to cut his throat, but Holmes went lily at the idea. So we told the geezer that this was his last day in the village and kicked him out. He took his marching orders with a little bow and sneaked off over the rocks.

I slept like the dead that night. Then, at first light, I had a few cigars sent to my room and sauntered out for a smoke in the street to watch the goings-on. They were good tobacco, those tent-pegs, and I was heading back in to ask the guv'nor what the orders were for the day, when I saw him about a hundred yards off, close to the rail platform. There was a set of steps going down in the direction of the village boneyard, and he was standing at the top. But the queer thing was that he wasn't on his own. Holmes hoved into view, and they were chumming around like brothers-in-arms. Then they went down the steps together.

I didn't like it. I didn't like it at all.

So I found a decent observation point along the edge of the plateau where they wouldn't easily spot me and watched for a bit. Luckily the air was clear during the day. They were down there for nearly half an hour chatting together, and at one point Holmes laughed loudly enough for me to hear it on the wind. Well, that did it for me. I crept, belly to the ground, right to the edge so I could eavesdrop.

'... more years of this?' I heard Holmes say.

'If that is what you desire.'

'It brings a degree of challenge to my life.'

The Professor rested against a headstone. 'Were you subject to unusual conditions as a child?'

'What sort of conditions are you suggesting?'

'Extremes of heat or cold. An uncomfortable existence.'

'The heat and cold to which I was exposed are in line with the commonplace of southern England. And it was perfectly comfortable. I thank you for asking.'

The guv'nor shrugged. He did that when he was irritated by a reply. 'Then it is quite inexplicable. But to your point: you are quite aware that I have no equal in my chosen field and that the detective force of Scotland Yard – or the Pinkerton Agency, or the Sûreté – is no more a match for me than a beggar child. I admit that can be irksome at times.'

'You are going some way, Professor, to agreeing to what I suggest.'

'I make no agreement. Merely express interest.'

I saw Holmes turn and stare out over the cliff edge. 'It will not be forever – cannot be forever. There will come a time when things must end. There will be a place, too. But until then, a moratorium on permanent measures would suit us both.'

'Where? When?'

'For the finale? That we can decide when the juncture arises. We will both know when that time has come. But as for a location . . .' He spun around and even from where I was, twenty yards away and half-hidden by a snow drift, I saw the gleam in his eye. 'There is a place in this very mountain range. A waterfall. Your body, or mine – or both – would never be found.'

There was silence for a while. Then the Professor spoke. 'Then that shall be the place.'

Holmes went right to the edge of the plateau and looked down. I watched the Professor walk slowly towards his back, and I knew what he could do and I wanted him to do it. We didn't need these nancies. We'd been in tighter spots and come out nicely as you like. When the Professor was only two or three yards away, Holmes suddenly spun round and stared at him. The guv'nor, of course, just carried on walking right up to him as if he had been wanting a word and pointed out one of the graves.

'Do please wait your turn, Professor,' Holmes said. 'I do not wish to be disappointed in you.'

When I went in to luncheon, the fat manager, Albert, walked to the centre of the room and cleared his throat. 'Messieurs,' he began. 'I am afraid I must inform you that the current weather has cut off the railway line.'

'Are we able to leave?' the Slav ambassador asked.

'No, your Excellency. There is no other way down.'

'Are we to starve here?!' The stupid foreign Johnny could have taken a look at the bloody turbot on our plates and come to the conclusion that we weren't going to have to turn cannibal quite yet.

'This has happened before, your Excellency. It usually lasts no more than a week.'

'A week? I have appointments to keep! There must be a way to communicate. A telegraph?'

'I regret that there is not.'

The Slav chucked his napkin on the floor and chugged out, as if he might find someone in the bleeding lobby to say that there was a telegraph after all and the manager must have just forgotten about it. Not a bright spark, that one. I leaned back in my chair and saw him charge up to the front desk, where the flunkey shook his head. *There you go, old chum*, I thought. *There's your second opinion.* The Frenchie shogged off, and I noticed the Habsburger princeling on his own at a table, with two plates heaped with meat and cheese in front of him. There was bacon, eggs, kedgeree. Brown and white cheese. Hard-boiled eggs. Enough to feed a platoon on manoeuvres. I pulled out the chair opposite his.

'Did I say you could sit down?'

It takes a lot to make me stop and stare. But this fish, who'd been a poltroon the day before, was just about inviting me to step outside. I checked myself. I have never backed down and wasn't going to now. I placed myself into the seat.

'No. But I'm sitting.' Stone me if I didn't see him grip his meat knife like he was about to stick me with it. I got ready for that. A blade in a coward's hand will cut you just as much as if he had stones. 'Careful, laddie.'

There was something changed about him that morning. There was a look in his eyes, like he was staring right through me. And I knew that look. I've seen it a score of times. It's the one a man gets after his first battle, after he's tasted blood and seen death for the first time.

'Where did you get to yesterday?' I asked him. 'When that Frenchie took you away?'

He just gave me a sneer that said he'd never tell. 'He says we're stuck here.'

'He does,' I said.

'That's a lie. A claim for cowards.'

For cowards? Who was he now, a dragoon guard? 'What do you suggest?'

'We climb. The peasants around here have been climbing up and down from this hole for a hundred years. We're stronger men than they. We climb.'

'We don't even have ropes.'

He glared at me. 'We are going down. We don't need ropes.' Well, there was a queer turn. The day before he'd been a milksop. Now he was ready to scramble down the Mönch like a mountain goat. I didn't like it. I was about to give him a piece of my mind, but he stopped me with a raised hand. 'I can see you're no man of substance.'

And at that, I had a flash of red. The last man who called Sebastian Moran a weakling is still lying at the bottom of the Limpopo. I leapt up, ready to drag him across the table and knock his jaw out of place. But he jumped up himself and had such a glint about him that I held myself in check.

'I'm ready for death. Are you?' he barked.

'I've seen it many times.'

The room had fallen silent. We were being watched by everyone.

'Have you? From within?'

I clenched my fists, ready to put one across his temple, then the other into his gut. He squared his thin body to me.

'Messieurs!' Albert was hurrying in. 'Gentlemen. Herren. *Please.*' He lowered his voice for the last word as if he could keep all this a secret from the rest of the room.

Lucky for the Habsburg dog, the guv'nor was close on the Frenchman's heels. He shook his head, and I knew that this was the first fight of my life that I'd be ducking.

But then a light came into the fat bloke's face. 'Messieurs, I have an excellent idea.'

'Spill it,' I said. None too friendly, neither.

'Since we are to remain here for some days, an entertainment.'

'What did you have in mind?' I was keeping a beady eye close on the poltroon-turned-warrior. He was breathing like a tiger in a pit.

'A boxing competition. Gentleman's rules, of—'

'Count me in against him!' the Habsburger snarled, staring at me.

'Nothing I want more,' I replied. 'I hope you have no girl waiting for you in your nice palace back home. What's left of you won't be much use to her.'

At that, he seemed to crank up a notch. His lips actually curled back like that tiger. 'You'll be begging me to end you.'

Any other time, I would have laughed in his face or

smashed his nose then and there. It was only the guv'nor's stick rapping me in my chest that stopped me from doing the latter.

'You'll eat those words,' I growled.

The Frenchie looked as pleased as punch at the outcome. It was hard to say whether he was a sporting man or just wanted a bit of entertainment that night to distract all his toffee-nosed guests from the fact that we were all about to do a five-day stretch in that jug. And a jug's a jug, even when it comes with soft beds and lace table covers.

He hurried to the front of the room and lifted his paws. 'Messieurs! I am very pleased to inform you that tonight we will have an entertainment of sport. Two gentlemen will be engaged in a fine contest of skill and energy. Boxing, messieurs! A sport of noble men. According to the rules of . . .' He broke off, trying to remember.

'Lord Queensbury,' I prompted him.

'His Majesty Lord Queensbury.'

'He's a Marquess, not the king.'

'His Marquess Lord Queensbury, at eight o'clock this evening.'

'We won't be using his bleeding rules, anyhow,' I added.

Albert looked baffle-headed at that. 'Why?'

'Because for one thing, he says you have to wear gloves, and we don't have any. And for another, I don't want to use 'em. I want to knock this puppy's teeth out with my bare knuckles.'

'You can try,' the little prince said back. And I think he meant it, too.

'Tonight!' the manager yelled. And stone me if there

248

wasn't an absolute roar at that. Yes, every man jack in that room was cheering.

Well, you can't top that. So I just cocked a snook at the pup and took my leave.

I told you before that I like an uneven fight. I like it when one big bloke is pummelling seven types of the stuff out of a little 'un. So I was looking forward to that match, not just because it gave me a chance to teach the little fool a lesson or two, but also on what you might call an aesthetic level.

'Try not to kill him, Moran,' the Professor instructed me. 'There is no advantage in drawing undue attention to ourselves.'

'I would enjoy it.'

'I know. But it would bring me no gain, and that is all that concerns me.'

He could be straight with you, the guv'nor. The problem was that you never knew when that was. There isn't a gamesman on any of the five continents who could match him for chess, I swear. So you're thinking to yourself, *I'm glad he's playing a fair bat with me this time*, and you find out the next day that he's tied a noose around your neck while you've been looking the other way.

His hands were folded on top of his cane, and he was resting his chin on them. He has a pretty, girlish way of doing that. Though I suppose not too many little coquettish wenches carry a sharp shiv concealed in a walking stick.

'I'll just teach him a lesson.'

He sighed. 'I suppose you must. It is the way of your class of man.'

I was a bit crabbed by that, I'll tell you. 'Eton and Oxford, Professor,' I said, with some challenge in my voice.

'I know your educational background. I am speaking of your class of man, not societal creature. You are of the class that enjoys bestial employ and pastime. I have no feelings as to whether this is a good or a bad thing. Merely that it *is*. Much as the morality of four fours equalling sixteen escapes analysis. Four fours equal sixteen, and that is an end to it.'

'But . . .'

'Do not trouble yourself to attempt further elucidation. You and I will gain nothing from it. I recommend you do nothing but prepare for your fight. It will advantage me little if you beat your opponent to the pulp that you propose, but it will disadvantage me greatly if he should do so to you.'

'He'll be chewing the carpet before he's lifted his fives.'

Chapter 27

It is a strange thing that even in the midst of such situations, there are always moments to think, moments when one latches on to thoughts that have been sitting at the back of the mind, demanding attention here and there. So it was that as I gazed up at the peak of the Jungfrau – clear now, as the clouds seemed to have moved on – I realized that I had been there the best part of an hour in the afternoon and had thought of little but my wife.

There is nothing crueller than wondering what might have happened if ... But it was a different speculation that had been running about in my head for a while: what should I do now that I was alone in life? I hadn't just loved my wife, I had loved being married. Having someone at my side day and night had made me twice the man I was. I could go back to my bachelor days, living at 221b Baker Street and charging around the country – and other countries – with Sherlock Holmes. But I did not want to. I wanted a companion of my soul, not just my days. And then I could hear Mary's voice, gently laughing at me: 'No more moping, John. God didn't make you for the solitary life. Make someone else happy. Make yourself happy.' Yes, I knew it was her voice; so, as I sat with the cold air blowing around and the ceiling of the world stretched before me, I knew that love and laughter would one day come into my life again.

Chapter 28

I could hardly sit still, waiting for eight to roll around. I was ready a full hour beforehand. My shirt cuffs rolled back and my tie off, I warmed up with a bit of shadow boxing and some hopping on the spot.

Now, a good gamesman never underestimates his opponent. So I went through what he might attempt. He was of a hellish pugnacious bent that day, so he wasn't going to try any cold-fish tactic. No, he was going to come in like the cavalry. He would have no cool, so I had to keep mine. A bit more bouncing about the chamber, a quick roar in the looking-glass and then I was off to the dining hall.

I'll tell you, I wasn't quite ready for what I saw when I kicked those double doors open. It was like the Madison

Square Garden. Those nobs who'd been so buttoned-up during the day were screaming blue murder. Everywhere they were punching the air, yelling at each other, shaking hands on wagers, jostling so they could get to the edge of the rope. A bunch of bank-men turned into banshees for the night. Who would have thought it? But there they were. And then I saw *him*.

He was stripped right down to his waist, already sweating like a monk let loose in a nunnery. I'll swear his eyes were swivelling out on stalks like a lobster's. I decided to have a little fun with him. 'Come on, little girl, I'll let you off your challenge if you show me your sweet rump,' I yelled over and kissed the air.

Just as I predicted, he turned red as a tomato. It took three other fellows to hold him down.

'*Ich bring dich um! Ich bring dich um!*'

'You can try, matey. Though you won't be boasting after I've ripped your tongue out your head.'

At that, you could see the steam spurting out of his ears.

'Knock him out!' I heard a good English voice cry.

'*Zeig keine Gnade!*' a hunnish bloke yelled out.

Well, I know 'show no mercy' in about fifteen languages, so I knew that command well enough too. 'Don't worry, old lad, I won't,' I returned, though I knew he hadn't been addressing me.

I saw the guv'nor slip into the room and stand in the corner to observe. I quite wanted Holmes and the lapdog to witness what was about to come, so they could see what my fists could do. I pushed my way through the crowd – some of them slapping me on the back, others trying to shove me off. I stepped into the ring and gave my opponent a flash of my pearly whites to show him just how much I was looking forward to turning him into cat meat.

This made him roar again and the blokes holding him back started to struggle. He fought his way closer and closer until we were toe to toe and snarling at each other.

'Messieurs!' Albert was jumping up and down and doing his best to squeal above the hubbub. 'Messieurs! I want this to be a fight between gentlemen. It is to be—'

But he was cut short when I socked my left up into the Hun's ribs. 'Weren't expecting that, were you?' I dropped into his ear as he doubled up. And never one to miss an opportunity, I took a bite out of his lug while I was there and spat the wobbly bit of flesh aside.

'Monsieur!' Albert burst out, forcing his way between us. 'That is not according to the Marquess of Queensbury!'

'I was at school with Queensbury,' I said. 'He once forced a first-year to strip naked and run about in the snow with a rose glued to his buttocks.'

He looked utterly vexed, and his mouth opened and closed like a halibut until I told him to get on with it.

'Then . . . then begin!'

And he and the four blokes holding the Habsburg monkey back all leapt out of the ring like their lives depended on it.

I'll tell you what: I knew what to expect. I knew he'd come straight at me. What I hadn't banked on was the sheer speed that it happened. The kid was like a bull charging at a matador. Before I had a chance to lift my dukes, his crown was smashing straight into my gut.

'Prince ... I mean, Herr Schott!' the manager was screeching. 'That is not according to the ...'

'Oh, shove it,' I growled as I squirmed, trying to get a purchase on the slick flesh of the man. Skinny he was, but every ounce of him was going at me.

I gave him a good kick in the knee that crumpled him down, and before he could get up to his haunches, I was on top of him doing crack-and-repeat with my right fist. I fight southpaw, always have. It puts some blokes off, and that's always to the good. Each time he lifted his face, I'd smack it back down.

'Monsieur, will you please ...'

'All right,' I said, standing up off the Hun. He burbled something through his swollen lips, but me putting my boot right into his kisser put an end to that, and he was back down, then it was a few left hooks that spread his nose right across his face and extracted a couple of teeth that he wasn't using.

'That should be enough, Moran,' I heard spoken in my ear. I know the Professor's voice better than my own mother's. 'Oh no, apparently not.'

The princeling had managed to pull himself up and spit out one more coffin peg. Now he was lifting his fists with a howl once more.

'*Vorbereiten auf—*'

I had had enough by that point and gave him a quick hoof in the stones. Down like a sack of spuds. A boot between the hams will always finish a fight, Whitechapel-style. What, you think when some hottentot is trying to stick you in the ribs with a four-foot spear you fight all nice and gentlemanly? Hardly. Anything that gets the job done.

'Yes, yes, not according to Queensbury,' I said as the Frenchie hurried over, looking aghast. 'Well, what're you going to do about it?'

I had him there. And the crowd lost their minds. Some were roaring for me, others were spitting in anger.

'Who is he?' gasped the Habsburger as best he could. 'Who *is* he? What is he here for? He isn't one of us.'

Weird thing to say. My ears pricked up. Not just mine, neither. 'Find out what he means, Moran,' was muttered in my ear. The guv'nor again.

'Yes, do.' That was in my other ear. And it was a very different voice to the Professor's. I turned my head. It was Sherlock Holmes whispering little nothings in my lug hole. Well, I could take a little demon on one shoulder, but not his pal on t'other at the same time. And they looked to me like nothing so much as two little Old Nicks together. 'Goad him on. Make him forget himself. Make him sing like a canary.'

'Do it, Moran,' the Professor said quietly. And I'll tell you, that berserker Habsburg didn't make me start one tenth as much as the idea of the two of them on either side of me.

'Not one of you?' I called out in challenge at the princeling.

'Not one of us. You haven't seen what we have seen.'

'Go on,' Holmes urged me.

'Yes. Again!' demanded the other demon.

'What have you seen?' I shouted.

'We have been reborn as Solomon was reborn. We have . . .'

But the crowd closed around him, some of them casting nervy glances in our direction. And he was swallowed up and carried off. The atmosphere towards me had changed. One or two were still offering their congratulations – those men who had won a stack on me, I guessed – but most were now muttering among themselves and casting suspicious looks. Aye, things had changed all right. From then on, I'd be watching the shadows while I walked.

'You have made few friends,' Holmes muttered. 'I should go for a gentle evening walk and give these gentlemen a chance to cool a little.'

'He is correct,' the Professor dropped in my other ear.

Well, I was looking for a bit of a gloat, but I knew when to withdraw, too. So I took myself off for a mooch around that hole of a village. Not much to do other than peer into peasant hovels, so I strung it out for an hour, then stalked back in. Thought I'd get some sort of slap on the back from the Johnny on reception, but I just got a curious sort of stare. That didn't bother me.

It was freezing when I got back to my room – they must have turned the heating off for the night. And there was something waiting for me outside my door. It was a package about a foot wide, done up in brown paper and string. And I wasn't the only one to have been blessed. There were others just like it outside the rooms of my travelling mates.

Now, I haven't lived through half a dozen wars without being careful about ugly little packages turning up on my doorstep without so much as a by-your-leave. It was too light for a bomb, unless it was only strong enough to singe some poor sod's eyebrows off, so I carried it into my room.

I set it on my bedside table and had a good feel. Whatever was inside was solid and in the shape of a cube – except that one side was missing.

I cut the string with the machete that I keep under my pillow as a nice 'hello' for any cove who fancies stealing in on me during the night. And instead of pulling the paper off, which might have been a trigger for some surprise I wasn't looking for, I tore it away, piece by piece. It wasn't long before I ripped off the last big piece and saw that I was in the clear. But I was left with one of the weirdest things I've ever held.

It was a glass cube, all right, with one side missing, as I'd thought. And inside was a hollow yellow wax model of the hotel, complete with the mountain that it was carved out of. Only it wasn't just the hotel, because stuck on the roof were waxworks of four spiders, each about six inches long. Ugly blighters. Even their own mother would have thought so. And it wasn't helped by the fact that whoever had made the waxwork hadn't done the best job, because the wax had dripped down their legs and made nobbly little pools on the building. There was nothing else inside the package, and I was dead-beat, so I left it on the table and put myself down to doss.

Now, I'm not one for dreaming. That's for kids and fat-heads, if you ask me. But that night, something came at me while I was slumbering like the dead. If I remember rightly, I was out on the veldt. I was stalking a man-eater and had my rifle ready to pop him, but he was too far off and the sun was shining in my eyes.

I woke up to find that it was dawn and I hadn't closed my curtains. I grumbled but I was awake, so I hauled myself out of bed to have a quick smoke before settling back down for another hour or two. I lit a fag and opened the window so the room wouldn't whiff too seedy. Now, my eye is trained to catch the slightest movement, so when something right at the edge of my sight twitched, I saw it. I spun around, ready for whoever it was that had crept into my room. But there was nothing. I stayed still, hunting about for anything that had moved. No, nothing to see. But then I spied something odd a few feet away. The previous night, when I'd put the model of the hotel on the side table, I would have sworn that all the yellow wax spiders had been rooted down, with their legs stuck into the roof. But now the one at the front looked like he was rearing up, with his front legs ready to strangle me. And what's more, I could have sworn just as much that it was *twitching*. I took it to the open window, the better to see. But no, no movement. No twitching. I tapped it with my fingernail. Solid wax. 'You're going fully Tom o'Bedlam, old boy,' I told myself. So I chucked the model back on the bedside table, finished the smoke, closed the window and took myself back to my perch.

This time as I slept, I was skipper of a ship – a whaler, I should say. And some leviathan was rising up at me out of the briny. Well, even when I'm asleep, I'm no white feather, so I grabbed a harpoon and fought my way through a storm to the bow, the better to hurl it through the eye of the beastie. I pulled the steel back behind me, tightened my grip on it and was ready to let it loose like an arrow. I shouted out, 'Avast!' and let it fly.

Well, with that I woke myself up – only to find that in my slumber I'd grabbed hold of the machete from under my pillow.

And it's a damned lucky thing that I did.

No, no prig had picked the lock or kicked in my door. No snakesman had slipped down the chimney with a stabber clamped in his jaws ready to stick me while I snored away. The vision that I saw was a sight more devilish.

A prissier man than me would have felt his hair turn white at the sight of that foremost yellow wax spider slowly, very slowly, beginning to lift his hundred eyes up to mine until I was staring right into them like they were Medusa's own.

'What the . . .' I cursed under my breath. Because I've seen men lift trees; lizards that track an injured beast for days, biding their time until it's too exhausted to care if it's eaten; bats taller than I am. But I've never seen a six-inch waxwork come to life.

And this one was beginning to cycle its legs in the air, reaching out to my face.

I watched pretty damned astonished as, one by one, its eight spindly legs detached themselves from the roof of the model hotel. Then it started to crawl in that evil way the little sods do, almost without moving their puffed guts and just rippling along. It was making its way down the wall of the hotel, ever so slowly, heading for the open side of the glass case. But since it was made of wax, each step it took made a tiny tap on the glass. Tap-tap-tap-tap-tap-tap-tap-tap, each leg, inch by inch. Making its way to me.

And then the others started up, too. First their eyes, then their front legs coming for my flesh, I knew. Prising their eight stumps up, they made like Old Nick's own train towards yours truly. Tap-tap-tap-tap-tap-tap-tap-tap. Each one with my murder in his hundred peepers.

Suddenly the first one sprang from the bally table, right onto my leg, and started crawling up as quick as if he'd been pricked with a hot iron.

But that wasn't the worst of it. The worst was when he reared up on his back legs like a bucking nag and spat at me. It was as red and foul-smelling as the rankest slime spilling from a month-old corpse. That first salvo missed and spewed into the empty air. Then he bucked up, ready to try again.

After a half-second where I wondered if this was the end of the bleeding world, when waxworks come to life and spit poison, my reflexes kicked in and I took the second lot of spit against the blade of my trusty slasher. Good thing I did, too, because I saw that stuff start bubbling on the steel like it'd eat right through.

And then I pulled myself together and brought the knife down, and the wax cut-throat was sliced into two. Four legs on each half. I eyed the other three behind him, which were still coming on like Zulus. So then the machete came down three more times, and the four bastards were cut neatly into eight. And I'll tell you what: the blood that squished out of 'em was as real as any other animal's.

I stood for a minute, staring at the beasts, before I realized.

One package open. Three others left for my travelling mates.

It would be no skin off my nose if Holmes and his lapdog were croaked by these eight-legged freaks, but if the guv'nor was gone, that would put me in a difficult situation vis-à-vis employment. So I headed out, with the blade in my hand, straight for his room.

Immediately, I saw his door was ajar. Now, those spiders weren't going to push open a jigger, so I knew something was up. I kicked it open and stone me if I didn't clap my peepers on Holmes and the guv'nor, sitting about like they were at a duchess's tea party, casually watching four of the little waxen bastards running about in a glass case that had been set on the table with the open side down so they couldn't get out.

'. . . come across this species before?' the Professor was asking. He might have been asking for another slice of Madeira cake.

'No, a fascinating creature, though,' Holmes replied, like he was pouring the Earl Grey from a pretty little pot. 'Ah, Moran, you have taken to join us. I wondered if you might. Watson is not abroad yet. Would you mind looking in on him?'

'Mind looking . . .? Am I his nursemaid now?'

'Moran,' the guv'nor cautioned me. And I knew his tone.

Well, I grumbled, but what was the use? I took my machete and knocked on Watson's door. Instead of any sort of 'come in', I was answered by a yell and the sound of something crashing and splintering. I thought of just leaving him to it, but the Professor had it in his mind that we needed them, so I put my boot to the lock and crashed the thing in.

There in the dawn light was the medic leaping about as if he'd dropped into a crate full of tacks, and it wasn't hard to see why. Well, four swipes of my knife and there was no more caterwauling from the great Jessie. I didn't say anything but just sauntered back to the Professor's room. Watson followed, blubbing like a girl and damn near holding on to my coat tails for comfort.

'Ah, there you are, Watson,' Holmes said. 'Kind of you to join us.'

'Join you?' he spluttered. 'I nearly joined my ancestors.'

'And very good company I am sure they are, too. But here we have an ingenious little design, don't we?'

I took up a place against the wall. I don't like to sit if there are blokes about that I wouldn't mind beheading.

Watson dropped onto the bed and poured himself a glass of water. I think it was to steady his nerves. The pigeon-livered dunghill.

'Holmes, all I know is that I woke this morning to find that that strange wax miniature that I perceive we all received had come to life and was threatening to take mine away from me.'

'Come, come, Watson,' Holmes exclaimed. 'A man of science such as yourself? Do you believe in witchcraft all of a sudden?'

The guv'nor tutted.

'I do not, Holmes, nor shall I ever. But can you tell me what in Heaven's name is going on?'

'You cannot?' He looked at the Professor, who shrugged like he was dealing with a child who can't add two and two. 'But surely you considered the time of day? The state of the wax?'

'The state of the wax? Whatever do you mean?'

'We don't have all day,' the guv'nor said. 'Do please explain. Probably using simple language.'

'Watson, we are all modern men,' Holmes said. 'And we do not believe in magic or that waxworks can spring to life like Pygmalion's statue of Galatea. So what do we deduce?'

'That they were no waxworks.'

'Of course, that they were no waxworks. They were merely living creatures covered in wax. We were presented with them at a time of day when the temperature was very low. The wax remained set. But when the dawn light burst in – you will notice that the glass sides of the case are not entirely flat, but subtly moulded to multiply the light and its subsequent heat upon the wax object within – the heat melted the thin wax, and the creatures were able to move.'

What I couldn't understand was why, when I woke up the first time, I saw the little blighter coming to kill me. But as soon as I plucked his house up, he froze solid.

'Describe in precise details,' the guv'nor ordered me. I told him every movement. 'It is quite obvious. When you first saw the model, it was in the sheer sunlight and warming by the second. The wax softened, and the creature began to fidget. But then . . .'

265

'... you held it beside the open window and the blast of chill air turned it back into a solid statue,' Holmes charged in. I could see the two of them beginning to think together. I didn't like it. 'Certainly a novel little trick. Ever seen anything like it, Professor?'

'I have not. Although the Shah of Persia once consulted me regarding his eldest son, whom he wished to permanently remove from the line of succession. I suggested something not wholly dissimilar. An apparently dead sea snake would be suspended in a chilled jelly that would liquify at room temperature and allow the perfectly alive snake to slip out.'

'And the outcome?'

'That prince shall never sit on the throne.'

'Only to be expected.'

'So who sent 'em?' I asked, breaking in on their nice little fireside chat.

Holmes replied. 'I think we can surmise that your impressive display of boxing prowess last night brought things to a head, Colonel. I had hoped it would. Our presence has been felt, and questions have been asked about us. Someone here suspects that we are a danger to this institution.'

'We bloody well are.'

'Well, quite. And this is their response. The next question, of course, is who exactly are they?'

'I shall have Moran extract the information from the hotel manager, as he does it so well,' the guv'nor replied.

Holmes put up his hand. 'Oh, come come, Professor. That will hardly do while we are his guests. Where are your manners? Besides, for now, it might be to our advantage if he is unaware of our continued existence on this mortal plane.'

The guv'nor looked especially stoic at that. I know that look. Like a freezing-cold statue. It means he doesn't like something but he accepts it all the same. 'As you say.'

'Good. Now, what to do with these little specimens?' Holmes pointed to the eight-legged bastards in the glass box.

'Moran.'

'Only too pleased to help, Professor,' I said, lifting my machete, ready to stab it down into the bleeders. 'I sent two of 'em running home yesterday, and I'm happy to send as many as I can to meet their maker.' I brought the blade down.

'Stop!'

I stayed my hand, the tip of the blade half an inch from the first of the little cut-throats.

'Professor?'

He was standing. 'You say you sent two of them "running home"?'

'Yesterday. A few of 'em fell on my bed. I snuffed one, and the others took off.'

'Where to?' I pointed with the knife to the floor-level grille that brought hot air in from some furnace room hidden in the building. 'And you did not think to inform me?'

'They were spiders,' I grunted. 'You get 'em everywhere. No reason to think these three were anything special.'

'Idiot. We need to know where they are coming from. And wherever they ran to is likely to be that exact spot.'

'It seems to me,' Holmes added, 'that we need to trace where these pipes lead. And even Colonel Moran's great experience as a game tracker will be useless in this instance.'

'Do you have an idea?' the guv'nor asked.

'Not at this moment.'

'Then,' said the Professor, 'it is fortunate that I do. As you said, Moran's performance last night has brought affairs to a head. Whatever the secret of this hotel is, there are men here – men of whom the Habsburg boy is now one – who want to keep it secret and consequently sent us unwelcome gifts to secure that outcome.'

'You think that Habsburg molly sent them?' I said. 'I'll wring his neck.'

'More likely his more level-headed comrades. But either way, it would be to our gain to discover just where they are hiding themselves. Come, Moran.' He took his coat. Before we left the room, he stopped and glared at the others. 'I do not intend to allow you the freedom of my chamber.' And they stood and left, red-faced.

'Where are we going?' I asked as we left the hotel.

'The shack that serves as the local shop,' he replied.

Well, it was as good a place as any, I supposed.

We walked into the place, which was stuffed with food and household goods. 'Hmm,' he said, stepping over a few baskets full of eggs and bread, into a section that had kids' toys in a mess on the shelves. 'Not quite what we ... Ah.' He pulled things out of a cardboard box. 'This is what we want.' It was a simple wooden toy car, three or four inches long, without a roof. Cheap thing painted red. He tested the wheels, and they went round easily enough. 'Good.' He stepped out of that corner, selected a tub of glue, three candles, some string and a box of long cook's matches, placed them all on the counter and bought them.

Back in the hotel, he collected Holmes and Watson and brought everyone to my room. 'Remove the grille,' he said, pointing to the hot-air vent at floor level. It was easy to pry off. 'Hmm, no, there is a turning in the pipe; it will not do. We shall try Dr Watson's.' So we tramped two doors down and tried again. 'Good. Perfectly straight as far as we can see. Now, give me six of your bullets.' Well, I don't question the guv'nor, though ever since Dutch Calhoon had been knocked off, I'd become accustomed to keeping the Webley loaded with manstoppers. So I unloaded the pistol and handed over the rounds, but wasn't happy about it. 'Now, find me some rags.'

'Ah,' said Holmes. 'I understand. Yes, a neat solution to a knotty problem.'

'Rags?' I said, looking around the room. Did he think I had a supply of 'em, like a chambermaid?

'Tear up one of your shirts.'

I grumbled but took one from my room, shredded it and handed him the strips of cloth. Then he cut down the three candles and placed them in the roofless toy car. He broke the heads off six of the long matches, then stuck the shafts together to form a cross-rigging, like a galleon. He glued a large square rag onto it to become a sail, which he angled over the candles, and then stuffed the rest of the rags inside the car. After that he placed the bullets inside the rags, then soaked a length of string in oil, coiled one end into the rags and tied the other around one of the candles. Finally, he placed the car as far into the vent as he could reach and lit the candles.

We all crouched and watched. Nothing happened. I wasn't sure what he was expecting, but just as I was about to say something, damn me if it didn't start to roll forwards.

'The hot air from the candles rises into the sail and forces it forwards,' Holmes explained. 'That propels the toy on.'

I understood what the device would do. As soon as the candle burned down to the oily string, the string would light and that would spark the rags. The bullets would cook off and shoot all over the drum. There'd be a hell of a shindig.

We watched as it slowly rolled along the pipe, the light from the candles showing us how far it was going – three, four yards. Five. Six.

'We can only hope that it remains a straight path to its destination,' Holmes said.

'Indeed,' said Moriarty. 'I considered methods of turning the item – staked strings, falling side anchors – but they were unreliable. We shall discover first if this suffices.'

'Then it is time we take up observation points.'

'Quite. Moran, you shall be in the lobby. I shall be in the dining room.'

'My place will be in front of the hotel, and Watson, please place yourself outside in the corridor here.'

'What are we watching for?' he asked.

'You will know it when you see it,' Holmes told him with a grin.

We all hurried off to our places, and I took up a spot in the lobby with a copy of *Le Monde* for cover. I was watching all the fellows in that room making out like they were all up this mountain for nothing more than a holiday, when suddenly I heard those six manstoppers blasting. It made a damned racket, I can tell you. Reflex made me bob my head down and reach for my own gun, but it was empty, of course. The other blokes in the room just stared in the direction of the sound, and then a section of the wood panelling behind the reception desk blew open and some cove dressed all in white fell out with a dripping gash on his thigh. *Oho*, I said to myself, *a secret door, eh?* There was a lot of claret spilling from the bloke's leg, and you didn't need to be a doctor to know what caused it. He fell to the floor, swearing in German, and a flunkey on the reception desk grabbed him and hauled him back into that secret wing, locking the door behind him.

Too late, old chum, I said to myself. *I saw everything.*

'Aha,' the guv'nor said when I reported back to him.

'And I would wager that that hidden chamber is where the vertical shaft we found in the cave dwellings gives access to,' Holmes piped up.

'No doubt,' the Professor said. 'Well, we can hardly stride into the lobby in broad daylight to use their door, even if we have discovered it. Moran, I believe we are therefore in need of a rope ladder. It is good fortune that the village shop sells such mountaineering supplies. Go out and procure one.'

In, out. In, out. It was becoming bloody tiresome. Well, I did as ordered, gave the owner of the shop a look that told him if he spoke to anyone about what we had been buying he would regret it, fixed the ladder to the new bracket we had found at the top of the vertical air shaft in the cavern at the old village, and soon we were stepping off the bottom rung and onto a hard rock floor.

Hello, I thought, *this wing's a devil's stride from the rest of the hotel.* The other parts were carpeted and plush as a pasha's palace. In here, though, we were in a big dry cave where the floor was just flagstones on the solid ground and the walls had been whitewashed but not plastered. The ceiling was hard rock, not much more than a foot above our heads. We had come down in a corner of the cavern, and there were low natural walls of rock all around. It would be a tight little drum for a firefight. And the air was stifling – four big braziers were stuck around the place, burning charcoal to give the place a dark red glow and heating the rock so much that it was warm to the touch.

'Hot down here,' I said.

'Well, certain species need a warm atmosphere,' Holmes whispered back.

There were two doorways cut into the side of the chamber with modern doors installed, so the owners of the place had added some proper rooms. They had also put in a gas supply and a new ventilation shaft, so there were lights burning on the walls and you could breathe. Still smelled like the grave, though. I once saw something just like it under a prince's gaff in Rajasthan and that blag didn't end to anyone's good, so I didn't like it this time, either. I cursed the guv'nor for using up all my bullets on his mobile bomb.

They all followed me. The thing about places like that is that they're so bleeding quiet, your footsteps sound like cannon fire. It's hard enough for me to move on the hush-hush. A thick-headed fellow like John Watson might as well be beating a drum as he goes. I gave him a black look, and he got the message and made it a bit quieter.

A quick scout about, and I saw the set-up. One of the doors was locked – the knob had some fancy lock that held it fast so you couldn't even turn it. I could have kicked it in, but we were looking to stay quiet then, and the guv'nor opened the other one without bother. 'We shall search this one first,' he said. Queer thing was that right behind the door, there was a heavy curtain across. We pulled it back, and when we'd lit the gas lamp on the wall, we saw a desk, two chairs, a writing bureau and so on. Pictures on the wall, a Persian rug on the floor.

I set about searching the desk. No gun or ammunition in there, which was a pity.

Now, the Professor rates Holmes. He's not on the guv'nor's level for intellect, the guv'nor says, but he's no cloth-head. So when I saw him staring at the curtain, then feeling around a painting of the mountain on the wall, while the rest of us turned the place upside down – as quietly as we could – looking for anything of use, I got ratty with him and told him to buck up and do something useful.

'Why screw a picture to a wall?' he mumbled without so much as turning around to look at me. Well, I left him to it. Nothing in the bureau apart from some letter paper with the hotel's name on it and a few pens and ink.

And what did that tell me? It told me that the important stuff was hidden away.

One thing you can say about a cave is that there are precious few hiding places. I could see there was nothing in the walls, so that left the floor. A quick lift of the rug, and there it was. An iron compartment set into the floor. Strong lock on it, but it took me no more than a minute to pick it with a couple of pens and a paper clip I found in the desk. What did I find inside? A buff folder of papers. Not my bag, so I chucked 'em on the table and went back to the box. There was some cash in there, which no one else wanted, so it fitted nicely in my pocket.

Chapter 29

Moran had thrown a file of what looked to be important papers on the desk. I took them up. They certainly seemed pertinent because, like the page we had found hidden within Ridge's violin, they were in a cypher that looked like a string of randomly chosen letters. I handed it to Moriarty. He rubbed the sides of his head.

'It is a complete carbon copy of the report that we found in the musician's house,' he said. 'I shall decrypt it.'

Her Majesty's Foreign and Colonial Office. Report from our man Mercury in the Levant. First of October 1881.

On the orders of the section colonel, I joined the

expedition comprising Mr Benjamin Ridge, Mr Peter Jet and Lord Wyneth of Darlington. Our mission – and my presence in particular – were to be kept secret, due to the chance of the Turkish sultan taking anger and the very real danger of direct conflict. The balance in that region of the world is to be maintained until such time as we have the advantage.

We sailed first to the port of Haifa, via Salonika, arriving on the seventh of April. The local Ottoman authorities are indolent and corrupt, so that it took only a little minor baksheesh to be granted safe travel. The Governor of Haifa, indeed, presumed to request that his son be granted a place at Eton from the autumn and offered to pay the fees in silver coins, with a gratuity to ourselves of the same again if we could arrange said request. I assured him that I would put the matter in train.

Jerusalem is not the city that it was in the time of Jesus. The Roman and subsequent occupations that forced much of the indigenous Israelite population to depart has left it a ghost of what it once was. Ancient dwellings stand empty. The market places and temples of which we read in the Bible see but a handful of people each day. The Ottomans have erected their mosque-temples – often on the site of old churches, which themselves were built on the remains of synagogues – but they are as rarely used. The only renewal of life seems to be from the European Zionist communities that have sprung up, increasing some commerce in the town and irrigation-supported agriculture outside.

It was a representative of one of these projects, a Mr Levy, late of Paris, whom we met in a tavern, who made us aware of local rumour regarding the location of the palace of King David. The Biblical story, of course, documents David's rise from a life shepherding in Bethlehem to his defeat of the invading Philistine army, uniting Israel in a single nation and leaving his son Solomon to rule with famous wisdom. All this we learn from Samuel I and II, Kings I and Chronicles I. Notably, his first action as king was to capture the Palace of Jerusalem from the Canaanites, which he did by secretly entering through the palace's underground water system with a number of his soldiers. The attack was successful, and he became undisputed king of all Israel. But it has been a mystery where this palace lay. Until now.

Mr Levy informed us that a Zionist agricultural project had been exploring a ridge on the southern edge of the city, bordering the Kidron Valley, which contains the city's main source of water: the Gihon Spring. The members of this project – which numbered around twenty families – included engineers, historians and even a leading moral philosopher from the University of Prague. It was one of the engineers who surveyed the land closely enough to deduce the presence, under millennia of built-up soil, of large or very large building structures. The community had no time to excavate for the sake of curiosity, being more concerned with growing food enough to survive and trade, but they were delighted to show us where to dig ourselves. It was, they said, their ancestral heritage, and it would be a joyous occasion if these historical remains were rediscovered.

We hired labourers from the Arab population and dug with shovels, picks and, at times, our bare hands. We worked at night because of the heat, breaking at dawn to sleep until the afternoon. Little by little, we found broken pottery, then knives and implements, then a few Hellenistic-era coins, then walls, and finally, one night, as we pushed ourselves and our men to breaking point under a blood moon, we found a stone hatch buried under rubble. We lifted it and lowered a torch. The light showed us water: the water that had flowed for three thousand years. We had found our way to the home of the first king of Israel.

We entered the palace as David did: in the night, through wide pipes bringing water from the Gihon Spring.

It was hard going, wading through water that was at times up to our necks. We tried to preserve our lamps so we would have light, holding them above our heads. But one by one, as the water rose higher, they were extinguished by splashes or as we stumbled on the unseen floor and dropped them. Before long, we were blind, feeling our way along for hundreds of yards in the darkness. The place smelled of death. Each time we came to a junction, we chose the right-hand path so that we could at least guess which way we had come if we needed to return. Thus we frequently found ourselves in dead-ends, having to double back on ourselves. The time stretched on, but we could not see our wristwatches to check it – and they had probably stopped working anyhow, after being submerged in the ancient water.

We must have been in there for an hour, freezing. I was not worried that we would be lost forever, but there was a danger that one or all of us would fall down some hidden pipe underfoot or trip and knock our brains out on some unseen obstruction.

It was Wyneth who changed everything.

'Light,' he said. 'Light!'

I felt my way towards his voice. The water there was only knee-high. And I saw what he had seen. The wall of the passage was as sheer as the others, but there was a crack – no thicker than a blade of grass, but shining with light. And stranger, the fissure was L-shaped, five or six inches straight down, then a perfect corner to the right. It was no natural crack, but had been made by man's hand.

'What could it be?' Jet asked.

'It could be a way out of this sewer. Give me tools.'

Ridge was carrying the smaller tools and handed him a hammer and chisel. Wyneth did his best with them in the dark, but after a few minutes he gave up. 'No use,' he said.

'Let me,' I said. I had one of the heavy pick-axes. This was no time for delicacy. I pulled on a pair of gloves, made sure the others were out of the way and swung at the stone with all my strength.

The first blow struck with little impact, because I was too close. I took a pace back and tried again. This time, I felt the steel point of the pick chip away some of the rock. I swung again, and the pick went in harder and deeper. A piece of rock flew off into the water. The third time, I must have struck the point precisely into the crack, because it went in a full inch, breaking the rock apart along the line of the fissure, widening the light so that, for the first time in more than an hour, we could see our own hands and each other's faces.

Another swing, and more rock came away. Another, and there was a hole in the rock the size of a fist. I put my face to it and looked through. It was daylight coming down a narrow shaft in the ceiling to illuminate a chamber about five yards square. I must say, I was disappointed to see that the room was empty – at least, from what I could see in the dim light. I had hoped for the sort of riches that had been laid by in the Egyptian kings' tombs.

I handed the pick to Wyneth. He was a strong man for a lawyer and set about breaking down what turned out to be a doorway that we had exposed. Eventually, he had knocked away enough so that we could scramble through the opening.

I was first in. Yes, the room was bare. Disappointed, we rested, our backs against the wall. Our clothes were saturated – and that was what saved our mission. Because when we stood up to press on through the tunnels, the thin light from the shaft overhead picked out the spots where our wet jackets had wiped away some of the dirt of the ages. And the cleared patches showed bright paint under the grime.

We used our shirts as cloths, cleaning away millennia of soil, and soon we could stand back and see huge pictures emerging – pictures of life in the palace. Of meals and sports and a great battle.

There was something quite ingenious there, too. One scene featured a life-sized king – Solomon, we thought, due to him being pictured on a throne holding a scroll and a pair of scales, which are the eternal symbols of wisdom and good judgement. He was being presented with a large wooden chest. And the ingenious part was that the chest, when we put our hands to it, turned out to be a real box embedded in the wall.

Was this it? The treasure that men in London had dreamed of? Ridge forced open the wood and thrust his hands in. Immediately, he cried out in pain.

'What is it?' Jet asked.

Ridge pulled back his hand. There was a large green spider on his wrist. 'It bit me,' he said. Wyneth laughed and thumped the spider, crushing it. Ridge immediately submerged his hand in the stream of cold water outside the doorway to wash away or at least dilute any venom.

I looked into the chest. There were items in there, for sure. I put my gloves back on and carefully pulled out a host of small packages, all wrapped in grey linen. A few spiders came with them, but the gloves protected me, and they ran away to the darker corners of the room.

Among our findings were scrolls of parchment well preserved by the dry air, a copper candelabra of the Jewish type and a golden item they call a *mezuzah*, which contains a prayer that protects the home. I know some Aramaic and began reading the scrolls while the others brushed the dust from the other treasures.

'Give me your screwdriver,' Holmes instructed Moran.

'I don't take orders from you!' he snarled back.

Moriarty intervened, though. 'Do as he says.'

Holmes set about unscrewing the painting from the wall. 'And why have a curtain across the door?' he mused as he worked. The Professor, meanwhile, continued with his translation of the document.

'This is a poem,' I said, holding up one scroll. 'It describes the sea and—'

I broke off because Ridge had knocked it out of my hand as he fell to the floor. He was shaking violently enough to break his own neck.

We could do nothing but hold him down. His teeth were chattering, and he wailed like all the devils of Hell were torturing him. His forehead was burning hot, his eyes turned up so that you could see nothing but the white of them. And then, with one last scream, he fell silent. He was quite dead.

'My God,' Wyneth said. 'It was the spider bite.'

Ridge's face was a picture of pain, twisted almost out of recognition.

'Yes,' I said. And we all grabbed whatever we could as weapons and looked about in case there were any more of the creatures. When we were sure they were all hidden away in fear of us – the irony of the situation was that we had far more to fear from them – we put down our weapons and laid Ridge in a more respectful position before discussing what to do. It would be hard to carry him out. We could try the light shaft above, but how to get up to it? We did not want to just leave the man there. He might have been beyond suffering then, but he was our friend.

I was for one of us going back for aid, but Jet insisted we should try the shaft and I relented. But then something happened that made our discussion seem like a child's game. Something the like of which I had never seen before in my life and that shook my belief in the laws of this world. For just as we had gently put our hands beneath his lifeless body and lifted him to our chests, his mouth burst open, and he drew in a breath. 'It is only a muscle reaction,' Jet said, shocked. But then he stopped rigid, because Ridge's eyes opened wide. He stared at us one by one. And then his right hand shot out and grabbed my wrist . . .'

Chapter 30

'The lights!' the guv'nor barked at me. He was staring at Holmes, who had lowered the painting from the wall.

I knew better than to question the Professor and leapt up to turn off the gas tap. But that didn't drop us all into pitch black as I thought it would. Because where the painting had been, there was a light shining in.

We were staring straight through a pane of glass into the next room. And inside was the cove that the Professor had said was the Russian ambassador. He was standing bolt upright in a white room with a bed and a steel table covered with what looked like medical equipment, looking away from us, not moving a muscle. At the far end of the room was a campaign bed – a good one, made out of wicker. And it was occupied, too – a fair-sized bloke was kipping on it, but the rum thing was that he had a red velvet mask over his head, with two eyeholes cut so he could see. His wrists were trussed, and he was lashed to a water pipe to stop him moving, like he was a prisoner. He was moaning a bit, like he was dreaming.

There was another bloke in the room, too. He wore the uniform of the hotel and was sitting on an upright chair looking straight at us, a newspaper in his hands. Over his head was a chain, painted red, strung from the ceiling like the emergency chains you get on trains now. I got ready to scrap; the man was going to raise the alarm any second, that was for sure. I started for the door to take the fight to him, but the guv'nor grabbed my wrist. The one on the chair turned the page of his newspaper and went back to reading. 'He does not see us,' he whispered.

'He's looking right at us.'

'Idiot. Look at the glass.' I looked at it. 'The silver coating on this side is very thin, which allows light to penetrate, meaning this is a transparent mirror. If there is bright light in that room, but none this side, all that man sees is his reflection.' He pointed to the curtain across the doorway, too. It wasn't there to keep the room warm, it was there to keep it dark. We were in an observation chamber.

We retreated to the corner of the room so we could speak and not be heard – all except Watson, who stayed at the window, watching.

'We should depart and return later,' the guv'nor said.

285

'A return visit will merely double the chance of being found,' Holmes replied.

'If you think—'

He was interrupted by Watson clicking his fingers to gain our attention. Even with what else was going on, he was lucky I didn't break his jaw for treating me like a waiter. We all moved over, taking care not to make a sound, and looked through the glass. The cove in uniform had folded his paper, stood up and lifted the Russian's arm. He let go, and the arm stayed there in the air like the man was hailing a hansom. The Russian was just staring right ahead, not even blinking. The Johnny in uniform did the same with the other arm, and the fellow stood solid as a tree.

Holmes took us all back to the far corner. 'Watson? Your medical opinion?'

'I have only seen that effect once in my life. It was a subaltern in the Grenadier Guards who had been in Rome years ago to act as an advisor at the embassy. He was there during the outbreak of what the Italians called the "*Nona*".'

'Which was . . .?'

'It was an epidemic of people becoming living statues just like that. Only now we have a medical name for it: encephalomyelitis. No one knows how it spreads, and there is no cure. For now, the man in there is doomed to remain as he is: alive, but not living. And soon he will not even be alive. It begins with short episodes like this and slowly takes over. If the man on the bed suffers from the same affliction, he is also for the grave.'

'You say there's no cure?' Holmes asked.

'None at all. Nothing to relieve the symptoms, nothing to cure the disease.'

We all hushed then, because there were footsteps outside. They halted right outside our room. Then the handle began to turn down. I readied myself. How in the Devil's name we'd get down the mountain if we had to scarper was for another time. The handle went fully down, but before whoever was pressing it down came in, I heard the door of the room we were peering into creak open.

'He's ready, Doctor.' It was in French. The man we had seen in uniform had put his head out the door and had, thank the stars, distracted whoever had been about to come in and discover us.

'All right.' I recognized the manager's voice.

We heard them both go into the next room and silently went to the window to observe. I had no idea what that Ruskie could be ready for, unless it was a coffin.

Well, the manager – the doctor, apparently, though I've known a few men go by that title who knew less than your average village butcher – tramped in and started examining the Russian. He had a silver pen and started poking and prodding. No response. 'How long has it been?' he asked, taking a gold timepiece from the fancy little watch pocket on his waistcoat.

The orderly checked his wristwatch. 'One hour, fourteen minutes.'

'That's the limit. Get him on the table.' Between them, they lifted him up to the steel table, where he lay with his eyes staring up like a dead fish. The doctor took a syringe and needle and shot some stuff into his arm. Then he tied the straps that were attached to the table across the Russian's chest and legs and stood back.

The man began to stir, then woke up. 'You can remove the straps, Doctor,' he said, rubbing his eyes. 'I am quite in control of myself. More in control than I have ever been.'

The doctor checked his pupils. 'Yes, I believe you are.'

He and the orderly unbuckled the straps, and the Ruskie jumped up. 'I have never in my life felt like this!' he said. He had a bellow of a voice, that geezer. He went all round the room staring at things as if he had never clocked them before. He even went over to the other chap in the corner, whose wrists were tied, and took hold of his velvet hood.

'Don't, sir!' the doctor told him, nervy as a flapping fish.

'Why not?' He laughed right from his belly and ripped the hood off.

'Good God!' I heard Watson say under his breath 'It's . . .'

'Yes,' Holmes said. 'I thought it might be.'

Chapter 31

Standing there, staring through the glass, I was quite amazed to see that face. The last time I had seen it, the man was being bundled away unconscious on a horse on the other side of the Channel. But now, here he was in the Swiss mountains: our client, young George Reynolds, descendant of a deposed prince. His eyes were opening, but I could see the effect upon him of whatever strange drugs they had been using, and he was only half-awake.

Despite his sorry appearance, my heart nearly burst with joy that he was alive. I had almost despaired of seeing him again. The sight of two men being swarmed over by those spiders outside the British Museum, the looming presence of the cemetery below the village where we stood, the mysterious and threatening secrets of the hotel – they had all forced my mind to play out a scene where I broke the news to his beloved girl that he would never be returning to her. I had had enough of scenes like that, damn it. So the joy I felt when I saw him alive turned quickly to a force of resolve that I had rarely felt before.

'We must rescue him,' I hissed.

Holmes went to the door, opened it a crack, then closed it again. 'Not now. There are two more men coming.' I saw Moran lift a heavy walking stick from the corner.

I was worked up by that, I can tell you. There was George, right in front of us, and Holmes was saying we had to leave him in the grip of these criminals. I had no idea if we would ever get another chance to save him. 'We must!'

'No,' Holmes replied. 'Not yet. Even if we overpower them all, we have no way of escaping the village. We must wait until we have a plan.'

'But . . .'

He put his finger to his lips, and I held my tongue. We watched as the two new men entered the medical room. That was our cue to slip out and up the rope ladder, pulling it up after us.

'I know your blood is up,' Holmes said when we were in the upper cave. 'But he will be safe for a few more hours. We are outnumbered, so we must use night as our weapon. Especially now that we have some idea of what this place is truly about.'

I calmed myself. I knew he was speaking sense about

George, though I did not quite grasp his meaning about the hotel.

'Well, surely it is some sort of private hospital,' I offered. 'They have found a cure for encephalomyelitis, and the patients want their condition kept secret. Though I cannot understand why George is being kept prisoner.'

'Oh, Watson,' Holmes said. 'I do not think you could be more wrong. Why kill a government minister and a judge, then? What of the strange behaviour of those men before their deaths? Or the deaths of the villagers? No, my friend, I think the solution to this strange affair is quite the opposite of what you believe it to be.'

'Whatever do you mean?'

'I mean that this place does not prevent death, it supplies it. And the patients we have seen and met embrace it readily. Indeed, we have spoken to the dead.'

I shook my head with an utter lack of comprehension. 'I cannot understand you.'

'I know. But there is a man who can explain all.'

'Who?'

'The man in room fifteen.'

That man again! 'But if he knows so much, I don't understand why we haven't approached him. Is he a danger to us?'

'Watson, to my knowledge, dozens of men and women have posed themselves that very question, word for word. And in almost every instance, the answer has been "yes".'

'It's Brahms on the gramophone again. His little joke at my expense,' Holmes said as the four of us approached room fifteen. 'He does not often joke.'

'What is the joke?'

'I told you that I saw Ridge perform Brahms. It was this piece.'

'Are you saying this is . . .'

'Ridge playing? Yes. Listen to the reckless abandonment of orthodoxy in his notes. The soar of his ambition; his arrogance, almost.'

I listened. I have never heard in music what Holmes hears in it. But somehow there was something in that sound that was . . . I can only describe it as hubris. Yes, there was hubris in his performance.

But it was not the music that I wanted identified. It was the man listening to it. And there was something very different as we neared his room this time. Because as we reached the door to that room, I saw that it was ajar. 'But just who is inside?' I asked. 'Will you tell me now?'

'I will. It is the government agent they named Mercury,' Holmes replied. 'The man who stands behind so much of what we have seen.' And at that, he pushed the door further open, just enough for bright light to spill out.

Immediately we were blinded by two large lamps blasting their beams directly in our faces. But after a second, our vision adjusted, and we could make out the dark silhouette of a stout seated figure. I tried to shade my eyes, but it made no difference. It was like looking into the face of God: forbidden and painful. The figure shifted. I glanced at Holmes. He was looking straight at the other man. And I saw a strange smile play on his lips as he spoke.

'Hello, Mycroft.'

'Sherlock.' And Mycroft Holmes rose and strode towards us, surrounded by a corona of light, like a holy
vision. This hefty man who eschewed human touch and
company. 'I was wondering when you would call.'

'The time is now.'

'The time is always now.' Mycroft looked at Moriarty
and Moran with distaste. 'I suppose we must suffer their
presence.'

'You suppose correctly,' Moriarty replied.

Mycroft ignored him and snuffed out one of the lamps,
turning the other to illuminate the room. He went to a
bureau in the corner. 'You have been looking for this, I
expect.' He took something from a drawer and handed
it to Holmes. I saw that it was a bold-coloured panel of
parchment, depicting a man on his back, a spider crouch-
ing by his side. Above his figure, an anointed regal version
of him, lighter in tone and with a silver circlet around his
head, was flying down into his body. It was the missing
panel from the set we had found in Ridge's secret collection. 'We call this stage "resurrection". I hope our Saviour
will not begrudge us that word, he having largely made it
his own for two millennia.'

'In return, I give you this,' Holmes said. It was the photograph we had taken from the same secret room. 'It was
a pity you were the one taking it.'

Mycroft studied it with a nostalgic smile. 'I insisted that
I should be. A poor agent I would be if I left a record of
my presence. An interesting assignment, though.' He held
a corner of the photograph to the flame of his lamp and
dropped it in a glass ashtray to slowly burn.

'The venom. Out of interest, how much do you need to dilute it?'

Moriarty looked especially interested in the detail. Moran was surveying the room, as he usually did, presumably for vantage points or escape routes.

Mycroft settled in his chair. Strangely, he took up a piece of grey metal about the size of a matchbook and began shaving some of it off with a metal file, to produce a powder. He collected the powder in a paper wrap and poured in some white powder from a small box.

'The current mixture is one part venom to twenty-five parts animal blood and two parts the sap of a local tree. That way, death is less likely to be permanent.'

'Less likely to be permanent?' I said, astonished. 'What are you talking about?'

'Dear me, Sherlock, you really have not even suggested the truth to your friend?'

'I have not. I was not utterly certain until I saw your copy of Dante's *Divine Comedy* in the hotel lounge. A little research?'

'Let us call it comparative literature.'

'Holmes,' I insisted. 'What is this all about? For God's sake, tell me!'

'For once, you may invoke the name of God and he will appear,' Mycroft replied.

'Whatever do you mean?'

'I mean, my dear Doctor, that half the men in this hotel have known what it is to be a god. For they – we – have died and seen what comes after. And then we have been resurrected. We did not wait three days, as I believe is traditional, but only minutes or hours; that is our shortcoming. But the research continues, and with every attempt those scientific gentlemen make, they push it a little bit further and the subject sees a little bit more. To know what lies beyond, that is what makes us more than human.'

I stared at Holmes until he spoke. 'The venom is a unique compound,' he said. 'In normal quantities, it brings death. But in small enough doses, or diluted in the way that the ancients discovered and that was rediscovered on the famous dig, it brings on death and then recedes to allow life once more.'

'Extraordinary!'

'Nature is just that.'

Mycroft spoke. 'A fascinating piece of evolution. It means that the spider, by controlling the amount of venom it injects, can keep its prey near death rather than dead, and the meat therefore remains fresh.'

'And you have been using it for . . .'

'Knowledge!' Holmes cried. 'That most forbidden of all fruits. Knowledge that only an immortal possesses. The men who went through this process flew above all the world and felt invincible.'

'That is the case,' confirmed Mycroft. 'And that is why many died.'

The snow outside the window was whipping up, turning into whirlwinds, beating against the wall as if it was trying to knock the whole hotel to pieces.

'How?' I asked.

Holmes took up the explanation. 'Some of them in

accidents resulting from their own erroneous self-belief. Others because they were endangering nations with their caprices multiplied by the genius that they had gained – so they had to be stopped before they brought destruction not on themselves, but on innocent others. Think of Jet's mad idea of deposing the Queen and installing a new monarch on the throne, perhaps to be his puppet. Or Wyneth's wild revenge on the Professor here.'

These schemes had drawn Holmes, Moriarty, Moran and myself into this affair, and now we knew what even stranger events had led to their formation.

'So Jet and Wyneth were killed to prevent them furthering their plans?' I stared at Mycroft. 'Did you . . .'

He forestalled me. 'I see where your mind is heading, Doctor. But no, I had no part in their deaths.'

'Then who did?'

'Ridge. He saw what terrible consequences would arise sooner or later if they were let loose on this world. A powerful man who is not checked by fear of consequence is a pestilence awaiting a host.'

'And Ridge himself?'

'He invited you to his house to tell you everything so that you could expose this place. But the men here had no intention of allowing that and ensured his silence. It was they who sent Scotland Yard to arrest you for his death. It would have been a neat solution to their problems, I will give them that.'

'Did you know beforehand that Ridge was going to kill Jet and Wyneth?'

Mycroft picked up the metal file and continued turning

the block of metal into powder. A signet ring on the fourth finger of his right hand glinted in the light. He shifted the paper wrap of filings. 'There are times when it is best to close one's eyes to what is happening.'

'And when is that?' I demanded, wanting to know the truth as to how complicit Mycroft had been in the killings.

'I shall let you know when the time has come.'

Chapter 32

Well, after his fat brother had finished gabbling on – all right, his *meshuganah* explanation fitted, but I still didn't trust a word that buttery prick uttered – Holmes took a seat and started flicking his fingers like he was sewing a sampler.

'What a cat's cradle the world is, Watson,' he said. 'Each string pulls on another. You see how Jet's plan to foment revolt in Britain leads back to this building and what it holds – the courage or madness that he contained sprang from this well. And he believed that putting George through the same treatment could mould a suitably charismatic pretender to the throne. Now, let us recall that Dutch and Jan Calhoon, whom Moriarty tangled with, were reputed in the American underworld to have been cowardly disappointments to their tough father until they underwent a sudden and unexplained change in personality a year or so back. Well, I think we can guess where they came for that upheaval in nature,' he went on. 'Yes, the men behind this facility have their fingerprints on much that we have encountered recently. And only now do we see their silhouette behind the curtain.'

'It is all quite clear,' the Professor said. 'And now that we are fully apprised of the situation, it is time to depart. I presume you wish to bring that young man with us?'

'Of course we do,' the lapdog yapped.

'It is your choice. I presume also,' the guv'nor said to Mycroft Holmes, 'that you have a plan for departure that does not involve our hosts.'

'As it happens, I do. The train conductor who conveyed you all up here is in my confidence – or some of it – and tonight he will commandeer a small engine that can make its way up here and back. Take this, Sherlock. We might need it before the night is out.' He handed Holmes a large wrap of the metal powder that he'd been filing. 'I propose we rescue your protégé just before midnight. By that time, all the hotel staff will be safely ensconced in their beds and will be no danger to us. We can slip into the treatment block, free him, return to send the signal and quietly meet the engine. With any luck, it will be hours before they are aware that anything is amiss.'

'So what do we do in the meantime?' I asked. It left us hours to kill, and I wasn't in the mood to sit around twiddling my thumbs.

'It would be sensible to retain a low profile,' Mycroft said. 'We should all remain here.'

'I do not wish to spend so long here with nothing to stimulate my mind,' the guv'nor told him with a scowl. 'Your brains may remain idle without any noticeable effect upon you, but I live by mine.'

'And I was so looking forward to your company.'

'Oh?'

'Quite so. Indeed, I brought my favourite Go set, so that we might while away a few hours if necessary. I understand that you are quite the adept.'

Mycroft lifted a wooden game board from his desk. It looked a bit like chess.

Now, the funny thing was the effect of this on the Professor. He usually sets his mind, and that's it. But this time, there was a struggle – he wanted to leave the room, for sure, but he was drawn to the game. He tapped his stick on the floor. Then he gave in.

'As you wish.'

'Shall we play for stakes?' Well, my ears always prick up at those words.

'Stakes? Money? Pah, those of intellect play for nothing but proof of cognitive advantage.' He stared at Mycroft's forehead. 'Poor frontal lobe development, I see. A family trait.'

Mycroft smiled. 'I believe one of us will enjoy this immensely.'

Chapter 33

As time passed, the shadows outside grew longer. The white slopes turned blue, then grey. The sun, so white above us, dimmed and fell, eventually slipping down behind a mountain peak to let night cover us like a shroud.

All the while, I was thinking over the strange events that we had fallen into. As a medical man, I had always confined myself to the workings of our physical world of flesh and blood. But the idea that the mind could travel somewhere else, that the men who ran this place could unlock potential in it that the rest of us could only dream about, well, it unsettled me. It unsettled me greatly.

The clock struck the half-hour before midnight. The gas lamps in the room threw moving shadows over the

Go board. I could not tell which man – if either – was winning. Certainly, the edges of Mycroft's mouth were turned up in a smile. Moriarty was scowling, but it might have been concentration rather than irritation.

'Time, gentlemen, time,' Holmes said softly. Moran looked up with glee.

'We shall have to complete the game another day,' Mycroft said. 'I presume you are able to memorize your position?'

'Of course,' Moriarty replied.

We resolved that Holmes, Mycroft and I would go into the forbidden wing of the hotel. Since the staff were all asleep, we would enter through the hotel itself, by way of the secret door that was usually guarded by the staff at the front desk, rather than via the ancient caves above.

So we went to our own rooms to gather what possessions we could carry with ease. Twenty minutes later, we assembled in the corridor and crept through the hotel. Moran slipped the catch on the door with his knife and then he and Moriarty remained as our rear-guard while we rescued George.

We each carried an oil lamp, their shutters nearly closed so they gave only pencil-thin beams of light. Mycroft was at our back, but he was a more sprightly man than you would think by looking at him.

We spoke in whispers as we reached the room that had held George, hoping he would still be there – if not, we would have to search for him. There was a sound, but it wasn't coming from the treatment room. It was a rough noise coming in waves from the observation chamber alongside. Very cautiously, Holmes looked inside that room, then beckoned to me to do the same. The sound was the loud snoring of the orderly we had seen earlier, passed out in a chair, his arms folded. An empty half-bottle of dark wine stood on the table in front of him.

The door to the treatment room was bolted from the outside but not locked, and we eased it open. Inside was pitch darkness. I played the beam from my lamp about, picking out the chair and table we had seen before. There was something else we had seen before that we had not counted on: the Russian ambassador was on the table once more, but this time not strapped down. We would have to take pains not to wake him.

Holmes pointed to a corner of the room. A hooded man – by his clothes and shape, it was George for certain – was sat in a wooden chair with his hands and wrists bound.

Holmes indicated that we should free him. I carefully stepped around the table in the centre of the room, shining the lamp at the floor to make sure I did not kick something. Holmes and Mycroft followed, looking around cautiously.

I heard a sharp intake of breath. I looked to Holmes. He had found something that we had not seen earlier from our vantage point behind the one-way mirror. It was a large panel in the wall that swung open to reveal a sight that quite took my breath away with a horrible combination of disgust, fear and morbid fascination.

For embedded in the wall was a huge glass tank, a vivarium stretching four yards deep. And in the dim light from Holmes's lamp, it was pulsing with the movement of thousands of Green Lynx spiders, crawling over branches long stripped of their leaves, over each other and over the carcasses of the unhappy creatures that had been dropped into the tank as food. As the light flashed over them, they began to rush towards us, a horrible army. The first stopped an inch from the glass, watching us with their compound eyes. And then, at some unseen signal, they rushed again, some throwing themselves at the side of the tank and swarming up it in a murderous attempt to reach us, others spitting their red venom until it ran down the glass like streaks of clotting blood. I have never thought of any animal as evil, as having that human attribute. But without doubt, those creatures had something of the Devil in them.

The sight was terrible, but I could not help but be drawn to it, taking a step closer.

If only I had not.

If only I had stayed in my place! Then I might not have brushed my elbow against a side table, and I might not have knocked a large glass bottle to the floor, smashing it into pieces. I stared, horrified, at Holmes. He put his finger to his lips, indicating that there was a chance my mistake had not been marked. We stood stock still, listening as hard as we could. There was no sound from the neighbouring room.

No. Not from that room. For the sound, when it came, was a deep moaning from the man on the table. He was beginning to groan as he had done the last time we had seen him. In the weak lamplight, his face was dark and brooding. We stood still, and the moaning ended. He was back asleep, in whatever dreams had been induced in him. I said a silent prayer of thanks. But I was premature with my thanks too, for at that moment, a light blazed up. Suddenly the whole laboratory was clear in our vison, and standing in the doorway with a bright lamp in one hand was the orderly. In his other hand was a needle filled with red liquid.

'Get out of—'

He failed to say another word, however, because right then the man on the table let out a howl like a banshee and started clawing at his face as if it were covered in the spiders we had seen. He might have been possessed by a demon, the way he was writhing about. Then his eyes flicked open, and he was staring straight at me.

Holmes, ever an opportunist in a battle, took advantage of the distraction to knock the needle from the orderly's hand, sending it skittering across the floor. He struck the man's jaw with his fist, knocking him half-down, but the fellow was solid and came back up. I reached for the syringe, aware that the man on the table was starting to mutter words now. 'Careful, Doctor!' Mycroft warned me. 'You don't want that serum in your veins.'

The orderly was grunting as he made to grab Holmes around the chest.

I got hold of the needle, but before I could blunt its end to make it safe, the Russian had fully woken and sprung up from the table, his hands clutching at my throat. He was a strong man, and the evil syringe fell from my fingers.

Mycroft was attempting to help Holmes, and I was left

on my own with this animal. I truly believed he was going to choke the life out of me. But then something else rose at the edge of my vision. A black shadow sitting up and tearing a velvet hood from its head.

In less than a second, George, his hands still bound, threw himself a full three yards across the room, looped his wrists over the Russian's head and wrenched him off me. The two fell to wrestling on the table, with George holding his own by choking the man as the Russian had planned to choke me. As George pinned him, I strapped the man's wrists into the leather restraints attached to the table and tied him down.

By that time, Holmes and Mycroft had got the better of the orderly, too, and he was cowering in a corner, afraid of Holmes's fists and the needle of blood-red liquid that Mycroft had scooped from the tiles. I untied George's bonds and repurposed the ropes to tie the orderly to the water pipe. The Russian was huffing and puffing, but he would need to be superhuman to break through those leather straps.

I took hold of George. He had not said a word since he had torn the hood from his head. 'George, how are you?' I asked as gently as I could given the urgency of our situation. I was sorry to see that while he wanted to answer me – the mental effort was visible on his brow – he could form no words. 'Speech will come,' I told him. 'Soon, my boy.' He nodded. He could be a hothead, that young man, but that also gave him a determination that could not be broken.

'There is no time to waste,' Holmes said. 'We need to get out, hide ourselves and wait for the train to arrive.'

We hurried out, shutting and bolting the door behind us. Our lamps picked out the doorway to the hotel lobby, and we ran for it, George stumbling a little but able to keep up.

'What do they . . .' I began to ask Mycroft. But I did not finish my question, because as I reached that last word, the door ahead of us burst in. Three men followed: two burly guards with pistols in their hands and, behind them, the manager of the facility himself. His face was full of nothing but wrath. The guns were levelled at us, and I had no doubt they would be used.

Mycroft gazed at them. 'I expected you sooner or later, Albert,' he said. 'Your bumbling hotelier routine has been grating on my nerves.'

'I have been busy with a patient,' the Frenchman replied.

'Oh, the bank director? Has it gone well?'

'He will never be the same man. He will be better.'

'Oh, Albert,' Mycroft sighed. 'Nothing will shake your belief, will it? Neither evidence nor experience. You see, Sherlock, Albert is certain that he is improving our species.'

'Man must evolve or remain an ape,' Albert said. 'You have been too squeamish, Mycroft.'

'Mycroft,' Holmes said, 'I think there are a few details you have been keeping to yourself.'

'I do apologize, Sherlock. Force of habit, you might say. You see, once Ridge, Jet, Wyneth and I had all been through the process, we had died and returned from death with our minds expanded beyond anything we thought possible. We could think five times faster and a

307

hundred leagues deeper about any subject. Ridge and I saw the dangers of that, but Jet and Wyneth saw only the opportunities. They sought out Albert, who was gaining a reputation as a radical professor of the brain at the Sorbonne, and established this site. They believed that undergoing the process would be something akin to a new stage in evolution.'

'And it has been so,' the Frenchman insisted. 'The government ministers who have been through it have returned to their lives ready to lead and transform their nations; the scientists are already making breakthroughs in chemical processes and medicine – you have heard of Strazzeri's method for filtering blood? It would have taken him a lifetime to develop had he not been here. Instead, it took him six months. Delachair and Ramos's study of Occitan is groundbreaking. Yamaguchi in Tokyo will bring renewed prosperity to his country. In New York, Berger's salons are a river of creative thought. I could go on.'

'And the Calhoons?'

'An error. Some will occur. It is unavoidable.'

'How many patients have you had?'

'Close to a hundred men now, a few women.'

'You think these people are benign. Perhaps for now. But it also makes them unafraid of all dangers, and that is a terrible weapon. When conflict arises between them, it will mean wars on a scale we have never seen.'

'It is a risk, but worth it for the betterment of the species.'

So Ridge and Mycroft had sworn off the process but Jet and Wyneth had not. Thus, with Albert, they had built the hotel and put chosen individuals through the experience to create men who would lead the world in their fields. 'Those wax models were hardly very friendly, by the way,' Mycroft said.

'I must apologize. I was angry. I regained myself soon enough.'

I could see George tensing throughout all this, making ready to spring on our opponents. The treatment he had started really did give men the feeling of invincibility – but the lead in those revolvers would take no notice of his belief. I had to put a hand to his arm to steady him. He understood and shrank back a little, though I guessed he was unhappy at being warned off.

I wanted to know what had happened to Moriarty and Moran. Had they been captured? Were they lying dead outside?

'We have seen the effects of your work,' Mycroft continued. 'At best, it is men with immense power using it for their own caprices. At worst, they are turned to blood-lusting beasts.'

'We can keep such animals in a zoo,' Albert replied, then turned to me. 'Oh, so that amuses you?' he sneered. He had seen how I was smiling.

'Oh no, that repels me. I am amused for another reason,' I said.

For behind him now stood Moriarty and Moran, both armed. In the Colonel's hand, a revolver was pointing at the back of the taller of the two guards and, for his part, Moriarty had the blade of his sword-stick drawn and ready to plunge into the neck of the man in front of him.

I knew that Moran alone could end the lives of all three men before they could even turn around.

'Do not move,' Moriarty said. Albert did as he was told.

'Not so tough now,' I said.

But then, to my surprise, Albert began to chuckle. Then he moved to one side. I expected Moran to shoot. He has never been known to hesitate. But he did nothing.

'Now, Moran,' Moriarty said. The Colonel stepped forward between the two guards, and suddenly the gun was pointing at me. Moriarty slid his blade back into the stick. 'I am afraid, gentlemen,' he said, addressing us, 'that your presence is required here. It will not be a pleasant outcome.' I knew what he meant, what awaited us: those vile creatures in the glass tank. 'Bind them.'

'All of you, face the wall!' Moran snarled. It was clear that any sign of refusal would be the end of us.

So there it was. As soon as Moriarty had learned the secret of the hotel from Mycroft, he had gone to Albert, and they had come to an arrangement that betrayed us and benefited him.

'Oh, Professor,' Holmes tutted, shaking his head. And he looked to Mycroft. 'Is it the time?'

'*The time has come.*'

I understood what they meant and, as Mycroft had earlier instructed, closed my eyes.

The two brothers simultaneously threw their lamps, exploding glass and burning oil across the floor. In another second, they had drawn from their pockets the wraps of magnesium and sodium that Mycroft had prepared earlier and had cast them into the flames. The explosion was so loud, and the flash of light so bright, that even though I had prepared for them, I was left deafened and disoriented. But our new enemies had it far worse. Moriarty collapsed against the wall, and Moran was leaning against a doorframe, rubbing his face. I saw the Frenchman laid out on the floor, one of his guards stumbling about, the other on his knees, scrabbling for his gun, which had fallen close to my feet.

'Come!' It was Holmes, who was pulling me towards the door. I held him off for a moment, just long enough to grab the revolver. Moran aimed groggily at me and fired. The sound was like another explosion in that small room. I shot back, but my bullet went wide. 'Watson!' We charged out into the lobby.

Chapter 34

I've been hit with grapeshot, beaten down with cudgels and was once chucked out of a train going like the clappers. But I've never once thought I was fully snuffed – which I did until the smoke cleared and I could see I was back in that cavern. For about fifteen seconds, the ringing in my ears was so much that I wished I *had* been slotted. But then something else came to mind: I was going to bleed them dry.

I didn't wait for the Professor or the hired muscle from the hotel. I was up and running with my thumb on the hammer of my Webley, ready to blast the four of them apart.

'Moran!' The guv'nor was yelling like I was a mad dog. 'Moran! I know where to corner them!'

Well, I know when to hunt, and I know when to stalk. So I stopped, shook myself down and turned back. *Yes, get a grip of yourself, old man, you'll have 'em*, I thought. *You'll have 'em*.

Chapter 35

'Where can we go?' I shouted as if the hounds of Hell were at our heels.

'We can't escape,' George cried, looking around the lobby for a way out or perhaps a weapon to make a last stand. 'We must fight!'

It would have been impossible to run and make it to Interlaken and safety – a near-blizzard was blowing, and we would surely soon freeze if we tried to descend the mountain.

'Messieurs!'

It was whispered to our side. A crack of light had opened up. I recognized the face. The woman Ioana had opened the connecting side door from the chapel. 'This way!' I cried. And, as one, we made for the tiny church as our only haven from death.

We barrelled through – Holmes, George, then Mycroft and myself. I slammed the door closed and locked it. George and I pushed a heavy oak pew against it, too. It seemed a sturdy piece of wood – but not so sturdy that it could stop the bullet that pierced it a second later, grazing my arm. 'Get down!' I yelled, and we all dropped to the flagstones. Three more rounds burst in on us, but each one found its mark only in the wall, ricocheting off old memorial plaques with long-faded names.

I looked about. The altar resembled nothing so much as an omen as the moonlight fell across it. A silver cross seemed to cry out a warning of the forces that the men in these buildings had been defying. A brass goblet lay overturned on the table, a bullet-dent in its side. Thick red Communion wine had spilled across the white altar cloth. In that milky light, it loomed like something other than wine.

The room was probably twelve yards long, floored in dirty flagstones and with a few small windows set in the whitewashed side and rear walls. Those in the side wall were certainly too small to escape through. The one in the rear wall was itself big enough, but it was stained glass and reinforced with lines of lead curling through it. A depiction of the Passion of Christ on the Cross bore down on us, the suffering of the man fresh on His face as blood dripped from His wounds. I wondered if we, too, were destined to die in abject agony. The main door, at the opposite end of the chapel, was bolted and barred.

'I was praying,' Ioana said in her Romansh Latin, by way of explaining why she was there. 'For my husband.'

A hammering and kicking pounded at the side door.

'Come out or we'll kill you all!' one of the toughs screamed at us. And to make a point, he let loose another round through the wood. It thudded into the altar, making the table shake. The Communion goblet rolled off to the floor. The dregs of the wine seemed to congeal on the filthy stones.

At that, Iona snatched the revolver from my hand and pointed it directly at the door.

'Come in!' she snarled loud enough to be heard outside. In reply, the timber shook as a boot thudded into the wood.

And at that, she took aim two feet above where the impact had come and fired.

The gun reported, a puff of smoke rose from the barrel, a small disc of wood erupted from the door and a hard scream, the sound of a man wounded in battle, shook the room.

Holmes, meanwhile, was at the main door, easing it open, but the moment he cracked it a finger-width, he threw himself to the side, just in time to have a bullet fly past him.

'Moran won't miss again,' he said grimly, bolting the door once more.

I took the gun back from Ioana, while George and Mycroft scouted the room for anything else we could use as a weapon but found nothing.

'They will send for more men,' I said. 'Our best chance is to rush them now.'

'I'll tear them down myself,' George growled.

We heard a gurgling moan from the other side of the door to the hotel. So the fellow had not departed this world. Then there was the sound of dragging and more pained moaning, followed by another voice.

'Gentlemen, I would not do anything hasty. If you try to run, Moran will drop all of you before you even see him.'

We knew the voice, of course. It had dogged us for years and been our unwelcome travelling companion for this past week. And we knew it spoke the truth. We would barely set foot outside before the Colonel would put bullets through each of our hearts.

'Stalemate,' Mycroft said gruffly. 'He cannot come in,' he nodded at the pistol in my hand, 'and we cannot get out.'

'Just let me try!' our young friend demanded.

'And lose you to Moran? No.'

'Why does he warn us?' Holmes wondered aloud.

'Holmes?' I asked.

'Moriarty wants us dead, so why does he warn us that Moran is out there with a gun trained on the door?'

'I cannot tell.'

'Neither can I. That is what worries me. He wants us to stay put. But why?'

'We have no time for this!' George insisted. 'If we can't rush them, we have to be ready for them to come in. They'll have more men coming.' He stole to a window.

'Stay back from there,' I warned him.

He turned back to me. 'I can't see any— Ahh!' He yelled in pain as his shoulder erupted in a spray of blood and cloth. The window shattered into a rainfall of glass, and he fell to the floor. Another bullet cracked into the wall, having passed through the air where he had stood just seconds before. Had he not turned to speak to me, the first would have gone straight through his skull.

'Come here!' I yelled. George crawled over, hidden by the wall from the view of the notorious marksman outside. He slumped against a pew, and I peeled away his shirt to check the bullet wound. I spied the bloody bullet, bent and crushed by the impact, on the floor behind him. 'It passed right through the flesh. It will hurt like hell, but you will recover,' I said.

'If we get out of here,' Mycroft said grimly.

I tore off one of my own shirt sleeves to use as a bandage on George's shoulder. 'We can't just wait,' he growled. 'I know these people.' The boy was hot-headed but a brave one.

Holmes spoke to Ioana in her language. 'Is there any other way out?' She shook her head. No, no hidden exits, just what we could see.

We shoved what furniture we could against the doors and took up defensive positions, waiting for the assault. We were tense, our sinews taut.

'What's that sound?' George asked after a while.

I listened hard but could hear nothing. 'What sound?'

'I must have imagined it.' Another few seconds passed. 'No, there! A sort of scratching.'

And then I heard it, too. A very slight sound like pieces of paper rubbing together. It seemed to be coming from the wall. 'My God!' I cried. And I pointed. At the foot of the wooden wall between the chapel and the hotel, filtering through breaks and gaps between the planks, were half a dozen bottle-green spiders. I stared left and right. Everywhere I looked now, spiders were creeping into the room.

'Watson!'

Holmes and I had seen what a thousand of those creatures could do. At the British Museum, we had stood and watched the agonized death-throes of two once-powerful men who could do nothing to defend themselves from the poison those arachnids spat or bit into their victims.

'Sherlock, we must run!' I had never heard Mycroft as rattled as he was then. But he had known – and seen – the work of these little devils for far longer than we had. I looked over at George. His face, so sanguine just a minute before and ready to take on Moriarty's army, had blanched now.

'But why release them? They will kill Moriarty, too!' I said, unable to comprehend.

'I expect he and his men are outside now. These creatures cannot survive in the cold.'

At first, the spiders – a dozen, now two dozen, now three or four dozen – walked around without discernible purpose, exploring. But then their eyes turned towards us, and they began slowly creeping in our direction.

'Keep back, they can spit their venom!' Holmes yelled to Ioana as she stepped towards them, not knowing their deadly intent. At his words, she jumped back. Then, out of the corner of my eye, I saw the wall at the other side of the room begin to move. Little green bodies were pouring in through cracks there, too. And then behind us. On all sides, hundreds of the venomous creatures were slipping towards us like a tide. No matter how many we did murder to, some would survive to cover us in that poison that would leave us screaming in pain before paralysis robbed us of our voices.

'What now?' I yelled to Holmes.

'I don't—'

And then, astonishingly, what was meant as an assault gave us a glimmer of hope. The sound of breaking glass made us spin around. The stained-glass window in the rear wall was shattering. The face of the Messiah was breaking apart, his tears of blood turning to a rain of red glass.

A man I did not recognize, but who must have been one of Albert's patients, was smashing the glass and lead with a huge hammer. He was as fat as a bull and knocked half the window right out of the wall, dropped the tool and thrust his terrible face right through. Then, like a snake, he wound his torso through the opening. *He must be mad!* I told myself, even as I should have been thinking of defence or retreat.

Holmes was not so stunned. He had pressed himself to the wall beside the window and surprised the intruder with a hard punch to the temple. The man was possessed of a superhuman strength, however, and barely seemed to notice. He spun around and cracked a meaty forearm against my friend's chin. But then another body flew into the fray: George, matching the intruder in fury despite the bullet wound in his shoulder. The young man seized our opponent around the torso, grappling with bestial strength, and toppled him to the floor.

The man's fleshy head landed no more than a foot from the spiders, his jowls slapping down onto the floor. And I saw his eyes widen in shock as the first of the creatures spat its red poison onto his cheek. George, knowing the danger, hurried out of their reach. A second later, the fat man put his hand to his skin, testing the site. More spiders spat, and he began flailing at them with his hands, but they scuttled around his fingers and leapt onto his neck and bit in. He began to yell, then scream. A score more of the arachnids jumped on and injected their venom; and, horror upon horrors, where they had spat or bitten, his skin started to blister and boil away from the flesh, adding to his terrible pain. Within seconds, his shaking body became a magnet for the creatures throughout the room, which swarmed to overwhelm him and he fell into a pit of agonizing death.

'Watson!' Holmes called.

I dragged my eyes away from the dying man to find a sight of hope! The intruder had so broken the window and its frame that with some effort on our part to tear out more of it, there was now a route of escape. We helped Ioana climb through, then George, Mycroft, then me, and lastly Holmes, sustaining gashes to his hands from the broken glass and wood. And then, finally, we breathed sweet air that was not of that chapel of death. But Moran was on the other side of the building, we knew, and it would not be long before he realized that we had escaped.

'Holmes!' George warned. And without another breath,

he punched at my friend's shoulder – coming away with a smear of bottle-green flesh on his fist.

'Thank you,' Holmes said.

But shouts from the other side of the chapel, and coming closer, told us we had no time to catch our breath.

'Which way?' I said.

'The only way we can,' Holmes replied. 'The mountain.'

'Follow me,' Ioana ordered us. She knew far better than we did where to go, and we did as she demanded.

I ducked as another bullet was let loose from behind. Only this time, I felt the moving air brush my face. It had been but a feather away from me.

And that was it. The bare, freezing mountain was our only hope of survival. We ran for our lives.

The snow was like fog, whirling around us, grabbing hold of us, inviting us to drown in it – but our saviour too, I believe, cloaking us so that we could evade our pursuers. After twenty paces towards a path up and across the wall of rock, even steeper than the one to the old village, I looked back, the wind was dropping and the whirl of snow was thinning. There were five figures like black ghosts chasing us. I lifted my revolver and took aim.

'No!' Holmes's hand grabbed my wrist and forced the weapon down. 'You'll start an avalanche!' He pointed up to the pregnant drifts on the mountainside.

I nodded, and we ran forward again, towards the trail. Perhaps on the mountain we could lose them in the cascading white. The stone was wet and slippery. We climbed desperately, our hands raw and our feet numb. Ioana was still out in front, followed by Holmes, George, Mycroft, then me. There was another rend in the air, and a bullet cracked into the stone by my hip.

'Where are we going?' I cried.

'Up!' Holmes shouted back. 'Up!' And on we went. 'Do you see them?'

My face was covered in ice now – hanging off my eyelashes, freezing my lips together so that I could barely open my mouth to speak. I looked over my shoulder. They were about a hundred yards away, I thought, but through the sheet of snow I could have been sorely mistaken. They might have been two hundred yards away. Or ten.

'They are close.'

'Then on!'

Chapter 36

'Move faster!' the guv'nor growled at the Frenchie and his two goons. 'Unless you fancy hard penal servitude for life.'

'*Allez!*' the manager repeated to his men.

They didn't say much, but they knew one end of a shooter from the other and had a bully-bat each, so the mollies we were chasing barely stood a chance. What could they do? Hide out on the mountain? In the blizzard, they'd be dead within an hour even if we didn't catch up with them. I'd told the Professor we should stay back and track 'em – let 'em freeze to death, then recover the bodies. Chuck the corpses off the mountain so it looked like they got lost in the white-out. But he wanted to watch them die with his own eyes. Well, can't say I blamed him.

After that, of course, there'd be a bullet each for Albert and his boys, too. Did the fat bastard really think the Professor would let this little gold mine just waste away, controlled by a coward? No, the guv'nor had big plans for this place. It just needed a man who knew what he was about to run it. And more fool the Frenchie for trusting the Professor to keep his word about dividing the spoils. This sort of business isn't made for thick-heads.

The guv'nor and Albert were slower than the rest of us, and we left them behind as we chased the hares. It wasn't easy going, but I've had worse. The frost didn't bother me – when I get the bloodlust, I don't feel anything else.

We got to the bottom of the path they'd taken just as they were reaching the top. I was going to chase them all the way up, but then I thought to myself, *Why bother? Let the bullet do the running.* Well, they don't call me a crack shot for nothing. So I steadied myself, breathed, raised my pistol and took aim at the good doctor. Take your time. Squeeze the trigger, don't snatch it. Pull on the out breath for stability. That's my way. That's what bags the pretty prey. The first bullet missed because the game moved. No loss. It was a difficult shot, and I had enough rounds in my pocket to drop an army. I lifted again, squinted against the glare from the snow, allowed for the wind and fired.

Chapter 37

We scrabbled and scrambled for our lives. We were twenty yards now above the village plateau and, looking down, I could see the hotel. Below it lay the cemetery. I stared up. Beyond Ioana, there was a sharp ridge like the backbone of a feral beast. It led to the Jungfrau, that black peak where so many mountaineers had met their deaths in conditions far better than those we were fighting our way through.

'Holmes!' I shouted. 'It's madness!'

'We can make it!' George cried back.

Ioana could not understand our words but certainly understood their meaning.

'Madness or death, old friend,' Holmes called. 'We must choose.'

And then another bullet. And this one hit home. I felt it as a tearing apart of the flesh and bones of my left hand. It was only the numbing cold that prevented me from yelling out in pain. But I saw it – it is a sickening thing to see your own flesh torn to bloody rags.

I heard a voice behind us. Moriarty.

'. . . fool! You will bury us all in an avalanche!' I looked back to see him swing his sword-stick blade above him. Moran, some way ahead of him, looked furious and shoved his gun in his pocket.

Another hand came down and grabbed hold of my coat, wrenching me up. Had it not, I know I would have fallen. And then the men behind would have wreaked whatever pain they wanted upon me. I looked up to see George straining with my weight. 'You're hit.'

'My hand.'

He said nothing, but descended until he was beside me, then pulled my arm over his shoulders, supporting me as we forced our way up once more. Moriarty might have warned them off shooting more, but we were outnumbered and I was already injured, as was George. I saw our pursuers reach the bottom of the path. George threw down a few loose stones, forcing them to take cover.

Ten more strides up. Another ten. Each weaker and more painful than the last. But with each one, we came closer to that black ridge of stones. Where we would go from there, I had no idea; I could only trust that Ioana did.

The air was so thin that my head felt like it was being crushed in a vice. One more effort. I felt my muscles strain and George nearly fall under my weight. Mycroft tried to help, but it was hard enough for him to keep his own balance. I reached out for a rock and pulled myself towards the ridge, but the rock came away in my hand and I teetered on the edge. I grabbed again, with both hands, the blood from my left seeping out and then freezing on the ragged skin. And somehow I managed to drag myself up. And then the five of us were on the ridge.

Looking down on the other side, there was a sheer fall of hundreds of yards. How far it was in fact I couldn't say, because it was through the clouds and the cauldron of snow. The blizzard had wholly cut us off from the world of men.

But I heard them below us. Closer than before. They were not being slowed by an injured comrade. They were still coming for us. George threw down more stones, and I think that gave them pause once more. I looked around us. In each direction, the ridge was swallowed by the sea of white. 'Where can we go?'

'We must head for the mountain,' Holmes said. 'If we descend, they will lay their hands on us for certain.'

We moved crab-like sideways along the ridge, desperately clinging to the top of its spine; our feet finding footholds, our hands testing each one to see if it would bear our weight. It was slower going than climbing the path. Ten yards. Twenty. Thirty. I could hear the men below reaching the top of the trail up. Soon they would be in sight and following us along the bleak spine.

As we pressed on, the mountain loomed out of the storm. Now that we were upon it, it seemed like nothing so much as a malevolent wall of rock, stretching out of sight into the sky. 'My God,' I heard Holmes say. But it was more than just the sight of the mountain that made him exclaim. The ridge ended and widened into an out-crop that we had reached, jutting out from the Jungfrau proper. It was about two hundred yards long and fifty deep. Beyond, there was another. But between them was a break about fifty yards across. And this break was filled with something like a natural bridge constructed entirely of ice.

'Can we cross it?' I asked.

We looked back. Our pursuers had reached the start of the ridge and were making their way towards us.

'It is possible,' Ioana said in her own language, under-standing the thrust of my words even though they were in English.

'We have no choice,' Holmes added.

'I agree,' Mycroft said. George and Ioana just looked grimly determined.

We pressed on carefully to the edge of the ice bridge. Holmes tested it with his weight, although if it had cracked, we would hardly have heard it above the wind. He looked back at us, and put his full weight on it. I held my breath. It was solid. Even so, we should have gone one by one, but Moriarty and his thugs were so close behind us that we had no choice but to go all at once and pray that it would hold.

So we stepped forward tentatively, trying not to crash down with each step. Until something made Holmes stop. He was looking up at the wall of stone. I gazed up to see what had made him halt. And I saw.

'What the . . .' I said. 'What is he doing?'

There was a man on a ledge above. Behind him was a sort of natural cavern.

'Polin!' Ioana cried, upon recognizing her brother-in-law. 'What are you . . .'

'He's going to use that,' George said.

In Polin's hands was a large, black, double-barrelled shotgun. 'He's going to shoot us?' I looked around for natural cover.

'No, no. Far worse,' Holmes said. Polin lifted the gun and pointed not at us, not at Moriarty and his gang, but into the sky. And I saw what he intended. He fired once, then again. For a second, there was nothing but the howl of the wind and the echo of the shots. Then we heard it: the ocean-like rumbling. And we saw it, too: the snow above us pouring down the side of the mountain, ready to engulf everything in its path.

Before I could say anything, Holmes had wrenched my revolver from my pocket and begun shooting down. It didn't matter now. The danger was no longer from the noise of my gun, but from the deadly avalanche above us. Holmes shot again and again, blasting the remaining rounds at the ice bridge below our feet. Bit by bit, it began to crack. We felt it giving way and then collapse from underneath us. And then we were falling, sliding down a channel carved by ten thousand years of ice flow. I heard a bell somewhere below us toll hard and fast.

We tumbled with the waterfall of ice and rocks, not knowing where we would end up or if we were falling to our deaths. But staying to be buried under a thousand tonnes of snow would have meant suffocation even before we froze to death. A chance in a thousand was better than none at all.

The men who had travelled to this place had embraced death as a doorway to another life. For us, it would be nothing but an end to life. And so we clung to our lives with bleeding fingers.

I cannot tell you how long we fell. A minute or a year, it was all one to me. There was nothing but falling.

Chapter 38

I stared up. This white wall was coming down on us. I knew we were for it. There was no way out. Nowhere to run. The Professor glared at me. 'You foolish ...' he started snarling.

But I stopped his mouth. I stopped it hard. That was the last time he'd speak to me like a guttersnipe.

Chapter 39

'Are you alive?'

'Are you alive? Watson?'

It was a voice echoing through the cold, the ice and the snow that covered me, blanketed me, smothered me. Then hands began to pull me clear, into the air once more. Holmes.

'Barely.'

My eyes cracked open, and I saw Holmes, his brother and George standing over me. And smiles of relief on their bruised faces. I tried to sit up. A sharp pain in my torso told me I had broken a rib or two, and I must have been unconscious for few minutes, but I had had it worst, it seemed.

'Moriarty?' I asked.

'I doubt anyone up there survived.'

I struggled to my feet. We were back down on the village plateau – we had been lucky the snow had not swept us right down the mountain. George had a fractured wrist and Mycroft a gash on his cheek but nothing serious. Ioana sat on the ground a few yards away from us but she seemed largely uninjured. The village houses were still there, but the hotel was gone, buried under the white river. I saw, milling about, the guests who had been within it. They must have been alerted to the danger and taken to their heels. Some seemed shocked. Others had their wits about them and realized the new danger they were in: the danger of the law and exposure in the eyes of others. They were the ones attempting to flee, running to the train stop, finding it useless.

'It's the end for them,' I said.

'I shall see to it that it is,' Mycroft replied.

'Some men know the secret,' Holmes pointed out. 'But they would be fools ever to reveal it.'

'We shall know,' I said.

'Yes. We shall know.'

Ioana sat whispering with her eyes shut, praying, or perhaps speaking to the husband she had lost.

Epilogue

I have never seen such a day as New Year's Day in the year 1890. Every other New Year's Day that I could remember had been a quiet affair, a bit of a rest after a fortnight of stuffing oneself with goose and figgy pudding for Christmas. But that year was somehow different. From the moment that the bells rang in a new decade at midnight, every face had a look of hope to it. Men in their clubs, ladies in their salons, children in the parks. It seemed that every one of them was looking forward to a new start with optimism.

And they had good cause. Over the past month, the newspapers had run story after story of growing entente and shrinking pugilism between the great powers. The

Tsar of Russia was to visit France as a gesture of friendship, and the British Prime Minister was heading to Germany for discussions on improving trade.

Holmes and I were strolling along the north bank of the Thames. 'I received a letter yesterday from George Reynolds. He and the girl Devi are to be married in March. They intend to establish their own theatrical company.'

'I hope they stick to light comedies,' I said.

Holmes chuckled. It was not often that he did that. 'I hope so, too. I never saw him act. Was he any good?'

'He wasn't bad.'

'A leading man for our age?'

I considered. 'Unfortunately not.'

At that, he threw back his head and laughed from his belly. 'Perhaps he should have taken the Silent Conspiracy up on its offer. Once one is king, one has the pick of all the roles in the English canon.'

I smiled. 'Do you think they could have done it? Turned George into a king, I mean.'

Holmes tapped his stick on the cobbles three or four times. 'The process to which they were subjecting him was designed to open a man's mind to great possibilities. But if his desire was only to be an itinerant player, I doubt it could convince him to seize a throne.'

'No, I expect not.'

'The wisdom of Solomon.' I glanced at him. 'Oh yes, we are handed down stories of ancient kings, but within each there is a kernel of truth. I have my suspicion that that Hebrew monarch was indeed possessed of knowledge surpassing the sea of men, but it was of a chemical origin, not a divine one. Do not forget that it was his portrait on the wall where our intrepid archaeologists found the telling parchment.' That made me stop and think for a moment. 'Ah, here is our man,' he said brightly.

Mycroft was approaching us from the opposite direction. The three of us walked to the embankment wall, rested our hands on it and watched the boats on the river. Some were delivering coal, some transporting baked goods or grain. Some were full of day-trippers from the provinces, waiting to point out the Palace of Westminster or St Paul's Cathedral.

'I have completed my duties in Switzerland,' Mycroft began without so much as a greeting. 'All is, I believe, resolved. The Swiss authorities, under a certain amount of diplomatic pressure, rounded up the last of the organization, who were lying low where they could. I was permitted – again, after a certain degree of diplomatic insistence, backed up with a few hints of the consequences for Swiss banks with branches in London – to interrogate them myself.'

'So now you know all?' I asked.

'As much, Dr Watson, as one can ever be said to "know all".'

'Of course. And I am still a little unclear as to how deeply you were involved in the early stages of the affair.'

A steamer piled high with coke chugged past us.

He tapped his cane on the ground. 'As you know, it all began with the four of us who broke into that tomb,' he said. 'For years, we experimented alone with the effects of the spider venom process that we had stumbled across.'

I was appalled, but also fascinated. 'Can you describe it?'

'That is very difficult,' Mycroft said. 'Rather like describing colours to a man who sees only in black and white. But the outcome, the outcome you can understand much more easily. It allowed us to excel in our chosen fields – Ridge in music, Wyneth in the law, Jet in government.'

'And you in your own field,' Holmes said. 'One which, we might say, does not yet have an appropriate name.'

'You are correct, Sherlock, it does tend to defy definition. Anyhow, Jet and Wyneth saw only possibilities in this process – men could become supermen. Ridge, however, was more worried for the evil that it could do. He thought of Paganini's contract with the Devil. By then, I had decided that I had gained enough from it and that it was time to stop before it began to consume me, rather than vice-versa.'

I wanted to know more about the medical effects of this treatment. 'Can you describe what happened when you stopped undergoing the process?'

'Fatigue, an aching head, excessive sensitivity to sound and light, inability to focus on the task in hand. Well, you saw it for yourself.'

'I saw it for myself?'

He looked amazed at my lack of understanding. 'Doctor Watson, do you mean to say that you have not yet realized that when you attended me at the Diogenes Club it was for that very malady?'

'No, I did not,' I said.

Holmes tutted.

'Well, it matters not, as I had to resume the regime again soon after in order to keep track of my former comrades' plans. Jet and Wyneth had established the facility in Switzerland, but there were some very bad apples in the barrel. Rising political men from rival nations attended, determined to gain advantage over one another. I felt it was time to act. And Ridge had come to the same conclusion, so he ended the careers of Jet and Wyneth in that dramatic fashion.'

'Did our government know?' I asked.

'Tsk, tsk, Doctor. You know that I cannot reveal such details.' He turned back to the river. 'But if you were to suggest that certain select individuals in Whitehall were aware of the bare bones of the situation, I would not dispute your words too energetically.'

We wandered on a few paces and sat on an iron bench outside Temple Underground Railway Station. A newspaper boy was hawking the *Daily News*. The headline read: 'Bells ring as new year dawns.' Holmes handed over a penny and flicked through the pages as he listened.

'What about those who underwent the process?'

'We know who they are. We will keep a watch.'

'And what of the facility itself?' I asked.

'When it is dug out, it will become what it should have been from the beginning: nothing but a pleasantly remote hotel, suitable for a little walking and relaxation.'

'How nice.' We were silent for a while. Mycroft opened a gold cigarette case. I watched the boats. Holmes read his newspaper. 'When did . . .' I began.

But I was interrupted by Holmes. 'As expected,' he said quietly. He folded back a page of the *Daily News* and placed it in my hands. It was open at the small advertisements page.

Professor M. sends his compliments to S.H. He expresses his gratitude for the gentleman's aid in his recent travels. He begs to remind S.H. of their future appointed meeting at a certain location in Switzerland.

Holmes burst into laughter again. 'Well, now. It appears we have reached only the end of the beginning!' And he threw the newspaper into the Thames, to float away on the tide towards the North Sea.

The TURNGLASS
GARETH RUBIN

'Vivid, resonant, melancholy and beautiful'
Janice Hallett

1880s England.

Idealistic young doctor Simeon Lee arrives on the bleak island of
Ray, off the Essex coast, to treat his cousin, Parson Oliver Hawes,
who is dying. Parson Hawes, who lives on the only house on the
island – Turnglass House – believes he is being poisoned and he
points the finger at his sister-in-law, Florence. Florence was declared
insane after killing Oliver's brother in a jealous rage and is now
kept in a glass-walled apartment in Oliver's library. And the secret
to how she came to be there can be found in Oliver's tête-bêche
journal, where one side tells a very different story from the other.

1930s California.

Celebrated author Oliver Tooke, the son of the state governor, is found
dead in his writing hut behind the family residence, Turnglass House.
His friend Ken Kourian doesn't believe that Oliver would take his
own life. His investigations lead him to the mysterious kidnapping of
Oliver's brother when they were children, and the subsequent secret
incarceration of his mother, Florence, in an asylum. But to discover
the truth, Ken must decipher clues hidden in Oliver's final book, a
tête-bêche novel – which is about a young doctor called Simeon Lee . . .

'A stunning, ingenious, truly immersive mystery.
The Turnglass is a thrilling delight'
Chris Whitaker

AVAILABLE IN PAPERBACK, EBOOK & AUDIO

**SIMON &
SCHUSTER**